PATCHWORK PARADISE

INDRA VAUGHN

RIPTIDE
PUBLISHING

Riptide Publishing
PO Box 1537
Burnsville, NC 28714
www.riptidepublishing.com

Patchwork Paradise
Copyright © 2016 by Indra Vaughn

Cover art: Lou Harper, louharper.com/design.html
Editors: Carole-ann Galloway, Kate De Groot
Layout: L.C. Chase, lcchase.com/design.htm

ISBN: 978-1-62649-381-0

First edition
March, 2016

Also available in ebook:
ISBN: 978-1-62649-380-3

PATCHWORK PARADISE

INDRA VAUGHN

RIPTIDE
PUBLISHING

This is to everyone who has had their butts kicked by life, and who kept going anyway.

TABLE
OF CONTENTS

 CHAPTER
ONE

Ever since we'd left high school, Saturday nights had been holy. Untouchable. All-night happy hour at the Nine Barrels was something none of us skipped. The bar was known for its paella and port wine, but we went there to drink cheap beer and gyrate to Latin music while hitting on anything that moved.

Or, well, the others did the hitting. Not me. I'd found the love of my life when I was sixteen years old. He was being incredibly stubborn at the moment. Or maybe I was being a bit of a brat.

"But it's Saturday," I complained for the tenth time that day.

Sam sent me a look with a hint of annoyance, and I knew I was running out of brat-credit. "It's one time, Ollie. It won't hurt," he said as he straightened his tie.

"I don't know about that." I threw myself back on our perfectly made bed and luxuriated in the duvet with the ridiculous thread count. "I might injure myself. You know like how those marathon runners or professional cyclists can't just stop doing exercise or their overlarge hearts will explode? I bet it's the same with me. I stop drinking abruptly and—"

"Your liver will explode?" Samuel smiled at me in our stripped and repainted mirror—an old piece of shit I'd found on one of my digs through Antwerp's flea markets and that Samuel had completely turned into a work of art. "Now there's a sight I'd like to see. Besides, there will be alcohol at this party. Better alcohol."

It was mostly his eyes that laughed at me. Samuel always laughed with his eyes. His dark eyelashes were so long. They'd lift as his eyes narrowed in mirth, and the pale blue of his irises would glint with mischief and promise.

"But—"

He spun on his heel, and I snapped my mouth shut. We'd known each other since we were ten. We'd started dating when we were sixteen, we'd had sex for the first time two weeks later, and we were getting married in one month. And still he took my breath away. Samuel always looked gorgeous, but Samuel in a suit threatened to melt my brain.

"Hi," he murmured as he walked up to the bed.

"Hi," I said. I sat up so I could touch him—his lapels, the white shirt underneath, the luscious burgundy tie. He kissed my nose.

"Get dressed, Ollie. We go to the opening, I show my face, do some brownnosing, and then we'll go to the Nine Barrels."

"Really?" I sprang up and hugged him—lightly, I didn't want to crease him. "You're the best."

"That's why you love me." He grinned, and his eyes crinkled.

God. All mine.

"I do," I whispered and kissed him. He smelled of cinnamon toothpaste—which I thought was disgusting to brush with, but somehow on him it tasted divine—and of my favorite aftershave. His dark hair was carefully gelled away from his face, and I wanted to mess it up but didn't. I knew how important hosting this event was to him, his first as manager of the gallery. So I let him go, lifted my own suit off the hanger, and began to dress.

Samuel sat on the bed and watched me. I felt like making lewd jokes, but something fragile hung in the air, something to be treasured. A little moment in time I'd remember forever.

"You look gorgeous," he told me when I struggled with my tie. He rose to his feet, squeezed my hands, then gently moved them aside. With long, deft fingers, he did my tie for me. He stared into my eyes the entire time. It was sappy. I didn't care.

"You sure they'll be okay with me being at the gallery?"

Samuel shrugged one shoulder. "They all know."

"Knowing and seeing are two different things."

He'd been working for his current boss at a huge gallery for over three years, but this was the first time she'd let him organize an opening party, and he'd managed to snag one of Antwerp's most up-and-coming talents. I'd been to the odd Christmas do, but this felt different.

Samuel cupped my face. "It's fine, Ollie. I'm not the only gay person who works at the gallery. This is Antwerp, after all." The right side of his mouth lifted. "Stop looking for excuses."

I rolled my eyes. "Okay."

He opened his arms, and I walked right into them, sighing deeply. Samuel was taller than me by a good four inches, and broader—not that that was hard.

"You make me feel so safe," I murmured. His cheek lifted against my temple, and I smiled too.

"That's good to know," he said and gently let go. "We need to leave soon. Are you ready?"

"As I'll ever be."

"You'll be wonderful."

One last attempt to get out from under this. "But I won't know anyone and I'll look sad and pathetic." I fluttered my eyelashes at him, knowing it wouldn't work.

"All the women will fawn over you as they always do because you look like a blue-eyed Labrador puppy."

"Thanks." I pouted, and he laughed, ruffling my hair. Unlike his, mine didn't have any gel in it, because while it was thick, it was straight as a pin.

"Let's get going."

We trudged down the marble steps of our ridiculously oversize home. We lived in a three-story house with a large garden right on the edge of Antwerp South, as the area was known. No twenty-six-year-olds should've been able to afford a place like this, but Samuel's grandmother had been filthy rich and he'd been the only grandchild, so . . . lucky us.

His parents had been less than happy with Grandma's choice and had tried to talk Sam into giving up the house for a while, but the will had been solidly drawn up, and they quickly let go of any objections. Sam and his parents had gone through a tense couple of months after that, but everything seemed to be forgotten now. He didn't talk to me about it all that much. I always felt he had a strange attachment to the house, an intense connection I didn't entirely understand.

We actually didn't use a lot of the rooms. I'd suggested more than once that we should rent out a room or two to students, since we were close to a few colleges and a hospital, but Samuel didn't like the idea.

The early June evening was fresh but not cold when we stepped out, and we walked arm in arm toward the tram that would take us into the center. For once it didn't look like rain, and I squeezed Samuel's biceps. Despite my earlier little tantrum, there was nowhere I'd rather be.

"You'll be great tonight," I told him, and he smiled down on me.

I probably drank more at the gallery than I should have—but I managed to make small talk and be polite and appear interested in the women who descended on me, as Samuel had predicted.

I was proud of my fiancé. He looked cool and competent as he guided guests inside, welcomed them, made sure they had something to drink while he chatted briefly here and there. He was always sending people off to see a particular piece of art. He checked on caterers, sufficiently calmed the artist—who looked one shattered glass away from a nervous breakdown—so the twitchy prodigy started chatting to potential buyers too. I noticed Sam managed to gather a collection of business cards along the way. His boss would be pleased.

He was born for this. A true people person. While I, on the other hand, loved hanging out with our close group of friends, but needed downtime afterward to recharge. Events like this made my knees knock together.

I kept my straight face going for most of the evening, but when it neared eleven and the party didn't seem to be winding down, I began to worry. I really didn't want to be stuck here all night. I was pretty sure two old ladies had squeezed my butt, and one scary bald guy with a scar through his top lip had given me his card in case I needed "a real man."

I shuddered as I wondered what someone like that was doing at an art gallery. I remembered Antwerp had its very own mix of Mafia and decided I didn't want to know.

As if my thoughts had summoned him, Samuel appeared by my side.

"I need to talk to one more person," he told me, "and then we can go."

"Really?" I tried not to look as happy as I sounded. I probably failed.

"Really." He grinned and touched my sleeve. "Angela can take over from here. Everyone's getting drunk now and just talking. Hardly anyone is looking at the art, and the doors are locked, so no one new can come in. Why don't you go get our coats and I'll meet you at the back?"

"You're my favorite person in the world."

"Lies. Stijn is your favorite person in the world."

"Only for five minutes on Sunday mornings when I buy chocolate croissants from him. The rest of the time, I'm all yours."

He smiled and his eyes twinkled, and suddenly I was reminded of the first time he'd looked at me that way, after our very first kiss in my bedroom. It had been a fraught moment because I didn't know what I was doing or if he wanted it too or what it meant that I wanted it with *him* and not Cleo, our other best friend. His mouth had met mine. He'd opened me up from the inside out. And just like that, the world had stopped being a scary place.

"I won't be long," he said, and I nodded. The coat check was on the other side of the building, but I lingered a minute so I could watch him walk away. *Damn.*

When I looked up, one of the old ladies gave me a lavish wink. I offered her a little wave before scurrying away.

"Why do elderly women like me?" I lamented as we walked toward the Nine Barrels. The walk was maybe three miles or so and the air had turned chilly at last, but I didn't mind. Antwerp was gorgeous at night, the traffic negligible, and we held hands as we crossed the cobblestone streets on our way to the harbor.

"It's your personal charm," Samuel said. He glanced down and smirked, and I knew what was coming. "Or maybe it's the fact that you look like a mildly underfed young boy. You bring out their mothering instincts."

"Since two of them copped a feel, that's gross."

Samuel burst out laughing. I couldn't help it; I laughed too. "Well, it's because you're so beautiful they just can't help themselves."

I squeezed his hand, and he squeezed back. "You're not so bad yourself," I said.

"No, stop with the praise. It's too much. I can't take it."

We walked down the Hoogstraat, which meant we were almost at the bar. I loved this whole area, but mostly the small antique stores that lined the streets. They sold everything from absolute junk to the most gorgeous pieces of furniture I'd ever seen.

"We should come back on Sunday," I said to Samuel as I tried to peer through one shop's gated-up doors. "We could get breakfast and go shopping."

"We don't need any more stuff," he said. There was mirth in his voice, and I knew he'd come with me anyway. Partially to keep me company, but also because he liked strolling the Antwerp streets as much as I did. There could be something magical about this place. There was ugliness too, as in any city. Mostly it was pretty easy to ignore. Its seaport brought with it an industrial coldness, cranes standing out like silent monsters in the night. In contrast, the fashion, the art, and the students lent it a vibrancy that made my blood thrum.

"Maybe we'll find an old crib," I teased. "For all those babies we're going to adopt when we're married."

He pretended to glare at me. "No babies. Not even furry ones."

I squeezed his arm to let him know I was only teasing, and we walked on in silence. The streets grew busier, and when we neared the Nine Barrels, we could hear the music spilling out into the night.

As he always did before we went inside, Samuel pulled me close and kissed me lightly on the mouth. "I love you," he murmured.

"I love you too, Sam," I said. If I'd known it'd be the last time he'd ever hear me say it, I would never have let go.

The Nine Barrels itself was a tiny place, but the front door didn't open up straight into the restaurant. The building was old and gorgeous, with a little courtyard that had been covered with a concave glass roof two stories up. The owner had crammed in a few tables and chairs there, with small trees and flowerpots strategically positioned to give patrons the idea they were still outside.

The left and right of the courtyard held stores that had closed hours ago. Small groups of people were murmuring over their *porto* and tapas. We pushed our way past. As soon as we entered the restaurant, loud music assaulted our ears, and my eyes fell on Cleo dancing on top of the bar. Simultaneously we looked at each other and laughed.

"Night shifts?" I asked Samuel, and he grinned.

"Most likely."

Cleo was an ER nurse with a brutal schedule, but she figured she needed to work the hardest while she was young and childless. Her boyfriend Imran stood in the corner of the restaurant, chatting with a bunch of people I didn't know, but as soon as he saw us, he excused himself and made his way over.

"Where's Thomas?" I asked as we hugged hello. Imran nodded toward the other end of the bar from where Cleo was dancing. Thomas was patiently waiting for the bartender's attention. He turned and gave us a little wave, as if he had heard me.

"You want something to drink?" Samuel asked.

"Sure." I dug for my wallet, but Samuel stilled my hand.

"I got it," he said, and I bit my tongue. Money was the only real argument we'd ever had, and we'd only had it once, but that didn't mean I could always keep a lid on the trickle of embarrassment I felt whenever he paid for me.

"What's yours is mine," he'd told me once, *"and what's mine is yours. We're going to be married one day, so what difference does it make now?"*

Since we'd only been eighteen at the time, that counterargument had shut me up effectively. But these days I had a decent wage of my own as a medical software consultant. He'd been asking to make our accounts joint since we moved into his grandmother's house four years ago, but I wanted to wait until we really were married.

He winked at me like he knew exactly what I was thinking and then walked up to Thomas to take over the drink ordering.

Cleo and I had played naked together in the paddling pool when we were three, so she was pretty much considered my sister—and Samuel's too. Imran had joined our little triumvirate when he began dating Cleo. Their affair had been the dirtiest gossip her nursing school had ever known. Imran had been a resident at the hospital where Cleo had started her first practical, and needless to say, the authorities were not pleased. They'd lasted, though, and I wouldn't be surprised if he popped the question at our wedding. The thunder stealer.

Thomas de Ridder had been the last addition to our group of friends. He had slipped in almost unnoticed three years ago. As head of IT at one of the hospitals where I'd had to install new software and familiarize everyone with it, he'd spent a lot of time with me. When I'd asked him to join us for a drink after a really late night, he'd agreed. He'd been quiet, and I'd wondered if I'd made a mistake not warning him about my having a boyfriend. But he'd agreed to join us again the next time, and after that he never left.

I watched Sam and Thomas kiss each other on the cheek, then talk for a minute before Thomas grinned and lifted his hands. *If you want to stand in line, be my guest.* Or something like that. He scanned the crowd, spotted someone, looked in our direction, and winked before moving in for the kill.

My fears about Thomas being homophobic had long since proven to be grossly unfounded. As he wove through the crowd, I had no clue who his target would be. The gorgeous brick of a guy who looked like he could be a professional triathlete? Or the short girl with a blonde bob and an impressive—even to me—pair of boobs? It didn't matter who it was. Thomas wouldn't be joining us again for the rest of the night. He was an unapologetic, self-proclaimed slut who would *"settle down when I find the one, and how can I possibly find the one unless I try them all?"*

I shook my head and left him to it, watching as Samuel fought the crowd to the small table I'd been able to secure.

He put everyone's beers on the laminated wood. Thomas's drink would most likely go untouched, so I appropriated it with a cheeky smile. Sam kissed the top of my head and straddled a chair. "You going to join Cleo soon?"

"I need some liquid courage first," I said and pushed the lime into one of my beers. Imran tapped the neck of his bottle to mine, and we drank. "Water, Sam?" I asked when I saw him sip his glass.

He smiled at me and ran a hand through my hair, tugging it lightly. "Yeah. Don't feel like drinking tonight, but you go on. I know you've been looking forward to the weekend."

"Not to mention all the mimosas I've had already." I sniggered into my beer, and Imran laughed.

"Good show?" he asked Samuel.

"Not bad." Samuel hooked his arms over the back of the chair, resting his chin on his wrist, and I couldn't tear my eyes away from him. His eyes twinkled with pride, and I squeezed his knee. He didn't like to brag about anything, ever, but he'd done well and he knew it.

"You were amazing," I told him, and beside me Imran made a gagging noise.

"You two put all the couples in the world to shame," he said. "I'm disgusted." He drank his beer, and Sam tugged my hair again. I threaded my fingers through his. Yeah, we were sappy, and I couldn't care less.

Out of nowhere Cleo dropped into Imran's lap and snatched Samuel's water, which she downed in one go.

"Darlings," she said and blew us kisses. "How did opening night go?"

"It was perfect," I told her.

"So you hated every minute of it."

Sam laughed at my indignant "No!"

"He did. You should've seen him, Cleo. Pressed against the wall like a frightened little flower."

I sniffed when they all laughed at me. "Well, those old ladies have very sharp nails. And that bald guy was either going to make me buy illegal art or force me to become a running boy for his Mafia diamond-trade operation."

"I think he just wanted to make you his bum boy," Samuel said, and I felt my cheeks stain red while the others hollered at me in glee.

"Come dance," Cleo said, and she gripped my hand. She was sweating head to toe, her dark hair hanging in thick strands to her collarbones, and she still managed to look radiant. I fought her tugging long enough to kiss Sam, because I knew once I was on that dance floor with her, I wouldn't be coming back anytime soon. Our mouths brushed together, and for a moment the music seemed to dim, the noise around us fading into nothing. There was just me and him.

"God, Ollie," he whispered, and then he let me go. The noise returned with a *bang*, the music heaving in the sweltering heat. I lifted my free hand, gave in to Cleo's tugging, and whooped. She laughed and swung her arms around me. Out of the corner of my eye, I saw Thomas making out with the buxom blonde, and after that my world dissolved into the hot rhythm of Latin music and Cleo's lithe body against mine.

Around three in the morning, the music slowed a little and Imran came to steal Cleo away. Right behind him was Samuel, and we slipped into a slow dance as if we'd rehearsed it. He didn't say much and neither did I, but I felt the moment deeply, like a comforting weight in the center of my soul, grounding me to earth. I closed my eyes and smiled as I laid my head on his shoulder.

"Can we go soon?" he asked me when the song ended. "It's been a long day, and I'm tired."

"Yes," I said. "Of course. Let me just go grab a glass of water. I'm parched."

"Sure. I'll be waiting in the courtyard. I need some air. Thomas said we can take his car." He held out a bunch of keys, and I was relieved we wouldn't have to walk home.

The place was still busy but not packed anymore, and I got my water pretty quickly. Cleo and Imran were snuggled up in the corner, so I just gave them a little wave. When I saw Thomas standing all by himself, I went to go say hi.

"What's up?" I asked. "Where's your girl?"

"Her name's Liesbeth. And she's in the bathroom," he said. A strand of his long brown hair had gotten stuck between his lips. He'd pulled it back in a bun, but a lot of it had come undone and clung to his neck in sweaty peaks. I plucked the hair out of his mouth.

"So you won't need our couch?" Thomas lived outside of Antwerp in a small village by the Schelde. He always talked about moving to the city so he wouldn't have to deal with traffic on the E17 anymore. So far he hadn't made real plans yet.

His gaze trailed to the bathroom, and I followed it, seeing the girl emerge. She waved, and we both waved back. He smirked at me. "Doubtful, but I'll call if I do."

"I'll leave you to it. Good luck." We hugged quickly, and he rubbed my back.

"Take care," he said.

I nodded and walked away.

Samuel was waiting for me by the big wooden door that led to the street. "Ready to go?" he asked as he held up his arm. I walked underneath it and snuggled close.

"Yes. Did you have a good time?"

He smiled down at me. "I had a great time. You know I love watching you have fun."

"Yeah, but I don't want you to sit through these evenings because you have to."

"No, I had a good time talking to Imran. His hospital stories are always incredible."

Thomas had left his car by the docks. We crossed the Ernest Van Dijckkaai, a wide road that hugged the water. The night smelled of the sea air the river brought with it. A cool wind had picked up and made me shiver, and Samuel hugged me tighter.

Little light covered the parking lots, and we fell quiet as we hurried along. Samuel held Thomas's key out, and in the distance a car beeped once as its indicators flashed.

We walked toward it, and a chill ran down my spine. Every single hair on the back of my neck rose. Either my eyes were playing tricks or the world was turning darker. The foreboding hung so thick I could taste it. "Sam," I whispered.

"I know." He grabbed my hand, squeezed it, then tugged me forward. We half ran toward the car. I'd never figure out why, but I understood something terrible was about to happen. My heart tried to claw its way out of my throat.

"*Sam*," I said again, and a dark figure stepped out from behind a van. "Oh no."

"Your wallet," the man said. His eyes were wide and his gaze kept darting from me to Sam to the street behind us. It was hard to see his face, but every now and again the dim light caught the sweat on his forehead or the brown of his rotting teeth. "Both of you. Car keys, phones, watches. All of it."

"Oh God." I began to tremble, and Samuel took a careful step away from me. The mugger's frantic eyes followed him, which must have been Sam's intention, but I didn't like it one bit.

"Do what he says," he told me calmly. "It'll be okay."

I nodded and tried to keep a hold of myself as I undid the watch on my wrist. It had been a gift from my dad, but in that moment it could've been a gift from the king and I wouldn't have cared.

By the time I managed to take my phone and wallet out of my pockets, I was trembling so hard I fumbled and dropped them. Then it all happened at once.

"Oh God," I said again, bending to pick them up.

The guy yelled, "Stay where you are!" and Samuel stepped between us.

I heard the guy swear, ripping something from Samuel's hands. Samuel turned around, his eyes wide.

"It's okay," he said.

"Yeah, we can get new wallets." I tried to laugh, but my eyes were wet and my voice was hoarse. I looked up to see the man running away. "He's gone. Should I call the police?"

"I think you need to call an ambulance," Samuel whispered. He was clutching at me, dragging me down with him. I didn't understand.

"Sam? Sammy? Oh my God. Oh my *God*." I tried to ease him down slowly, but he was so heavy we both fell. The gravel bit painfully into my knee, and his head lolled to the side.

"Sam!" I grabbed his face and righted it. He looked at me and mouthed something, but all that came out were bubbles of blood. "No. No no *no*, Samuel, oh please, God, no." He was clutching his abdomen and I pried his fingers away. A thick pool of blood darkened his shirt. I made a hoarse noise. Pressing my hands over what must be a stab wound, I looked up and saw a couple walking. "Help me!" I yelled. I fumbled around for either of our phones, but my vision was cloudy with panic and tears, and I couldn't find them. "Somebody help me!"

When I looked back down at Samuel, his eyes had filmed over.

I screamed as his blood seeped under my fingernails. And because grief is, intrinsically, a selfish emotion, all I felt was my own heart bleeding.

 CHAPTER
TWO

I sat in the hospital, unaware of anything but the loud buzzing noise between my ears and the glaringly bright lights. I had no idea how I'd gotten there. Someone in a police uniform was kneeling in front of me. His mouth was moving, but I heard nothing. Eventually he shook his head and stood. I watched him go toward a nurse. They talked. He pointed at me. She looked over and nodded. Her mouth pinched together in what could've been sympathy. I averted my eyes. I didn't want to see anyone's pity. That meant acknowledging something was wrong.

Someone rubbed my arm. I looked down at the hand. Wrinkled fingers stroked the fabric of my coat. I knew the fat golden ring on the index finger, but my brain didn't work. I looked up. It was Sam's mom. I quickly looked away again. Cleo sat on my other side, sobbing so hard I suddenly understood why the chair I sat in seemed to be moving jerkily. I looked away from her too.

Something cold pressed to my cheek. I startled.

"You have blood on your face."

They were the first words to penetrate the fog in my mind since Samuel told me to call an ambulance.

"What?"

Where the cop had been, Thomas crouched. His eyes were swollen and red, his cheeks tearstained. There was such enormous pain in his gaze, my heart flinched.

"There's blood on your face," he said again. "Here, let me . . ."

He pressed the wet paper towels to my temple. I watched them come away dark with brown flecks. *Sam's blood.*

I lurched out of the chair and barely made it to the bathroom in time to throw up into the sink. I didn't look at myself. I couldn't look at anything, because everything would bring me closer to acknowledging the truth. I rinsed my mouth and walked out.

"Ollie? The police have to ask you some questions, darling."

Oh no. I shook my head, not looking at Sam's mother either. "I want to see him," I whispered. "Can I see him?"

A nurse stepped into my line of sight. "Yes. You can come with me."

"Do you want anyone to go with you?" Cleo asked.

I glanced at Sam's mom, but she was staring into space. I shook my head.

I should've felt something, surely. But there was nothing at all as I kept my eyes on the nurse's white shoes and followed her down the stark hallway. Her soles squeaked with every step. I had no idea where we were going.

She opened a door leading to a small, single-bed hospital room. "Will you be okay?" she asked me.

I looked around the sterile space, the huge window in it, the crisp, clean floor, the table with its retractable leaf, the handrails, and finally the unmoving shape in the lonely bed. He was in a bed. Did that mean he'd still been alive when the ambulance brought him in? I wished I could remember if anyone had said something, but my mind was completely blank. I couldn't even recall the ambulance ride.

No, I thought. *No, I will never be okay again.* "I'll be fine."

She nodded, touched my shoulder gently, and left me to it.

I took one step and then stood nailed to the floor as the door quietly fell shut behind me. It felt like I should stand there forever, like this moment should never move along.

What lay ahead of me anyway? Nothing at all. I tried to imagine, for a second, what life would be like without Sammy in it. My brain recoiled and slapped that thought away like it was an angry wasp. I stood there until my toes cramped.

I caught sight of Samuel's hands, and my gaze snagged there. I wasn't ready to look at his face.

His hands lay on top of the sheet, by his sides. They were pale and a little bit dirty. I stepped into the bathroom to my right and grabbed a few paper towels. I wet them under the tap and slowly walked over. His hand was still warm. Maybe not as warm as it should've been, but warm enough to pretend.

"I'll clean you up," I said. "I know how much you hate dirt under your fingernails. Unless it's paint. You never seem to mind paint. Although . . ." I lifted my head and smiled as I stared out of the window. The sky was turning gray in the distance. I didn't want there to be a new day, or a new dawn. It reminded me of every morning lying ahead of me when I'd wake up without . . .

I pushed that thought away too. "You could only bear the paint on your hands as long as you were actually painting. As soon as you were done, you'd scrub and scrub until it was gone."

When I'd cleaned the dirt from one hand, I stood to get fresh paper towels and sat down on his other side.

"You never told me what you've been working on lately. I'm sorry to say I'm going to have to take a peek now." I cleaned his fingers and his palm. "You always used to let me see all your paintings, no matter what stage they were in. So I could only come to one conclusion, you know. It's a wedding present, isn't it?"

Oh God.

I dropped his hand. I dropped the towels. Automatically, like a reflex, I raised my head and looked at his face.

"Sammy?" I asked in a very small voice. My hand trembled when I lifted it to swipe his hair aside. The gel had all come out, and it looked so soft. My favorite time of day was when he'd exit his evening shower and I could run my hands freely through his locks.

An ugly hiccup of a sob tore itself free from my mouth. I covered it to make sure no other noise escaped. His eyes were closed. His lips were pale. I dropped my hands. "Sammy?"

Nothing. Of course, nothing. Because Samuel Mathieu was gone. He'd been gone for goodness knew how long, while I'd been sitting in the waiting room, trying to change the course of time.

It was my fault. If we'd left earlier, if I hadn't insisted on going out, if we'd stayed at the gallery and gone home from there . . .

My fault.

I shook all over when I rose to my feet. Tears leaked out of my eyes and fell onto his cheeks as I leaned over him. I tried to wipe them away, but it was no use; they kept on falling. The pain was immeasurable, a giant beast in my chest, and I thought it wouldn't ever stop roaring. I gave up, pressed a gentle kiss to his lips, and carefully lay down beside him, where I cried and cried until someone came to take me away.

I couldn't remember anything between that moment and the funeral. Most likely I slept a lot on my mom's couch. She lived in a small apartment on Linkeroever, on the other side of the Schelde. After my dad died when I was eighteen, and as I got ready to move on to college life, she'd downsized and never looked back.

The weather was undecided on the day of the funeral. A few raindrops fell when we entered the Holy Ghost Church, and as I sat through the service, I kept listening for a downpour on the roof but heard nothing. I don't remember what the priest said. Afterward, a lot of people offered me condolences, one or two ignored me completely—I couldn't have cared less even though my mom was outraged—and then I was in our home, with people eating and laughing and reminiscing.

I hadn't been here since Sam died. It didn't feel like my house without him in it, and part of me wondered if I'd have to give it up now. Did he have a will? I didn't know. I hadn't even been able to answer the question if he'd wanted to be cremated or not. His mother had thought so, and so did I, even though the idea of it had made me cry for hours. Imagining that beautiful man wasting away in a coffin six feet under had been ten times worse, so cremation it was.

"Ollie?"

I blinked. Somehow I'd made my way to our bedroom. From here the noise downstairs was a dim murmur. I couldn't begrudge them their laughter, but it cut my soul.

Cleo stared at me, and her bottom lip began to tremble.

"Hey," I said. When I looked down, I noticed I was holding one of Sam's soft cashmere sweaters. I brought it to my nose and inhaled. His scent hit me like a sucker punch. "I can't do this," I whispered. I looked at Cleo and held the sweater out. "How do I do this? Help me, Cleo."

Her face cracked and she ran at me, hugging me hard and crushing the sweater between us. I wanted to shove her away and fold it, but she wouldn't let me.

"We're here," she whispered. "Oh, Oliver, we're here for you. I'm so sorry. I'm so fucking sorry. If I hadn't insisted you come out that night . . ."

Her grip on me loosened, and I pushed her away, holding her arms tight so I could look at her. "No," I said firmly, giving her a little shake. The awful urge to shake her really hard washed over me, but I didn't. "This is not on you."

It's on me.

Work gave me a week off for bereavement leave, and I took another three weeks' vacation because there was no way I'd be fit to join the general population after seven days. I stayed with my mother for a while, but I grew antsy there. I kept thinking our house still smelled like us, and I was missing it. Soon he'd fade away completely, and I wouldn't remember his scent, or his voice, or what he looked like. I'd never know him when he was old. I'd never get to see him with gray hair.

I went home and slept a lot. I received a ton of phone calls I continued to ignore. My mom stopped by a few times, and I managed to pull myself together for long enough to shower and see her, but as soon as she was gone, I went back to bed. I could tell she was worried about me. It bothered me in a vague way because I knew she was grieving too, but I didn't have the energy to think too much about it.

I wondered what was going to become of me. What about the house? It belonged to Sam. We hadn't bothered signing any sort of contract because we were getting married anyway. I had no idea what would happen to his bank accounts or his savings, and I honestly couldn't care in that moment. Sam would've wanted me to have it all, but he wasn't here to stand up for me anymore.

"I miss you," I whispered into his pillow, and I could hear his voice, almost clear as day, telling me, *I know.*

Crying again, I pulled my phone from underneath my pillow and dialed his number. Apparently he had fallen on top of our mobiles. The attacker had only taken my watch and Sam's wallet. An onlooker had grabbed our things and given them to a paramedic. Sam's battery had gone flat a long time ago, but I hadn't canceled his service yet.

"You've reached the voice mail of Samuel Mathieu. I'm not available right now, but please leave your name and number and I'll get back to you as soon as I can."

I cried until my throat was sore, with my mouth wide open, until his pillow was drenched in tears and snot and saliva. I really needed to change the sheets, but the idea of washing even part of him away was enough to make me throw up with anxiety. I couldn't do this. How was I supposed to do this?

Then, a few days before I was supposed to go back to work, I couldn't stay in that bedroom a moment longer. I didn't know what came over me, but the urge to get out was so overwhelming I ran down the marble stars, almost slipping on the runner on the landing. I stood panting in the hallway, looking at my front door, where a pile of mail should've been gathering on the doormat. It was empty.

I opened the double doors to the living room. In Sam's favorite chair sat my mom, blanket over her knees, book facedown in her lap, asleep with her lips parted. Cleo lay stretched out on the couch, her feet stuffed under a fat pillow. I had no idea what time it was, but it was definitely not the middle of the night.

"Guys?"

Mom jerked awake and smacked her lips. "Oh, darling. Finally."

"How long have you been here?" I asked, keeping my voice down as I eyed Cleo. She was out like a light, and she looked awfully thin and tired. I tried to dredge up the slightest bit of concern for her, and couldn't.

I walked over to hug my mother. She patted me gently on the back before pushing me away. "We've been here for two days. If you hadn't come down by this evening, we'd have dragged you out of bed. Have you eaten? You look so skinny. And darling, no offense, but you need a shower. Desperately."

"Okay," I whispered, shamefaced. "I'll go do that now."

Mom rose to her feet. "Is it . . ." She wrung her hands. "Is it okay if I refresh your bed? I peeked into your room last night, and the smell is terrible."

"Yes," I said. "But you don't have to do it. I will."

She patted my shoulder. "Don't feel bad, Oliver. No one's blaming you for wanting to hang on. We're here for you, and we want to help." She smiled a little. "And trust me when I say I've washed worse. You go shower. I made lasagna, so I'll go turn on the oven, and I'll have your bed made by the time you're done."

She was right. When I stepped back into the bedroom, the stale smell hit me like a brick. In an attempt to hide at least some of it before Mom came upstairs, I opened the curtains and the windows, even though a light drizzle was falling. I found myself some fresh clothes—fighting the urge to reach for one of Sam's shirts—and turned toward the bathroom. As always, I had to wait forever for the water to heat in this old house. I vaguely wondered if I'd enjoy the novelty of having instant hot water in whatever new place I ended up renting.

Oh God, I was going to have to move. To someplace where Sam had never been, where his presence had never lit the rooms. I stepped under the stream of water to halt that way of thinking, even though it was still too cold. I shivered and waited for the heat to come.

One step at a time, Ollie.

I nodded and reached for the shampoo. "Okay, Sammy."

Cleo looked terrible by the time she went home, and I knew I should reach out to her and the others, see if they were okay, but I lacked the strength.

Mom had wanted to stay another night, but I sent her home with the promise I'd call first thing in the morning. I mentally prepared myself to return to real life: work, grocery shopping, and eating meals at regular times. Everywhere I went, people would look at me with pity. I'd have to smile and go on and pretend I was already healing, because no one liked to be reminded of death and loss for too long. And each day I'd come home to an empty place.

The huge living room felt small for once. The walls closed in on me, and my clothes were too tight. I struggled upright and ran into the kitchen, where I threw open the back door and breathed the summer air. Sweetly, agonizingly familiar, our garden, and all I wanted was to scream.

I kept my mouth shut. Silently I closed and locked the door. Time stretched out in front of me like a dark abyss. Just like that, the sleep that had given me solace for all these weeks became elusive.

From the bay window seats in my living room, I watched night fall. The vibe of the city around me changed, but I remained safely in my cocoon. To feel less lonely, I turned on the TV, but in my mind I walked through the house and thought of all the things I'd have to go through at some point. Decide what to keep, what to give away, and what to throw out. In a self-flagellating way it made me feel better. The thought that I'd have to part with his things fed an anger I had no idea how to deal with. It churned along with the guilt in my stomach. I tried to cry, and couldn't.

Am I already feeling less sad? I thought. When I reached within to find that hard core of hurt, that monster, I touched a tender scar. The gaping wound was gone. Surely I should mourn him for longer than this?

CHAPTER
THREE

"**D**o you think he sees us?" Cleo sat in the chair opposite mine, bare feet curled in my lap, and she managed to rub my belly with her toes.

"Sam? I don't know." Throngs of people passed by us. We'd left for Antwerp's city center at the busiest hour, and I felt like an exposed nerve. "Do we have to do this?" My head throbbed with lack of sleep, and my skin crawled with claustrophobia.

She eyed me darkly. "You haven't breathed fresh air in three and a half weeks. Yes, we do."

I scrunched up my nose at the diesel fumes wafting toward us. "I'd hardly call this fresh."

She huffed and ignored me as she sipped her coffee. We were sitting on the Groenplaats, outside one of the only cafés I really didn't like. The inside was huge and cold, designed to hold a lot of people. I preferred the cozy little treasures that were hidden throughout the city, with their rickety wooden tables and surprisingly delicious foods.

The terrace of this place was normally not so bad, but shoppers had descended en masse on Antwerp's July sales season. It seemed as if everyone stared at us while they sat packed around the tables, enjoying the summer weather.

I decided to ignore them all. "You doing okay, Cleo?" I asked. She looked better than she had the day before. Maybe all she'd needed was a good night's sleep.

"Yeah, I have a whole week off next week." She stretched her arms above her head with glee.

"How about Imran?"

She faltered for a second, then plastered on a smile so fake I could've peeled it off. "He's been great. He took the week off too. But this whole thing has been hard on him. We've all been friends for such a long time, but he understands that it's . . ."

"Extra hard on us," I finished.

"Oh, babe." She sat up so suddenly she gently hit me in the balls, and I made a squeaky noise. She gripped my hands tight. "I don't mean to imply that my hurt is as big as yours."

It's not; it can't possibly be, I thought, flinching at the anger behind the thought. I pushed it aside and took a deep breath. "I know that, Cleo. But you've been friends . . . You were friends with Sam as long as I was."

"Yeah." She stared out over the market square, and I saw her eyes swim.

Oh please God, don't start crying. "How's work?"

"Tough. I had trouble dealing with blood for a little bit there, but I'm doing better now."

For a second I wanted to tell her that every time I closed my eyes last night, I'd seen the blood bubble up out of Sam's wound all over again, just to see what she'd say. I looked out toward the crowd. "We should go out sometime."

Cleo's head whipped up, and she stared at me. "What?"

"Not to . . . not the Nine Barrels. I don't think I'll be able to go back there. But maybe dinner, or something. Get everyone together again. I don't want us to . . . splinter." I thought of Thomas for some reason, the look on his face as he'd wiped dried blood off my cheek.

"That's not a bad idea." She chewed her lip, and her eyes narrowed. "How about we do a barbecue at your place? Backyard. Like we used to."

"I don't know." *That's our place. Ours.* The anger caught me by surprise. I'd been incapable of feeling it until now. The idea of losing the house hadn't shaken me. Now, imagining anyone coming over and laughing and wandering around like they belonged . . . I studied my hands. They'd knotted themselves around my coffee cup, and I hadn't noticed it was still hot. My palms stung, so I let go. "I don't know how long I'll be living there."

"Oliver!" Cleo gaped at me. "You're not thinking about giving up that place, are you?"

I shrugged, confused by this urge to shock her, hurt her almost. What was I doing? She was my best friend, and I wanted to make her feel bad. "I don't know what's going to happen to the house. We weren't married yet. He had a will but . . ."

"Did he leave it to you in the will?"

"Yeah." It was his, it had been ours, but it didn't feel like it should ever be just mine.

"I'm sure you'll be fine. Don't go looking for trouble, Ollie. And, oh." She sat there with her hands covering her mouth, eyes finally spilling over. "Your wedding day," she whispered.

"Yeah." I lifted my coffee, but my hand shook so hard it spilled over the rim. I carefully set it down again. "It would've been this Saturday."

"I know. We got . . . we got the cancellation notice. Did you contact everyone? The caterers and stuff? Do you need me to do anything?"

I shook my head and looked away. I could see it in her eyes, the doubt and hurt that I hadn't asked her for help, but I'd needed to do it all by myself. For once, Cleo didn't press. We sat in silence and watched city life pass us by.

"Oh my God," Cleo said, pointing toward the square. "Look at that."

The benches placed around the Groenplaats were known for their homeless occupants during the day. On one of them, a disheveled, long-haired man with an unmistakable hard-on under his sweatpants was staring at a girl waiting for the tram. She didn't know where to look. Poor thing was maybe twelve or thirteen. My heart began to hammer in my chest, and I'd half risen to my feet when I saw someone stride toward the pervert.

"Hey!" My back straightened, and a smile lifted my cheeks. "Isn't that Thomas? Check him out!"

Cleo and I watched as Thomas ripped the guy a new one. He was too far away for us to overhear what he was saying, but his gestures and the man's hasty retreat were obvious enough. Thomas went to the girl, crouched beside her without touching her, and asked her something.

She nodded. He pointed to a policeman who was cycling up the street. She shook her head. He asked her something else. She nodded before she got on her tram.

By the time Thomas stood, Cleo and I had jumped to our feet, and we were cheering so loudly, he heard us. He gave us a quick smile. Then he saw who his audience was and bowed extravagantly. With a ridiculous swagger in his step, he walked up to us and bowed again when he stopped a few feet away from our table.

"A real knight in shining armor!" Cleo said, clapping her hands as she bounced. "What did you tell him?"

"You don't want to know," Thomas softly said. He always spoke pretty quietly. I'd liked that about him from the beginning. He wasn't timid. It was . . . soothing. His eyes fell on me, and he sobered. "Hi." He stuffed his hands in his pockets. "How are you?"

My heartbeat slowed. "Good," I said, and was shocked to realize I meant it. For a whole two minutes I had been free of the weight of death.

Cleo glanced between us. She smirked and sat down. "Join us," she said. "Want a drink?"

"Sure. Is that all right?"

I frowned at Thomas. "Of course. Why wouldn't it be?"

He shrugged lightly but wouldn't meet my eyes. I didn't get it.

"Hey." I put my hand on his shoulder, and he looked up. His dark eyes were a little bloodshot, as if he hadn't been sleeping well. "I'm sorry I never returned your calls, okay? I didn't mean anything by it. I was just . . ."

"Oh, I know that," he said and offered me a half smile. "It's fine." He was wearing his hair loose today, and he dragged his fingers over his scalp, lifting the thick strands off his shoulders and back. In the sun, the brown gleamed with gold and red.

The waiter interrupted us. I watched Thomas flirt with him, feeling the sadness creep up on me all over again. Life went on after death, sure. It just went on a little faster for the others than it would for me.

When the waiter turned his back, Cleo lifted her phone off the table and said, "Oh, Imran wants to meet me for a late lunch." I stared at her. There hadn't been a message on her phone. "See you guys later, okay?"

"Cleo—" I began, but she gave me a little wave, kissed Thomas on the cheek, and darted away.

"What was that about?" I turned to Thomas, who was fiddling with a napkin.

"No idea." He glanced at me, then went back to the napkin. "So . . . how have you been?"

How did I answer that? When I'd started accepting calls again the day before—from those who still bothered calling—I'd mostly fended off with a fake smile in my voice and an *"Okay, all things considered."* But this was Thomas. One of my best friends. Still, this whole situation felt really awkward, and I had no clue why.

"It's been a pretty shitty month," I said. He met my eyes, and I grinned weakly. "All things considered."

He snorted and shook his head lightly before he reached out and squeezed my arm. "I feel like I should've been there more," he said. "But I had no idea how—"

"I know." I patted his hand, and he let go. "It's fine, really. I'm . . . heartbroken, obviously. And for the past month I've basically buried myself under my blankets. But I can't go on like that." That was what people expected me to say, wasn't it?

The waiter interrupted us again, but this time Thomas thanked him absentmindedly and stirred his coffee. "Did Cleo drag you out of bed?"

I threw my hands in the air. "Literally. There were threats." He laughed, and I shrugged. "She looked pretty bad last time I saw her."

"You noticed that, huh?"

I looked at him, latching on to this chance to talk about anything but me. "You saw it too? What's going on?"

He stuffed some of his thick brown hair behind his ear and drank his coffee. "I don't know what I should tell you," he said. "I don't want to talk behind their backs, but there's been some trouble with Imran."

"What?" I leaned forward and pushed my empty cup aside. "What kind of trouble? Is he okay? He's not sick, is he?" Shit, I really had been completely self-involved.

"No, nothing like that. Ah man, I shouldn't be gossiping about this."

"You're not gossiping. Cleo would've told me, but she obviously thinks I need to be handled with care right now." I rolled my eyes.

"Well, she was convinced Imran had cheated on her with another nurse."

"No!" I gasped. "That little shit. I'm going to rip his balls off and—"

"Okay, whoa, no. He said he didn't, she didn't believe him, they broke up for a little bit, but they sorted it all out. Apparently he didn't cheat." To my utter astonishment, Thomas went puce to the roots of his hair.

"But that's not all."

"Um. No." He spun his coffee cup around and around and wouldn't look at me. "We, uh—" Thomas glanced at me and then looked toward the Groenplaats as if he was hoping he could go save another girl from harassment to get out of this conversation.

"Jesus, you're killing me here. Spit it out already!"

"We slept together," he whispered.

"You and Imran?" I squeaked.

"No." He laughed once, covering his face with his hands.

My mouth fell open. "You and *Cleo?*"

He nodded.

"Shit." I sat back, reached for my cup, realized it was empty, and drank from his instead. I gagged. "Oh my God, how many sugars did you put in here?"

He winced and let his hands fall away. "I was too nervous to pay attention."

"Nervous? Why?"

"I don't know, Ollie. I was afraid I wouldn't know what to say to you, that I wouldn't be able to be the friend you need right now. But what was I worried about? Five minutes and I'm spilling my darkest secret."

"Yeah, we're coming back to the friend bit in a minute. I can't believe *you slept with Cleo.*" I hissed that last part under my breath, and he flinched.

"I know, okay? Believe me, I've been beating myself up about it for a long time. I . . . I was lonely, and she was angry, and— I know she's been your friend forever, Ollie, but that girl is seriously messed up emotionally."

"Cleo? No, she's not! I mean, she's a character, sure. But she's got a heart of gold and she'd never hurt anyone on purpose."

"I know that, but she's also incredibly insecure and . . . you know what? That's not up to me to talk about. But yeah, Imran found out, and they're fighting. I don't think they'll break up, but you can imagine things have been . . ." He shrugged.

"Ah shit." I tilted my head to the sky. While I was caught up in my own grief, Thomas had been all alone. And in their own ways, Cleo and Imran must've been too.

"And for the record, the only friends I need right now are you, Cleo, and Imran. This doesn't have to be . . ." *Weird*, I almost said. But of course it would be weird. A huge chunk of me—of us—was gone. And this thing between the three of them would make things even weirder. Shit. What if we were falling apart? What if I lost them all?

A shiver ran down my spine. One half of me wanted to be left alone, and the other half was terrified my friends would do exactly that.

"Sure," he softly said. He bumped my knee with his and pulled away.

I stared into nothing. I needed to fix this somehow, but smoothing over quarrels had always been Sam's strength. "Can you take Monday off from work?" I asked him.

He blinked at me. "Next week? I guess. Summer holidays are pretty quiet at work."

"Okay." I picked up my phone and texted Cleo and Imran in one thread and said aloud, "Pack a bag with swim trunks and some hiking gear. We're going on a long weekend trip."

"Don't you have to go back to work?"

I gave him my best sad face. "I'm still mourning. I can take an extra day unpaid."

A slow smile began to light his face. "Welcome back, Ollie," he whispered as he gave me a one-armed hug. "I've missed you."

Warmth spread through my body. I realized how deprived of touch I'd been for the past month, after over a decade of having Sam's arms around me whenever I craved them.

"I'm not completely back yet," I admitted as I surreptitiously buried my nose in his shoulder. I missed the feel and smell of a guy so badly, I wanted to close my eyes and take a little nap in that circle of safety.

The first thing I did when I made it home was get in touch with Sam's parents. It was a grossly overdue phone call. My knees were trembling so hard, I had to sit down at the kitchen table as I listened to the dial tone.

"Martine Waterslagers," Sam's mom answered.

I sucked in a breath. "Martine? It's Oliver."

"Oh, Ollie. I'm so glad you called. I'm . . . Are you okay? We tried to get a hold of you, but—"

"I know. And I'm sorry I didn't return your calls. I was . . ." I trailed off. If there was anyone to whom I didn't have to explain how I'd been feeling, it was Sam's mother.

"I know, love. We completely understand, but there are some things we need to sort out. Are you ready . . . to talk about them?"

"Yes. I'm . . . That's why I'm calling. I mean, also to say I'm so sorry for the loss of your s-son."

She was quiet for a second, and I thought she was steadying her voice. "You don't have to tell me that. I know how much you loved him, and I know how much you're hurting too. Are you back at work? You could always come for dinner tonight."

"I'm not, no." My heart tripped with nerves. "But dinner sounds good."

"Let's say about seven?"

"Sounds good," I said, and my voice cracked. I winced and tried to cover it by clearing my throat.

"It's going to be okay, Oliver," Martine told me gently.

I murmured something trivial and ended the call.

For a while I sat and stared at the warm country kitchen we'd spent so many hours in. This house we'd shared for years had started to feel like a temporary place over the past month, like a dream that would dissolve as soon as I opened my eyes and returned to the real world.

But it wasn't a dream, and while it wasn't ours anymore, I knew Sam would always be here with me. In the paint we'd chosen and the off-white kitchen cabinets he'd picked out. In the grout between the bathroom tiles and the roses we'd planted together at the end of the yard. Suddenly the thought of having to leave all this behind suffocated me. I squeezed my eyes closed and tried to breathe past the constriction in my chest.

"I miss you so much," I whispered.

A breeze touched my face, and I glanced around. The window above the sink was cracked slightly, but I didn't remember opening it. Since I'd be going out that night, I closed and locked it. In the distance, a siren wailed, and I shut the noise out.

A strange energy crackled under my skin, light but undeniably there. I felt like I needed to do something. Although packing for this impromptu trip seemed like a good idea, I wandered up toward Sam's art room instead. It sat right under the roof and got hot in the summer but, because of opposing windows, remained bearable when there was a breeze.

It was stiflingly oppressive in there now, so I opened the windows and inhaled the fresh air as it mingled with the scents of paint and turpentine. The smell reminded me so much of Sam and how he'd always made me feel when I found him working on his art, paint-stained and focused. Arousal built in the depths of my stomach as I remembered how we'd ended up on the colorful tarp more than once, sticky with paint and our release, because I couldn't keep my hands off him.

The liquid heat in my belly felt strange at first. It had been almost a month since I'd experienced anything like it. At least I hadn't lost that. I vaguely planned to have a lazy evening with a bottle of wine, a hot bath, and my right hand soon.

Paintings lined the walls, some framed, some not, all stacked together to be given away, painted over, or thrown out. Sam never sold his work. That wasn't why he painted. I had no idea what to do with them all now. Even touching them seemed impossible. Maybe I'd leave them here and they'd be forgotten until, in fifty years' time, someone opened up the attic and found them.

In the middle of the room was his easel. On it stood a large covered painting: his gift to me for our wedding. I took a hesitant step forward and touched the white cloth. I closed my eyes and let myself imagine for a moment.

In another world, an alternate universe maybe, one where I hadn't insisted on going to the Nine Barrels, where we'd gone home and curled up in bed and made love until we fell asleep—in that world, I saw us standing here, our hands entwined, wedding rings still heavy, unfamiliar weights on our fingers.

Close your eyes, he'd say, and I'd obey him. I'd do anything for him, this handsome man whom I loved more than life itself. Maybe his tuxedo shirt would be unbuttoned. Maybe the bow tie would hang loose over his shoulders. Maybe his pupils would be large and his smile would be crooked the way it always was when he got a little inebriated. *Close your eyes*, and he'd guide me over and remove the cloth and stand behind me and hold me and say, *Open*.

I opened my eyes. I was all alone. Nothing had changed. The world hadn't shifted on its axis. I was still responsible for the death of the only person I'd ever loved with all my heart. The breeze ruffled my hair. I couldn't lift the cloth. Not yet.

Instead I went down to our bedroom and cried a little over the fresh sheets that smelled only of me now. I pulled one of his sweaters out of a drawer. I savored them like a pile of stolen candy. Only when I couldn't bear the loneliness did I take one out to smell and hold close. I knew his scent wouldn't last forever, so I was careful with it. Made sure I didn't get used to it, so every whiff of it was the sweetest torture.

When I had my breathing under control, I tucked the sweater back and closed the drawer tightly. I packed a bag for myself, indulged in spraying the clothes with Sam's cologne, and took a shower when I noticed my face was blotchy and puffed up.

I could drive to the Mathieu-Waterslagers household with my eyes closed, I'd been there so often over the years. They lived outside of Antwerp, in a village where cows still crossed the streets to their stables, and the farmer still brought milk to people's houses.

Their house was quaint but beautiful, surrounded by the most immaculate garden I'd ever laid eyes on. White roses climbed a trellis and provided a roof above the path that led toward the front door. I parked my car in front of it, pushed the little yellow gate open, and walked on a cloud of geranium scent.

Closer to the front door, mint grew in a tight bush, kept low to the ground. It sneaked between the steps up to the door. As I brushed it, I thought of summers spent in the south of France, like I always did. My parents never traveled farther than the Belgian coast, but once I became friends with Sam, his parents had taken me on their annual vacation every year. Even during those hot drives down the Autoroute du Soleil, our being together had seemed inevitable.

As kids we'd bounced in our seats for fourteen hours straight, giddy on excitement and whatever sugary treats we'd stuffed our faces with. As we grew older, the excitement had turned inward, to a darker, more forbidden place. A combination of yearning and fear that would lead us to find hot, dry places, the earth cracked from lack of moisture, the typical herbal scent thick in the air as we learned to know each other in whole new ways.

A bee buzzed through a bunch of lavender. Martine opened the door before I could knock.

She didn't say anything. She looked at me and began to cry as she threw her arms around me. I held her as she tried to speak, but it took her forever to get the words out.

"I'm so sorry," she managed eventually. "I promised myself I wouldn't do this, but seeing you is like seeing a little bit of him again."

I nodded as I tried to stop myself from crying. I vowed I'd come see her whenever I could, no matter where the future took me. These people had been in my life since I was ten years old. They were like a spare set of parents.

"Martine, let the boy inside."

I looked up to see Simon standing there. His eyes were a little damp, but otherwise he was smiling. He looked thinner. Older. I'd never know if Sam would have aged the same way. Martine let go of me and dried her eyes as Simon shook my hand. He held it fast between both of his for a long moment.

"It's good to see you," I said, starting to feel choked up again. Those damn Mathieu eyes.

"Let's get the awkward stuff out of the way first," Martine said as she guided me through their gorgeous villa. Simon followed us into the kitchen and gave me a Stella when he grabbed one for himself. I didn't particularly like that beer, but I said nothing and sipped it. Martine put grapes, cheeses, and crackers on the table. I would have protested, but this was what she always did when we came to visit. It was nice, in a way, to know some things never changed.

"We know Samuel left you the house," Simon said, "but we wanted to talk to you and see if we couldn't come to an agreement."

My spine stiffened. I set the beer bottle down on the table. I glanced at Martine, but she resolutely kept her eyes on whatever she was fiddling with by the cooker.

"What kind of agreement?" I asked carefully.

Simon pressed his lips together and swallowed hard. "We talked to a lawyer, and we stand a good chance to win if we contest the will."

I stared at him. "Contest Sam's will?" I asked, hating how small my voice sounded.

"Obviously we don't want it to come to that," Martine quickly said. "We just want to talk to you. See where you stand on the idea of giving up the house."

Simon sent her a badly concealed look of irritation. "The point is, it wasn't fair of my mother to cut me out of such a large part of my inheritance and pass it on to Samuel. I could've fought it harder back then, but Sam is my son . . ." He winced and took a sip of his beer. "But now it's being passed on to you while you two weren't even married yet. Can you see how that's not really fair?" He sighed and gave me a sympathetic look. "That house is far too big for just you anyway, Oliver."

My heart was thudding so hard I could see my chest move when I looked down. Sam had drawn up that will long before we had any kind of money to our names. There hadn't been any mention of his bank accounts in the will. So his money—a substantial amount—had gone to his next of kin, his parents. I hadn't minded, at the time. With a roof over my head and a steady income of my own, the money had seemed trivial.

"What—what do you suggest?" I croaked. Part of me thought he was right. The house was too big for me, and maybe it shouldn't be mine. It'd been in their family for generations. But the idea of giving it up . . .

"Maybe we should do this some other time," Martine said. She stood by the cooker, a dripping spatula forgotten in her hands.

"We want to sell it and give you half of the profit," Simon said. "But we won't make you move until you've found something you like. You can pay us a little rent."

Until he mentioned the word "sell," I had felt completely numb. Now, a low-grade rage burned in my belly. They weren't even planning on keeping it? I would have to pay to live in my own house?

I lifted my head. Simon looked slightly mulish while Martine looked scared. "What happens if I say no?"

"We go to court." Simon's voice hardened. "We don't want to take that route, but we will if we have to, and it will cost us both a lot of money, Oliver. So think about that carefully."

"If all this had happened a month later, the house would've gone to me anyway and you wouldn't have been able to fight it."

"But you weren't married." Simon's fist was tight around his beer bottle. "We're trying to be reasonable."

"Simon," Martine said, pale and on the verge of tears.

My heart beat harder, faster, the blood thrumming through my veins. "You want me to leave the house that was ours. That we were going to share for the rest of our lives. And you expect me to be happy with a lump of money?" I shook my head. "It's my home."

"Ollie," Martine implored, her eyes darting between me and her husband. "Please don't make any hasty decisions. Think about it first."

I nodded slowly. My eyes felt dry and gritty. I couldn't even tell anymore if that meant I was about to cry or if I'd completely run out of tears. I whispered, "What do you think Sam would say if he knew about this?"

Martine began to sob quietly, and Simon gave me an angry look. "Maybe you should go." Simon stood. "And think about this, before either of us says anything we'll come to regret."

I opened my mouth to snarl something mean, but I felt the ghost of a handprint on my shoulder, the whisper of a breath against my ear. *Easy now.* I rose to my feet. Without saying another word, I left.

I got in my car, drove a hundred yards, and pulled over. I stared into nothing. This was a side of Simon I'd never seen. Back when Grandma had left the house to Sam, he'd dealt with most of the fallout. I knew at the time it'd been happening, but it hadn't seemed all that urgent. Not to me, at least. We'd both been young and on the verge of starting our adult lives together. Back then I didn't care what house we lived in. Now, thinking of Sam facing his parents like this made my stomach turn.

With shaking fingers I dialed Cleo's number. I told her the whole story and finally began to cry with anger.

"I don't even want it!" I yelled. "I don't want the house or the money. I want Samuel. I want my *Sam*." And it hit me, truly hit me, maybe for the very first time with full force, that I'd never, ever see him again. That his body had been burned, his ashes collected and spread on the wind in the backyard of his parents' house. He was gone. Completely, utterly, gone.

I heard Cleo cry on the other end of the line. "I know," she croaked. "I know, honey. But don't give up on the house. You do want it. You love that place."

I felt terrible after I calmed down. Both in body and in mind. These were his parents, and I'd expected to share my grief with them. Instead I dragged it around all by myself.

"I'm sorry," I whispered, and Cleo sobbed in my ear.

"Don't be. They're being assholes. You loved him so much. It should be a relief to them to know he was loved like this. That he had someone like you in his life. Instead they're ruining his memory."

"Maybe I should just let it go," I mumbled, suddenly exhausted. "The house is too big for me. They're right. Maybe it's not meant to be mine."

"Well," Cleo said firmly. "Samuel disagreed."

 CHAPTER
FOUR

"I'm coming!" I yelled the next morning, as if Thomas could hear me through the house, onto the street, and into the car he was honking from. I hastily poured coffee into a travel mug, nearly tripped over my bag, almost forgot to turn off the coffee machine, had to go back for my keys, and finally pulled the heavy front door shut behind me.

Thomas had managed to squeeze his Peugeot into a spot the size of a handkerchief. I hurried over, tossed my bag in the trunk, and claimed the passenger seat when I saw it was empty.

"Hey!" I said, then noticed the backseat was empty too. I met Thomas's steady gaze. "Where are Imran and Cleo?"

"They're driving separately," Thomas said, and he winced slightly. "Cleo said they had a lot to talk about."

"Oh." I settled in my seat and pulled the safety belt across my chest. "Well, that's good, right? I mean, maybe they'll have argued themselves out and made up again by the time we get to the Ardennes."

"Or they'll kill each other on the way there."

"They won't." I hesitated. "Will they?"

Thomas gave me a crooked smile. A flop of his thick brown hair fell over his left eye, and he pushed it away. "No, probably not. Listen, Cleo told me what happened with Sam's parents yesterday. I'm really sorry."

"Yeah, thanks."

"Are you okay?"

I shrugged. "It stinks. But I'm not rolling over without a fight." I looked back at our—my—white front door, and my resolve tightened. "This is my home."

"Yes, it is," Thomas said. "And if there is any way I can help, you let me know." I nodded but said nothing, so he let it go. "You have the address? I can put it in my phone."

"Oh, yes." I lifted my ass and groped in the back pocket of my jeans until I managed to extricate the rumpled brochure.

DON'T MISS OUT ON KAYAKING AND HIKING IN THE ARDENNES, it read.

I spelled out the address, and then we were on our way to Bouillon, a beautiful town in the French-speaking half of Belgium.

My first vacation without Sam.

Just like that, the hustle and bustle of the morning was forgotten, and my good mood evaporated completely. I stared out of the window as we left my house behind.

"He would've wanted this for you," Thomas said. His hand hovered in my direction, but he pulled it away again and put it on the shift stick. "To get away for a bit, I mean."

"I know," I said. It didn't comfort me at all.

In no time we hit the E19 and cruised along with a minimum of traffic—for Belgium. Thomas didn't say much, and I preferred it that way. He hummed to the music every now and again, but seemed to catch himself each time. It never took long before his fingers began to tap on the steering wheel and he was humming again. He had a playlist going with all my favorites. The National, Editors, Iron & Wine. I wondered if he'd known, or if our tastes were really that similar.

After about an hour, I was humming too, and we softly sang the lyrics to my favorite song together. We weren't looking at each other, but I could tell from the note in his voice that he was smiling.

"Why Bouillon?" he asked when we had passed Brussels.

"I went there on a school trip once," I said. "I was a sulky prepubescent boy who didn't care about anything." Anything but Samuel. "But I cared about that place. I didn't tell anyone, of course."

"Of course," Thomas said. I glanced at him, and he was grinning at the road ahead.

"It's beautiful," I simply said. He nodded, like he didn't need anything but my word to believe me.

The playlist came to an end. Because the silence felt so natural, neither of us noticed until we drove into Namur and hit a traffic jam.

Thomas fiddled with the radio for a bit to see if he could get an update on whether it was an accident or everyday madness, but in the end he smiled sheepishly at me.

"My French is shit," he admitted. "Flemish and English are the only languages I can manage."

"I can listen," I said, turning the volume up a little. "Sam's—" I choked on his name, and Thomas's expression was full of sympathy. For some reason that made me push on. "Sam's family on his mother's side is from Dinant. When his grandparents were still alive, they came over sometimes, and they were very strict about him being able to speak French. Every Saturday his parents spoke only French all day long." I shrugged. I'd been subjected to that from age ten, and it'd helped me tremendously in French class.

"That's pretty cool," Thomas said. "My mom's American."

I whipped my head around and stared at him. "I had no idea," I said. He spoke so very little of his family.

"Yeah. Dad met her when he went on a cross-country camping trip when he was twenty-one. He traveled from New York to LA, met her in Chicago, and she tagged along the rest of the way. They dated long-distance for a year while she finished college, and then she came over here to work at the American embassy."

"But that's in Brussels," I said. "How did you end up in Bazel of all places?"

The traffic jam moved a little, and he eased off the clutch. "She went back to the US when I was five. My dad was heartbroken. He couldn't stay in Brussels anymore, so he got a new job, new house, new everything. He went into construction and made good money, really. He's pretty pleased with his retirement anyway."

"Your dad raised you all alone."

"Pretty much."

"That can't have been easy."

Thomas shrugged, but I saw the ache in his eyes. "I don't remember any different. I don't remember her apart from the odd photograph. She never contacted me."

"I'm sorry." I put my hand on his over the stick shift and squeezed lightly. He offered me a small smile.

"Can't miss what you don't know," he said, but I wasn't so sure about that.

"Thanks for telling me." I realized I was still holding his hand and let go. "I wondered why you didn't talk much about your parents."

"What about you? You lost your dad young too, didn't you?"

I nodded and stared out of the window. He misunderstood my silence.

"I'm sorry." He turned the radio down. "I didn't mean . . . to remind you. Of more pain."

"It's okay." A raindrop landed on my window, and I traced it as it raced down. More drops fell. Traffic sped up, and instead of rolling down, the rain ran sideways. "That's an old pain. I'm used to it. I still miss him, but . . . he didn't . . . die in a nice way. If there is such a thing. When he was gone, it was a relief." I'd had a long time to say good-bye to my dad, at the end, he was so ready to go, it hurt to see him fight to breathe.

"Was he sick?"

"Yeah. Colon cancer." I didn't want to talk or even think about that, because facing the fact that someday that could be me . . . I wasn't strong enough just then.

"I'm sorry, Oliver."

I gave him a little grin. "It's okay, Thomas."

He laughed. "This is all very heavy, isn't it?"

"Yes. Do you think Cleo and Imran have killed each other yet? Maybe I should text them."

"I bet they've pulled off the road to screw in the backseat."

I'd been reaching for my phone and gingerly put it away again. "That's a visual I don't need."

He looked at me curiously before turning his attention back to the road. "So you've never? With a girl?"

"God no." I shuddered. "Never even considered the notion. Besides, when would I have? I was with Sam from . . ." My voice died out.

"When you were sixteen, I know." He shifted in his seat. His voice sounded odd when he said, "It's going to come back to this for a long time, isn't it?"

This? Did he mean pain? Loss? Five minutes of reprieve before remembering I should be in pieces, not enjoying a mini road trip with a good friend?

"Yeah," I said, grinding my teeth. "It's going to come back to this for a long time."

Thomas sent me a contrite look, but I didn't want his apology so I looked away. When I didn't say anything else, he turned the music back on. One song in and he was humming again. I relaxed a little and closed my eyes.

I dreamed of Sam. There'd been snatches of him in my sleep before, but not this vivid. The scene felt like an overexposed photograph, with a sharp light—the sun?—surrounding us in a crisp white halo. He didn't say anything, and neither did I. I couldn't even tell where we were. I thought I felt sand under my feet, and maybe there was the taste of salt in the air. My head was resting on his shoulder in a way that would be uncomfortable soon, but in that moment I didn't feel it. The light danced around us, and we watched it. I felt his warmth. I heard his breath. Forever and ever we remained suspended in timeless silence. Peace I hadn't experienced in weeks enveloped me. Then his touch—on my cheekbone, down my jaw. His thumb skirted my chin.

"*Ollie?*"

"Hmm." I smiled. His voice sounded deeper, softer than I remembered.

"*Ollie?*"

His fingers in my hair.

"Ollie, we're here."

I sat up with a jerk and stared into Thomas's eyes. "Oh. Shit. I dozed off. Ow." I rubbed my neck, and he winced.

"Yeah, you didn't look comfortable, but I figured you could use the sleep."

"Thanks." I felt self-conscious for a moment, wondering if my contentment had bled through into the real world. I waited for the crash of reality, but it didn't come down as hard as it had in the past month.

Thomas still stared at me, worry lines creasing his forehead. His deep, dark gaze traced my face. I could tell he wanted to ask me if I was okay, and I was oddly grateful he didn't. He'd pulled his hair into a bun at the back of his head. A few wisps escaped and drifted along his slightly stubbled jaw. Which was when I noticed the windows were open. The sweet herby fragrance that spilled into the car betrayed we were indeed no longer in Antwerp.

I broke the strange moment and looked around me. Bouillon sits tucked in the arm of the river Semois, and over it presides the gorgeous Château de Bouillon. On my school trip years ago, we'd wandered the dripping underground passages that disappeared into the hillsides, imagined the worst of dank prison cells buried in the bowels of the beast. It'd been built in nine hundred and something—I couldn't remember the exact year—with Godfried of Bouillon its most famous occupant. We used to like imagining what it would've been like to live in the Dark Ages. It had all sounded wonderful to two adventurous little boys. Knights, horses, romanticized wars. Now I realized it must've been pure hell.

These days people could visit the castle at night if they liked to scare themselves, or during the day to see bird shows with hawks and eagles. I didn't think it bore much resemblance to the reality of the castle's heyday.

"We can go see it if you want," Thomas said, and I startled guiltily. I'd almost forgotten he was there.

"Yeah," I said, even though I didn't want to diminish my perfect childhood memories by realizing the castle wasn't as grand and impressive as I'd thought back then. I smiled at Thomas. "Maybe." I took a closer look around. "So this is it?"

"Yep." He grinned. "You did good."

We were parked on the Boulevard de Vauban, the road that followed the river. On one side the water looped around the town, while on the other side, buildings and houses hugged the foot of the hill upon which the castle perched like a slumbering dragon. Our apartment waited in one of the white houses to our right. To be honest, I'd spent a lot more money on it than I usually would, mostly because it was high season and everything else was booked, but also because I wanted my own bedroom.

"Ready?" I asked Thomas. When he nodded, I stepped out of the car.

The apartment that was ours was a top one, a sea of white and gleaming silver fixings. When we entered, we walked under a huge arch that led into the kitchen, which was open plan and gave way to a living room with a view that made us both gasp. The river seemed to run at our feet underneath the floor-to-ceiling windows. Beyond that lay the impossible green of one of Belgium's biggest forests.

"Jesus," Thomas breathed. I didn't think he noticed he was clutching my arm, and I didn't draw his attention to it. When I turned to him to share the ecstasy of the view, I saw he was pale as a ghost.

"Oh my God. Are you okay?"

Sweat pearled on his lip and his suitcase slipped from his fingers.

"Yeah. I'm really..." His eyes flicked to mine and away again. "I'm a bit afraid of heights."

"A bit? We're not anywhere near the window!" I wanted to laugh, but he started to turn green. "Okay. Look at me." His dark-chocolate eyes zeroed in on mine. "Are you fine with stairs?"

He laughed reluctantly. "Yes."

"Good. Let's go pick your bedroom, and I'll see what I can do about these windows."

He bit his lip. "I'm being ridiculous, aren't I?"

"No, man." I gripped his shoulder and turned him around, dropping my own luggage so I could pick up his. "Everyone has something they're afraid of."

For a second I worried he'd ask me what my fear was, but he didn't. Maybe he didn't need to.

The staircase that led up from the kitchen to an open landing was a work of art, a spiral made of oak, sanded and stained with extreme precision. We found him a bedroom that faced the hill and the castle—it was actually the biggest and nicest one, but Imran and Cleo would have to deal. While he got settled, I hurried back downstairs and drew the huge voile curtains across the windows. We'd still be able to see the view, but it was less *there*. I grabbed my own suitcase and picked the smallest bedroom, since it was just me.

Above the bed hung a gorgeous painting of the view Thomas would be avoiding so desperately. Such an exact copy had most likely been painted by someone who'd stayed here at least.

Sam would've liked it, the rough oil brushstrokes from up close, the fragility of the leaves on the trees from afar.

I wish you were here, I thought.

I know, he said in my mind.

The room was nice, but hot, since it sat under the roof, and I opened one of the slanted windows. I unloaded my suitcase into the white double-doored closet, changed into a fresh T-shirt, washed my face, and brushed my teeth. The four-poster bed with its gently swaying curtains and thick yellow bedding looked really inviting, but instead of falling face-first into blissful oblivion, I made my way downstairs.

Cleo and Imran still weren't there, but I found Thomas rummaging around in the kitchen.

"Not much here," he said. "We have water and some cans, but nothing fresh."

"Want to go find a store while we wait for the others?"

He emerged from the fridge. He'd wet his hair and pulled it back in a ponytail that sat low on his neck. A couple of strands stuck to his throat, and a droplet of water was running down his clavicle and into the V of his shirt. Thomas had the nicest body I'd ever seen on a guy, and it was easy to understand why he had no trouble going home with someone new whenever we went out.

"You look better," I said.

"Yeah, I feel better. Want me to google a supermarket?"

"Let's go out and walk until we find something."

He clutched his heart. "No GPS?"

I laughed. "It'll be an adventure."

 CHAPTER
FIVE

We wandered through Bouillon, and I felt that same sense of gentle happiness I'd experienced when I was eleven years old. Something about the water and the hills and the greenery called to me, along with the ever-present shadow of the protective castle reigning over it all.

"You're smiling a lot," Thomas said. When I glanced at him, I noticed his cheekbones were growing red. I needed to remember to buy some sunscreen.

"It's good to get away for a bit." The wind tugged at my hair and blew it in my eyes. I should get it cut soon, really. But Sam had always liked it longer.

Thomas shoved his hands in the pockets of his cargo shorts. "Are you doing okay? I mean, I feel like we haven't talked about . . . Sam."

"I know. It's still hard. I understand he's not coming back, but sometimes I feel like he's here. I'll be in the kitchen making dinner and I'll be ready to ask him something before I remember he's not around anymore. And I miss—" Jesus. Was I really going to say this?

I averted my eyes. Kayakers made their way down the Semois. I wished I could join them, flow on the current of the river until there was nothing but me, the water, and the hills.

"What?" Thomas asked me gently. "What do you miss?" He drew me to a halt in front of an alcove between two old, tall houses. They were stately, huge, bricked sentinels, standing watch over the decades coming and going. A chocolatier to the right made the place smell like heaven.

I didn't say anything, but the way I hugged myself must've given me away.

"Oh, Ollie," Thomas whispered. He reached for me, but I stepped back. I didn't even know why, really. A hug would have been better than the best piece of chocolate from next door, but something stopped me.

"I'm okay," I said. His expression shuttered, and I was sorry for it. I squeezed his arm. "You're a great friend, Thomas. It means a lot that you're here."

"Of course." He smiled at me. "Always."

We continued on our way in a not exactly comfortable, but easy enough silence.

"There." I pointed toward the end of the road. "That looks like a little outdoor market."

"Let's check it out."

We wandered the market stalls as the day wound down. The fresh produce was nearly gone, but it was nice to walk through stands and inhale the relaxed atmosphere, so different from Antwerp's beehive madness. On the way back, we stopped in a little grocery store and got some more essentials. By the time we made it to the apartment, I deeply regretted not taking the car. The sharp plastic handles of the shopping bags dug into my palms, and I was pretty out of breath when we reached the third floor.

"Next time Imran and Cleo can do the shopping," I said, and Thomas laughed.

"Speaking of, where are they?"

"I'm going to call Cleo."

Thomas began to put the groceries away, and I ran upstairs to find my charging phone in the bedroom. I had two missed calls from Cleo but no voice mails, so I figured whatever had happened wasn't too urgent. She answered on the second ring.

"I'm so sorry," she said, "but we're not going to get there until tomorrow, Ollie."

"Oh, is everything all right?"

"Yes, fine. We had a little, uh, complication."

I sat down on the bed and stared out of the window. The sun was beginning to set over Bouillon, casting the hills and trees in a rosy glow. "What kind of complication?"

"I'll have to owe you an explanation. For now. I'm sorry."

"Okay . . ." I waited, but the silence thickened and turned awkward. "Are you sure you're all right? I mean . . . Thomas told me what happened between you two. You're not breaking up, are you?"

"No." Cleo's voice softened. "No, we're not breaking up."

"Okay, well, that's good. So we'll see you guys tomorrow? It's gorgeous here. We already picked our rooms, by the way, but I left you the middle one. Did you know Thomas is afraid of heights?"

Cleo was silent for a moment. Then she slowly said, "Yes, Oliver. I knew that. We all knew that. How did you not?"

"It . . . never came up? How did you know?"

"From when we went to Walibi? And he refused to go on the Dalton Terror?"

"Oh. I think I was . . . a bit distracted that day."

Cleo laughed. "Yeah, I don't blame you. Only Sam could make a marriage proposal at a theme park romantic."

"It was, wasn't it?" I asked with a grin on my face.

"Yes, it really was."

I thought we'd say good-bye, but Cleo went on. "Ollie? You know how Thomas never really got into a relationship with anyone?"

I frowned a little, still too caught up on the memory of Sam, my beautiful, sophisticated Sam, kneeling in the middle of a roller coaster ride queue of *all* places. "Yeah?"

"Well . . ." She sighed. "Never mind."

"What? You think he found someone?"

"Maybe," she said. "I'll see you tomorrow, okay? Probably around eleven."

"Okay. If we're not here, I'll leave the key under the doormat."

"Yeah, because no burglar ever thinks to look there."

"Oh, shush."

Cleo laughed and hung up. I stayed where I was for a minute, running the conversation through my head. Had Thomas met someone? And how had I missed the fear-of-heights thing? My stomach felt strange and unsettled when I left my room. Thomas sat on the far-end couch, away from the window, and I could see him from the top of the stairs.

"It's just us for tonight," I said. "Want to go out for dinner?"

He looked up at me, head resting against the couch. His eyes were obsidian and unfathomable in the semidarkness. "Just you and me?"

"Um." I faltered halfway down the steps. "Yeah. Do you mind?"

"No." He shifted in the seat, and I could see his face better. He gave me a tight-lipped smile. "Not at all. But we bought all that food. I could make the fettuccine?"

"Sure."

"So why are they not coming down today?"

I shrugged. "Something came up."

I joined him in the kitchen and nursed a glass of white wine as he rolled turkey meatballs. I offered to help him, but he declined with a wicked little smile and started to chop shallots and garlic like a pro.

"Where'd you learn to do that?"

"I dated a chef for a while." He glanced over his shoulder and grinned. "There's something very hot about a woman who knows her way around a set of knives." I watched his hands as he worked the knife. They were strong, but oddly slender for a man his size. His fingernails were clean, broad, and blunt. "She taught me."

"Well, you can be the designated cook for the weekend."

"Sure. I don't mind. You don't cook at all?"

"I do, but Sam used to say cleaning kitchens was a waste of time when all we did was work during the day. So I usually made really simple meals."

"That makes sense," Thomas said mildly.

He grabbed a cast-iron pan, heated it, and tossed in a bunch of chopped peanuts. While those toasted, he snapped the ends of the peas and rinsed them. He removed the peanuts from the pan. He poured olive oil into it, waited while it heated, and tossed in the shallots and garlic. I was mesmerized. Within minutes the kitchen smelled so fragrant, my stomach gave an impatient growl. I was happy the noise of the exhaust fan drowned it out. I watched as he moved with spare grace and confidence. His shoulder muscles bunched under his T-shirt as he stirred the garlic, and just like that my mouth ran away with me.

"So do you prefer boys or girls?"

Thomas nearly dropped the fresh pasta he'd been about to toss in a boiling pot of water. "I . . . What?" He gave me a wide-eyed stare, and my cheeks heated.

"I'm sorry. That was super inappropriate. I was . . . curious. I mean, you obviously enjoy cooking, and I was wondering why you never had a steady relationship and—" *Oh God, stop talking.* "Never mind. Shit, can we pretend I didn't say anything?"

I couldn't read the look he gave me, but he laughed a little and turned back to the burner. "I don't have a preference," he said. "Sometimes I find myself attracted to a girl I meet, and sometimes it's a boy. I don't have any control over it. And I guess I'm not . . . ready for a relationship."

I worried my lip. I'd offended him somehow, and I had to bite back another apology. I wished he'd meet my eyes. "That's fine, obviously." I cringed at my stupidity but pushed on. "I was wondering if that's something you'd ever want, and who you'd want it with. But that's none of my business."

Thomas stopped stirring whatever he was stirring. "Well," he said. "I certainly don't want to be alone for the rest of my life. I haven't been able to convince anyone to stick with me so far."

You haven't tried, I nearly said, but I managed to keep my mouth shut. "Food smells good," I said weakly, and he laughed.

"Yeah, maybe I'll lure someone in with my cooking." He planted a plate in front of me. Fettuccine with snap peas, peanuts, and a delicate white sauce that made my nostrils flare. I took a bite as he watched me.

I moaned and closed my eyes. "Sold," I said, and when I opened my eyes, he was staring at me like I'd said something wrong again. "Uh, it's really nice, I mean."

He nodded and turned away to plate his own food.

I didn't understand what I was doing wrong, but it was something. "My dad was a good cook too," I told him. "Mom did all the work around the house, but Dad was responsible for grocery shopping and cooking. We were a bit lost when he died. I think my mother ate scrambled eggs and toast for dinner for months."

"Did you get on well with your parents?"

I shrugged. "We didn't fight or hate each other or anything, but we weren't close like Sam's family." Dull pain stabbed my chest, but I ignored it. "I actually have a brother who is ten years older than I am. I never see him or talk to him. I'm closer to my mom these days, though." Maybe because she knew what it was like to lose the person you loved.

Thomas sat beside me at the kitchen island. "I had no idea. I thought you were an only child."

"No, but I may as well have been. By the time I was seven, he was away at college, and I never really saw him much after that."

"What does he do?"

"He's an insurance broker or something. I'm not actually sure."

"Why did you fall out?"

"I don't think it was one specific thing. I remember he used to hate it when our parents paid attention to me. He kicked me once when I was a little baby."

"Aw jeez, Ollie. That's awful."

I shrugged. "It's not like I remember it."

I watched him take small bites from his food. As he bent forward, a thick strand of hair sprang loose from the tight bun. He reached behind him and undid it so a brown curtain covered his face. Without thinking, I lifted my hand and touched it.

"I don't think I've ever seen hair this thick on a guy," I said, and he went still.

"Yeah, I have my mother's hair. Dad has thick hair too, but nothing like this." He pulled his hair back again in a ponytail, and I let it slip from my fingers.

I squinted at him. "You ever think about cutting it?"

"All the time." He wasn't smiling anymore.

How did I keep messing up? I was missing something, and I didn't get it. Did he not want to be here alone with me? Did he feel awkward because of Sam's death?

Or was I acting inappropriately?

I sat back and stirred my pasta. "The food's really tasty," I repeated lamely, and stopped trying to make conversation.

Imran and Cleo arrived sometime the next morning, but I wasn't there to see them. If the world were a fair place, I'd have been at home right then. Probably tired after a nervous, sleepless night, but wired on adrenaline as I got dressed in a tuxedo for our big day, and Sam did the same.

The previous night with Thomas had unsettled me, made me question a friendship I'd counted on for years. I didn't want to spend the morning with him moving awkwardly around me, not knowing what to say. So I'd risen bright and early, put on my hiking boots, and found a trail that led up to the castle and beyond it. I climbed the hill and found a peaceful spot where I could watch the town wake.

Had I counted on my friendships though? Or had I lived in a bubble of bliss with Samuel, only surfacing a few nights a week to socialize and have fun? I hadn't been there for their troubled times.

Around nine my phone had buzzed, but I didn't look at it until past ten.

You okay?

Thomas. I sighed and swiped my thumb across the screen. His profile photograph was an off-center picture of him, laughing at something to his right. He was really gorgeous, in a rugged way. Samuel had been distinguished and elegant, but a little unavailable looking to people who didn't know him. Thomas, however, was lovely in a comforting, I-can't-stop-looking-at-you sort of way.

I closed my eyes and sighed. What was I doing here? Pretending I could move on? After one whole month? The ache for Sam burned in my veins. The scar inside me hurt like a fresh bruise. I never knew grief could fluctuate like this, allowing me to feel fine one day and wrecked the next.

I thought of Sam's painting in the attic. I thought of the tuxedos hanging in our closet, packed away in suit bags now that we'd never wear them. I knew what I was doing here. I was hoping being with my friends, away from home, would distract me from the horrible truth. My phone buzzed again.

I know what day it is today. Please tell me you're okay.

I'm fine.

Then come home. Cleo and Imran are here.

Part of me wanted to hide for the entire day, but what good would that do? It was just another day, an insignificant moment that would be part of my blurry past soon. Not the happiest time of my life. That had been snatched away from me for good.

I got back to the apartment at noon, finding the three of them on the balcony, eating tapas and drinking wine. Thomas sat with his back safely tucked against the wall, as far away from the railing as possible.

A lull fell in the conversation when I joined them, and while I didn't think they'd been talking about me, I knew what they were all thinking now. Cleo was the first to approach me.

"Ollie," she whispered and hugged me.

"It's fine. It's just another day."

"But it's not," Imran said. "You can't pretend it doesn't mean anything."

"We thought . . . we could do something." Thomas rose to his feet. "A little ceremony of our own. To remember him."

I shook my head. "I don't—"

"You need to share your grief, Ollie. Or you're never going to get over it."

"Maybe I don't want to get over it," I said. "Maybe I don't want to forget."

"This isn't about forgetting." Thomas reached into his pocket. "It's about remembering."

I stared at the white velvet pouch in his hand. With trembling fingers I took it from him and opened it. Two heavy platinum rings dropped into my palm, cold and glittering in the midday sun. I covered my mouth, afraid of the sound that might come out.

"Wait," Imran said. "Why do you have those? I was his best man." And Cleo had been my "best lady."

"He thought you'd forget them with your brain still half stuck in the hospital," Cleo said. "Or that you'd get called in for surgery and you'd forget to hand over the rings to me and they'd be standing at the altar, ringless."

Thomas was trying not to laugh at Imran's outraged expression but failed. "I'm sorry," he said—to me or Imran, I didn't know.

"No, you're right." I closed my fingers around the rings. "Let's go remember him. I know just the place."

I wasn't a religious person, but when I'd visited the Abbaye de Clairefontaine as an eleven-year-old boy, I'd been awestruck.

The church and cloister stood regally by the side of the Semois River, with a very green wall of forest at their backs and no houses nearby. The Cistercian sisters lived there and offered a space for peaceful retreat to those who wanted it.

When we left the apartment, everyone had been pretty subdued, but as we walked onto the grounds of the abbey, the silence grew almost reverent. Because I figured there was no hurry, we visited the church, browsed the little gift shop, and then walked the grounds until I found the spot I'd been looking for. A tiny beach hugged the shore of the Semois, and when I took off my shoes and socks, everyone else followed suit.

"So when I came here when I was eleven, Sam was here too," I said to no one in particular. "We were in the same class that year. In fact I think that was the last time. After that we were always in different classrooms. We'd snuck away from the tour guide and stuck our hot feet in the water. We'd been walking all day and were . . . tired of it, I guess." I walked up to the water and let it lap at my toes. "I remember having these weird feelings for him. He was my friend, but . . . at the same time I thought things about him that were confusing and a little bit scary and . . . he knew. I didn't think anything of it at the time, but he used to look at me in a certain way and tell me everything would work out fine. Even then he was looking out for me. Protecting me. And he was right. It did turn out fine. For a while." I fell silent, having to take a moment to let the burn in my throat subside. A hand came to rest on my back, and I didn't have to look to know it was Thomas. "I think he saved my life that night," I whispered. "He stepped between us, and the guy stabbed him. I think it should've been me. It should've been—"

"Oh, Ollie." Cleo wriggled her way under my shoulder and wrapped her arms around me. The hand on my back slid to my neck and squeezed slightly. "You can't think like that," she whispered.

"I know," I said. "I know." But in my darkest hours I wished that it'd been me. Sometimes I couldn't help feeling like Sam had it easy. He didn't feel any pain anymore, didn't have to go through the drudgery of getting up in the morning, or enduring those moments in the night when nothing seemed worth continuing for. I couldn't tell my friends that though. I couldn't tell anyone how I sometimes felt.

"He's gone and I'm here and that means I have to go on for as long as I need to. I . . ." I looked out over the river, the current sweeping past us and licking at our toes. "I miss you so much, Sammy. I'll never forget you. I'll never love anyone the way I loved you."

Cleo gently let go of me, and Imran hugged me and patted me hard on the back. Everyone said a few words after that, apart from Thomas, who looked too choked up to say anything at all. I pulled the white velvet pouch from my pocket and let the heavy platinum rings slide into my palm. For a fraction of a second I considered throwing them in the water, but I didn't. I'd have them turned into a necklace. Something simple and elegant, with maybe an infinity sign or something. I ran my thumb over the smooth metal of the smaller ring. I'd never tried it on. And I never would.

We stood at the water for a while longer. By the time we left, I felt oddly . . . cleansed. I even suggested going out for drinks that night, and everyone perked up—apart from Thomas, who remained subdued all night. Regardless of his near-silence, he pulled a pretty girl called Marjory and ended up bringing her home with us.

We drank more wine on the balcony—Thomas staying safely against the wall—until I was too tired to keep my eyes open. This day hadn't gone the way I wanted. In a different world, I'd be alone with Sam now. We'd retreat to our bedroom, where we'd make love as husband and husband, till death do us part. The death part wasn't supposed to come first, but I could do nothing but go on, one foot in front of the other.

# CHAPTER
SIX

I couldn't sleep, which was turning into a habit. Foreign bed, no one beside me. Too much strong coffee in the afternoon with added wine in the evening, resulting in a full bladder. That was why I heard the noise and crept out of my room to peer over the balcony leading to the stairs. I couldn't see much at first, but I heard something again, so I stayed where I was until my eyes adjusted to the darkness. I didn't think anyone was breaking in, but maybe someone else was suffering from insomnia. We could keep each other company.

Making sure I trod carefully on the creaky landing so I didn't wake anyone else, I eased along, barefoot and wearing nothing but my boxers, and looked down into the kitchen. No one. I shuffled the other way so I could see the couch tucked away from the huge windows. And what I saw took my breath away.

Marjory was straddling Thomas, both of them buck naked, their hair hanging loose and sweaty over their backs. She moved sensuously, slowly, guided by his large hands—dark against her alabaster skin— and I saw his cock disappear into her. His thighs flexed. I couldn't see his face because he was kissing her, but I heard him moan. I saw how his knees trembled slightly. I saw how his hands gripped her waist, her back, her butt. He pushed deeper, and she sighed into his mouth. His cock reappeared and the condom around it glistened. He kissed her harder, cupping her head as he bent her backward. His hair swung over his left shoulder and his neck was bared to me, oddly vulnerable.

Something sharp and unwelcome pierced my gut. I pressed my hand to my mouth and stepped back so I could lean against the wall out of sight. Why were my eyes stinging? Because they were so beautiful together? Because I'd never feel that way again? I inhaled a shuddery gasp and waited, but they hadn't heard me. Heartsore and shaken, I sneaked into my room again. I didn't sleep until dawn.

Marjory stuck around for the entirety of the next day. She was lovely and fun and had an accent to die for. I must've given her the impression I didn't like her, because every time I looked at her, all I saw was her naked body perched on top of Thomas. I could barely talk to her without turning scarlet.

"What's the matter with you?" Cleo snapped under her breath when we stood by the kayak-rental hut. The others were distracted with packing away their phones and wallets, and I'd been fiddling with a life vest that was too big.

"What? What do you mean?"

"If I didn't know any better, I'd think grief has turned you straight and you're crushing on Thomas's date."

"I— He— No!" I grabbed her arm and dragged her to the side of the hut. The guy renting out the kayaks gave us an odd look, but he'd proven solidly he didn't speak a lick of Flemish, so I didn't care about him overhearing us. "I caught them, okay? Last night. On the couch. *Doing it.*"

Cleo's mouth turned into a perfect *O* as her eyes widened. "No way! Oh my God, what did he say?"

"Huh? What did who say?"

"Thomas! When you saw him!" she said, as if I were slow.

"They didn't see me. I turned and ran back to my room as soon as I realized what was going on." Not entirely true. "But now all I can see when I look at her are . . ." I made an awkward cupping motion with my hands in front of my own chest. "And . . ." I repeated the move, but lower.

Cleo started to laugh. And she couldn't stop. And then she was clutching her knees, bent over, wheezing for breath.

"It's not funny," I hissed.

"What's not funny?"

I spun around and stood nose to chest with Thomas in his life vest. He was trying to look past me at Cleo. "I'm afraid of drowning," I blurted out, and his sincere, dark gaze landed on my face. Oh God, why had I said that?

"That's nothing to laugh about, Cleo," Thomas said gravely. He put his hand on my shoulder. "You and I can get a canoe and we'll go in together. I used to be a lifeguard in high school. I promise you'll be fine."

Behind me Cleo made a distressed noise, a sound I imagined might come from a dying seagull.

"You really shouldn't laugh at something like that, Cleo. I'm frankly surprised." He spun on his heel and was gone.

"Thanks a lot," Cleo said, still wiping tears from her eyes. "Now he thinks I'm a total asshole."

"Well, you deserve it."

"And you get to sit in a canoe with him for the next three hours while Marjory hates you a little bit."

"Oh my God," I groaned and followed her when she walked away from me, laughing again.

I stopped fighting Thomas when he squeezed me into the fifth life vest, determined to find one that fit me like a glove. Marjory kept looking at us speculatively, while Cleo was on the verge of another burst of laughter. Imran stood by and watched like we were all crazy.

Though I silently devised plans to tip Cleo's kayak when she least expected it, I remembered she was my oldest friend. I gave her a sideways hug. "Love you, Cleo," I whispered.

"Aw, Ollie." She hugged me back. "You're gonna make me cry."

The sun beat hotly on our backs when we finally took to the water. I'd kept my T-shirt on underneath my life jacket, but Thomas had slipped his off. His tan skin glimmered with pearls of sweat as he pushed our canoe into the Semois and jumped into the back.

"I take it you've done this before," I said, looking over my shoulder.

He gave me a toothy grin. "Yes, haven't you?"

"Well . . . not since I was eleven?"

He laughed and pushed his oar in the water. "Like riding a bike," he said in a way I didn't believe at all.

We did well for the most part, but when we hit a rapid, I panicked enough that if he hadn't bought my fear of drowning before, he would now.

"I swear, I'm fine!" I yelled over the rush of the water when he asked me for the tenth time if we needed to pull over to the shallower

side. "I thought we were going to end up going backward. I'm good."
My oar got stuck behind a rock, and I winced as it yanked my
shoulder back.

"If you're sure."

We were due to meet Marjory, Imran, and Cleo a little farther
down the river, on a secluded beach I remembered from the school
trip, but they'd struggled setting off, so they were pretty far behind us.

"You think our picnic will still be dry?" I glanced over my
shoulder, and Thomas nudged the waterproof container at his feet.

"It'll be dry and taste of plastic, no doubt."

"Yum. *Fromage au plastique.* My favorite."

Thomas laughed, then splashed me gently with his oar. I made an
outraged noise and flicked my oar back, sending a huge wave of water
over the edge of our little canoe. I stared at him, stunned as he sat
there, dripping wet, eyes wide with disbelief.

"I'm sorry! Oh shit, I didn't mean to—"

"Oh, you're gonna pay, buddy." Thomas dipped his oar in the
water, and I could see his chest muscles flex beneath the life jacket,
his biceps bulging and veiny as he fought the water, getting ready
to splash me in retaliation. As I braced myself to get soaked to the
bone, our boat slipped into a rapid, a narrow stream of fast-running
water tucked out of sight under tree branches and bushes. I wasn't
fast enough to correct our course, and we bumped into a large rock,
spinning sideways. Thomas's oar got caught in a bunch of weeds, and
our canoe tilted. The plastic drum with our lunch, phones, and wallets
bumped the side of the boat, and over we went.

I had enough time to think, *Holy fucking crap, this is cold,* and a
pair of strong arms wrapped around my waist. "I've got you!" Thomas
yelled over the roar of the water. "I've got you. You're fine."

"I know—" I managed. "I know I'm fine. Seriously, I can—"
The words died in my mouth. Thomas spun me around and held
me against him, and the noise that came out of my mouth wasn't
dignified. No one had held me this close since Sam died, and my body
craved it like air. I gasped for it as if I hadn't breathed in a long time.
He misunderstood me and soothed me as he dragged me toward
calmer water.

"It's okay. There's a little beach right there. Can you swim toward it? You should be able to stand soon. I'm so sorry, Ollie." He tightened his grip on me a little more.

I nodded, trying not to feel bereft as he let go of me. I knew I should've helped him drag the boat back in, but I felt weirdly paralyzed. At least I managed to rescue our lunch. I flopped down beside it.

"Are you all right?" Thomas asked me after he pulled the canoe onto our little refuge. "I'm so sorry. That was my fault." He sat down, reached for my hand, and grabbed it tightly. Maybe because I couldn't look at him. "I should never have played around like that knowing what you told me earlier. I feel terrible."

Ah fucking hell. I couldn't stand it.

"I lied." I stared at his neat fingernails, feeling every infinitesimal movement of his hand. The pressure of his grip grew lighter and lighter as I talked until eventually he let go. "I don't have a fear of drowning. Cleo was teasing me because I saw you and Marjory, um, on the couch. Last night. And you wanted to know what she was laughing at, and I saw your life vest and the first thing I thought of was drowning. I never meant to make you feel bad, and I'm really sorry."

We sat side by side, looking at our own hands like two bumpkins. "So," he said after a long, uncomfortable silence. "You saw us having sex?"

I ducked my head. "Yes."

"And you're not afraid of drowning."

"Well, I'd rather not, obviously. But being in the water or falling out of the canoe doesn't scare me, no."

"So I acted like a total idiot grabbing you like that. And telling you you were going to be fine. You were fine all along."

My heart ached. "Thomas, I really didn't mean to embarrass you or anything. I—"

"It's fine." He rose to his feet in short, jerky motions, dusting me lightly with sand as he walked to the water. "The others are coming down the river."

"Thomas . . ."

He shook his head, and I didn't press it, because there came Cleo, laughing as she saw us. "You guys tipped over? That's priceless. Hey, Imran! They capsized! Man, I wish I'd seen it."

We ate an only mildly plastic-y lunch. I kept quiet when Thomas suggested he and Marjory share the canoe the rest of the way. Imran thought nothing of it, but Cleo gave me an inquiring look. I didn't acknowledge her, I climbed into a kayak, heart heavy and a knot of feelings in the pit of my stomach I couldn't even begin to decipher.

The worst thing about holidays is returning to work afterward. I didn't mind work. At all, actually, but I needed to be in the groove, in the habit of it, and I hadn't been for over a month.

I was wrecked on Tuesday morning. The small hours had plagued me with strange thoughts again. I wondered if I should worry about thinking the way I did sometimes, but the worst of the darkness always fled when dawn came.

It felt weird to get ready to go in the morning all by myself. No one to squabble with over the shaving cream. Sam wasn't there to pretend to be grossed out when I used his deodorant stick. I could shower twice as long as usual and I'd still get to work in time. I ate breakfast by myself at seven thirty, and it tasted like ashes in my mouth.

Somewhat appropriately, it was raining when I stepped outside. The tram was dank with wet bodies. I had a car but mainly used it for driving to the hospitals I needed to visit. If I had to go into the office, it was easier to take a tram than wrestle through Antwerp traffic and search for parking.

At least school hadn't started yet, or I'd be squashed among a bunch of teenagers in badly put on uniforms. Instead I got to ride quietly, staring at my reflection as the tram entered the dark tunnels leading to the center of Antwerp. I had no idea what waited for me at work, but I doubted they'd send me out to a hospital on day one. I cringed when I thought of seeing my coworkers and their pity.

I wasn't wrong. Lesley, our receptionist, started crying when she saw me. Ben Dalemans, my boss, gave me an awkward pat on the back, and everyone else pretty much avoided eye contact. Most of them had been at the funeral, and they'd seen me at my worst. It was embarrassing. I was glad to grab my morning coffee and hide in my small office with its view of the central station beneath me.

If I squashed my face to the window, I could see the Antwerp Zoo, but I'd stopped trying that when I realized the windows only got washed once a year.

I answered emails all day long. Slowly my coworkers trickled in to offer me their condolences and to tell me I should let them know if they could do anything for me. An evil part of me wanted to take advantage and ask them to bring me coffee and lunch and more coffee. But I heard Sam's voice admonish me, so instead I smiled and thanked them and said that no, I was okay. Even the token homophobe came in to mumble sorry before he hurried away. He never set more than one foot into my office. Maybe he was afraid to get gay cooties.

Don't worry, I thought meanly. *The gays don't want your fat ass.*

And then it was evening, and I got to do the same bedraggled trek home again, only now the bodies were noticeably less well washed than they'd been that morning.

The next day I did it all over again, and so I went on week after week. I pushed through life as if it were a slightly monotonous and far too long novel, a page-by-page review of dreary, everyday details no one wanted to read about.

Simon called me once, asking if I had taken some time to think things through. I told him my answer was no. The house was mine by Sam's will, and if they wanted to fight me on it, they could. When he told me I was being ungrateful, that they'd treated me like a son while all I had ever done was take advantage, his words cut deep. Simon had been like a father to me, and yet here he was, throwing me out of my own home.

I heard the anger in his voice when he told me their lawyer would be in touch, and that he was disappointed Sam hadn't meant more to me than this. He said Sam would be shocked if he knew how much pain I was putting his parents through. When he hung up, I threw my phone across the living room in rage, but all it did was bounce harmlessly on the couch.

This house was my home. My last link to the man I had loved with more than just my heart. If Simon thought he could bully me into giving it up, he had another think coming.

And suddenly Sam had been gone for six months, and I awoke on an early December morning not reaching for him, not wondering where he was. That split second when I believed he was still alive was gone. I waited for the tears, the grief, the anger, the bargaining, the acceptance of this new loss, but they didn't come.

"You need to go on a date," Cleo told me at a bar one Saturday evening. I didn't go to the Nine Barrels anymore, and if the others did, they never told me. If anyone had asked me a year ago whether Sam held our group's friendship together, I'd have said no, but we'd undeniably seen a lot less of each other lately, and I felt guilty. I hadn't tried very hard to reach out to my friends.

Cleo and Imran had solidly made up during our trip to the Ardennes. Thomas had dated Marjory for another week or two before distance drove them apart. I had . . . worked.

"A date?" I wrinkled my nose. The music was loud in this bar, and not at all to my taste, but finding a new hangout was proving difficult. I liked the trendy interior with the gray walls and the wooden floor, but the acoustics were all wrong and the music grated on my nerves. I was glad we'd found a seat hidden away in a corner.

I looked around to see where the others were, stalling so I didn't have to answer her. Imran was getting us more drinks, and Thomas was . . . somewhere. The two of them had barely said a word to each other, and their awkward silence made me feel like I'd start to hyperventilate. "I don't know if I'm ready for that."

"You're not. But you never will be until you start." She set her wineglass down and leaned across the table to hold my hand. "You don't have to jump into a relationship, Ollie. You need to go for a few dinners, have a few drinks. Meet people. It's part of the healing process."

"You specializing in psychology or something?"

It was a joke, but she turned red in the mood lighting. "No. I may have read up a little bit on how to deal with grief and move on."

I bristled. "I'll move on in my own time, Cleo."

"But will you though?" Imran planted a Hoegaarden in front of me, and I made grabby hands at it. He slid it away from me. "She's right. You need to get out of your shell again or you'll be stuck in that house until it's a mausoleum."

I could feel my anger build. How dare they put a time frame on my grief? I had opened my mouth to tell them exactly that when someone behind me said, "It's been six months. Don't push him."

I jumped a little and glanced up at Thomas, who slid a chair out and wouldn't look at me. We hadn't seen much of each other since we went to Bouillon. I'd told myself it wasn't because of the canoe incident, but I'd been fooling myself.

When I finally caught his eye, I mouthed, *Thank you.* The corners of his mouth lifted, seemingly reluctantly, and a foot bumped mine under the table. I smiled and reached for my beer, but Imran's scowl made me uneasy.

"I'll think about it, okay?" I said, trying to appease them a little so we could just get on with our night like the friends we'd always been. "But I'm not promising anything."

Thomas studied my face, but I couldn't read his expression at all.

"Okay, good," Cleo said. "Now. On to Christmas. I need to know the when, the where, and are we doing secret Santa?"

All the men groaned. "It's Ollie and Sa—" Imran snapped his mouth shut.

"No, you're right," I said before the silence could suffocate us all. "It was our turn and we can still do it at our house. In fact . . ." I warmed to the idea. The thought of filling my too empty, too quiet house with my friends made my heart feel lighter. Maybe for the last time, if Sam's parents got their way. "I think that would be great. We could do it on the twenty-third or the twenty-sixth and everyone can stay the night."

"We're going to see my family on the twenty-sixth," Imran said, and Cleo nodded. "But the twenty-third works."

"In that case . . ." Cleo whipped her handbag out—or clutch, or whatever they called those wallet-sized things. Why she didn't just carry her wallet was beyond me. She removed four pieces of paper. She held them up to me first. "Choose."

I mumbled something rude under my breath and pulled a name. She did the same to Imran and Thomas, then folded open her own name. She made a face, looked at Thomas's, grinned, looked at mine, and snatched mine out of my hand.

"Hey!" Imran said, laughing.

"Well, what's the point of that?" I asked. "It's supposed to be *secret* Santa."

"I pulled that one last year. I want someone else."

I glanced at my name and frowned. *Thomas.* Hadn't she had Sam last year?

"So you know the rules," Cleo went on before I could point out her mistake. "Don't spend over twenty-five euros, and no gag gifts."

"Fine," Imran groaned. "Whatever makes you happy, babe."

She tucked her name in her purse, drained her wineglass, and held out her hand. "Dance with me," she said to Imran, and Thomas and I watched them go.

"You going to dance?" I asked Thomas.

He gave me a light shrug. "Maybe later." He sipped his beer. He'd let his beard grow a little bit, and his cheeks were scruffy and rough. A stark contrast to the soft swell of his full mouth. It made him look mysterious, and brought out the green in his brown eyes. He scooped his hair away from his face, and it drifted down again.

"Have you heard anything about the house?" he asked.

I made a face, not really wanting to talk about it. "I've been warned their lawyer will be in touch, apparently."

Thomas frowned. "You should probably contact your own lawyer just in case. To get some information and stuff."

"Yeah maybe," I said and looked away.

Thomas took the hint. "So, you really thinking about dating again?"

I sighed and put my beer down. "I don't know. I don't want to, but I can see how it wouldn't be a bad idea to try. I'm . . . I don't want to move on. I don't feel ready. But I know he'd want me to. And I don't—" I fiddled with the label on my beer. The words stuck in my mouth. Even though I'd thought them over the past few weeks, they still felt like a huge betrayal.

"What?" Thomas asked gently.

"I don't want to be alone for the rest of my life," I admitted.

He nodded and looked away. "No. Me neither."

"You?" I sat up in surprise. "Why would you be alone? You're Mr. Suave, with your door swinging both ways and the 'I don't want to settle down' speech you gave that first Christmas you joined us." He didn't say anything, wouldn't look at me. Unease made me shift in my seat. "Did you find someone?"

"No." He drained his beer. "But maybe I realized that I'm waiting for something that's never going to happen."

I didn't know what that meant. He jerked his thumb in the direction of the bathrooms, gave me an apologetic little smile, and left. I didn't see him for the rest of the night.

"You look like you swallowed a lemon."

I blinked and glared at Cleo, who pushed a cup of coffee across the counter and sat down on a barstool beside me. She and Imran lived in a large apartment on one of Antwerp's boulevards, high enough not to be bothered by the noise or smell of traffic. Imran was out with friends playing tennis all Sunday morning, so Cleo had invited me over to prove dating sites really did suck donkey balls.

"'My name is Johnny Deep,'" I read. "'I'm a nineteen-year-old gay male interested in group casual.' What does 'group casual' even mean? 'Johnny Deep'? Really? And he's nineteen! They're all either nineteen or in their sixties." I snapped the laptop shut. "I don't want to date. I changed my mind. I'm getting a cat. Two cats!"

Cleo stopped stirring sugar into her coffee and made a big show of opening the laptop again. "What about this guy?" She clicked on the one guy I'd been trying to hide because I knew she'd zone in on him. "Peter, thirty, veterinarian with his own practice." She whistled between her teeth. "And he's the only one with clothes on in his profile picture. Bonus!"

"He's got a big nose," I said sullenly.

"That's just a bad angle. And look! He's from Antwerp. Perfect! Email him."

"Cleo," I whined.

"Email him!" she repeated as her doorbell rang. She stood and pointed a finger at me. "Do it."

I huffed and I puffed and I clicked on the Contact Me button, dawdling as I heard her shuffle about the hallway, then muffled voices and pounding footsteps on the stairs.

Dear Peter, I wrote, and immediately deleted it. *Hi, my name is Oliver and I saw your profile on BoysOnly.* Ah, Jesus. Should I be judging him for making a profile on a site with a name that bad? He'd have to judge me for looking at it in the first place, and it wasn't like the Belgian gay population was swimming in dating site options. *I'd love to learn a bit more about you.* Oh God, how awful. I backspaced.

"Tell him his profile looked interesting, and you wouldn't mind learning more."

I startled and turned around. "Um, hi, Thomas." My cheeks flushed. He didn't look much better, only he was scowling.

"Are you emailing the veterinarian? He's a veterinarian," Cleo added to Thomas as she wandered back in. His scowl deepened.

"Yes, fine, whatever." I wrote something approximating Thomas's suggestion and hit Send, mostly because I wanted to stop these two gawking over my shoulder. "There. Done. If I get ax-murdered, it'll be your fault, Cleo."

She blanched, and Thomas gently hit my shoulder. "That's not funny. And if you do meet up with him, you need to text me where you are and where you're going if you're going anywhere."

"I'm not going to go anywhere with anyone on a first date!" I almost yelled, scandalized. "Oh my God." I clasped my hands over my mouth as something occurred to me.

"What?" Cleo asked. She seemed concerned, but I knew that sparkle in her eyes. I sometimes thought she was psychic.

"I have literally," I said slowly, eyeing first her, then Thomas, "never kissed anyone but Sam. In my life. Never mind . . ." *Sex*, I thought. Oh God. Sex with someone else. How could I even contemplate it?

"You should practice!" Cleo squealed gleefully.

"I'm not twelve, Cleo. And besides, you have too much going on up here and not enough down there"—I indicated the areas in question.

She zeroed in on Thomas, who looked like he was about to jump out of a window.

"I am not going to smooch my friends for practice. I'm just going to have to deal. Right?"

"Right," she said.

Somehow it felt like Sam was laughing at me.

We didn't talk about practice kissing anyone after that. Cleo dragged Thomas and me out on a reluctant shopping trip. We only agreed to go because we had Christmas gifts to take care of, and the weather was fairly mild for the beginning of December, so now or never.

I still had no clue what to get Thomas for secret Santa, but I got my mother and my secretary sorted out. Rather sadly, I thought I'd actually miss the excruciating task of buying something for Sam. Maybe Thomas saw what I was thinking, because he squeezed my shoulder as we waited for Cleo to try on her fourth set of boots. He gave me a lopsided smile.

"Anyone would be lucky to date you," he told me. "Whether you're out of practice with kissing or not."

"Hey!" I elbowed him, and he sniggered. "I'm a very good kisser, I'll have you know."

His hair slipped across the left side of his face, casting it in shadow. "Oh, I don't doubt it."

"What do you think?" Cleo demanded. We obediently looked down at her feet. The boots looked more like lethal weapons than footwear.

"I liked the other ones better," Thomas said.

She looked at the boot graveyard surrounding her. "Which ones?"

"Any that don't have metal studs and fifteen leather straps," I said, and Thomas laughed even though Cleo looked really offended. "No, but seriously. No studs, Cleo. I liked those brown ones actually. With the smaller heel."

"Me too," Thomas said.

She looked mutinous for a second, then relented and sighed before she sank down and began to tug off the boots. "And they say you should go shopping with a gay man," she mumbled.

Thomas rolled his eyes at me, and I grinned.

I had really enjoyed myself that afternoon. The sadness had hardly crept in and chilled the air.

CHAPTER
SEVEN

I hate you, I texted Cleo.

If that's what it takes, I'm okay with that.

I gritted my teeth and warily eyed the door of the Irish pub as it opened. An old man with a red nose shuffled inside and closed it on the torrential rain.

An Irish pub, Cleo. Of all places.

We can't all be trendy like you. Maybe this is a good thing.

I huffed and sipped my sparkling water. I hadn't wanted to sit there with a beer before knowing what Peter the veterinarian was going to drink, but in my extreme caution I was half an hour early and as nervous as a Victorian bride on her wedding night.

You'll let us know if you go home with him, won't you?

I AM NOT GOING HOME WITH HIM!

All right, calm down. Just be yourself. He'll love you.

But did I want him to love me? Well, I sure as shit didn't want him to hate me. I sighed and stuffed my phone in my pocket. I loathed dating already and my first one hadn't even started yet. I'd gone through my entire wardrobe, hadn't found a single piece of clothing that didn't remind me in some way of Sam, and had hurried into town for a last-minute, freaked-out shopping trip.

In hindsight, the jeans I'd bought might've been a smidgen too tight.

The door opened again, and I held my breath. To be honest, it was like a scene from a horror movie—which felt pretty accurate. Thunder rolled in, a flicker of lightning outlined a tall, dark shape, the few patrons in the bar seemed to pause their murmured conversations, and then the door closed. Fire crackled in the hearth, its orange light returned, and the room felt cozy all over again.

I didn't notice. My eyes were locked on the stranger who'd walked through the door. He was tall—oh God, was he tall—and handsome. I could see that from my little nook in the corner. He cautiously scanned the room as he unwrapped a huge scarf from around his neck. He took his coat off, fished his phone and wallet out of it, and hung it on the coatrack by the door. He shivered lightly, shook out his hair, and I could see the water flying. He was soaked through, poor guy. He checked the bar, checked his watch. His shoulders drooped a little. Almost knocking over my glass, I rose to my feet and hurried up to him.

"Peter?" I asked. He spun around. His tawny gaze landed on my face, and he didn't try the hide the pleased little flicker in them when he took me in. "Hi." I held out my hand. "I'm—"

"Oliver. Gosh." He wrapped my hand in his wet one.

Gosh? "My friends call me Ollie, actually. Um, I'm sitting over there if you want to join me." I tilted my head in the direction of the little table with the wraparound bench.

His eyes followed the movement, then landed on me again. He let go of my hand. "Sure. I'm sorry I'm late. There wasn't a tram for twenty minutes, and it's a fifteen-minute walk, so I figured I'd risk it."

"You're soaked," I said. Why? Why did I say that? In case he hadn't noticed?

"That I am." He was staring at me.

"Shall we, um, sit down?"

"Okay." He laughed a little bit when I turned and walked away, and I gave him a quizzical look as we sat down. "I'm sorry." He shook his head and folded his hands in his lap. A droplet of rainwater ran down his fringe and plopped onto the table. "I quite honestly didn't know what to expect. I've never been on one of these dates before, and you didn't have a profile picture up or anything. I almost didn't come."

"Me neither," I admitted. "I've never done anything like this before."

He laughed. "The online dating? It feels so awkward."

"Well, any kind of dating really."

His eyebrows rose quizzically, but he didn't ask when I didn't explain. I appreciated that. "So how about we pretend we ran into each other here and you didn't see my painfully awkward profile on that dumb site?"

"Oh, I didn't think it was painfully awkward. I mean, you're no Johnny Deep, but . . ."

He threw his head back and laughed again. It was a nice sound with a fluid move. He looked exactly like the kind of guy who laughed a lot.

"I'm going to get a beer," he said. "Do you want one?"

"Oh, sure, yes. I'll have whatever you're having. And the next one's on me."

He gave me a shy little smile and rose to his feet. I took advantage of his distraction with the bartender and subjected him to some scrutiny. Tall, yes, absolutely. A cheap haircut. His hair was dark with rain now, but I knew from the photo on his profile that it was blonder than mine. He had very broad shoulders and thick thighs stuck in a pair of comfortable jeans. He wore an off-white woolly sweater that looked prickly. Nothing like Sam with his tailored suits and manicured hands. I imagined Peter's hands would be rough and slightly callused, and oh my God, what was I doing thinking of his hands?

He came back with two Blonde Leffes and slid one over to me. "This okay?"

"Perfect." We touched glasses and sipped. "So how does this go? Do I ask you to tell me a little bit about yourself or is that a job interview?"

He smiled and leaned forward. The firelight beside us caught his face, and oh dear, his eyes were very blue. "In a way this is a job interview, isn't it? So yes, sure, ask away."

"Okay." I straightened my back, imagined what my boss had looked like all those years ago when I'd been interviewed, and asked him in a stern voice, "Well, Peter, why don't you start with telling me why you think you're perfect for this job."

Peter snorted in his beer and had to reach for a napkin to dab his chin. "Nice," he said. "Look what you made me do." My face heated but I stuck with the moment and raised one eyebrow at him. "Okay. Jeez, um. I think I'm a catch, all right? I own a house with a veterinary practice attached to it, I have two dogs and a cat, no kids, no skeletons in my closet, and only a mildly nosy family."

He looked so awkward I took pity on him. "What's your family like?"

He relaxed a little. "I have two older sisters and one younger brother. My parents are still together and we get along really fine." He shrugged. "Nothing out of the ordinary. What about you?"

"I work as a medical software consultant here in Antwerp."

"Oh. What does that mean?"

"I install medical software and help nurses and doctors become familiar with it." There was more to it than that, but I didn't want to go into the boring details. "It's fun, although I could do with less getting stuck in traffic."

"Do you live around here?"

"Yes, I live on the south side, close to the hospital."

"Nice. What about your family? Did you grow up in the neighborhood?"

"I did. I have a brother who's ten years older," I said. "My dad died when I was eighteen."

His face softened. "I'm sorry. That must've been hard." A lull fell in the conversation, and we drank our beers. Now what? Did I tell him about Samuel? Was that a second-date discussion? A third one? I had no idea. He frowned a little. "What's up?"

"I . . ." Well, this loss was part of me now. A big part. And while I didn't know whether I'd ever see Peter again, I didn't want to keep this a secret. The idea of talking about this to a stranger also appealed. I wouldn't have to worry about making him feel sad by mentioning Sam, since he hadn't known Sam and didn't know me. "The thing is . . . my friends made me go on that dating site. I was in a relationship for a really long time. Since I was sixteen, actually." My voice faltered a little, and I reached for my water.

"Wow, that's a long time. You broke up?" he asked me gently.

Oh, he was a good guy. I could tell. He'd be gentle with animals, and he'd be a sweet boyfriend. My heart lurched uncomfortably, and I began to sweat.

"He died," I said and wiped my palms on my too-tight jeans. "He was murdered six months ago."

Peter gasped. "Oh my God. I read about that. On the docks? The parking lot?"

I nodded. "Yes." Shit, I was about to lose it. I took a shuddery breath and wedged my hands between my knees. Behind him, the bar had started to fill up, and Peter looked around.

"Look, do you want to get out of here? Nothing . . . nothing like that," he quickly added when I gave him a sharp look. "We can talk about this some other time, if you want. Or we can have coffee at my place. I live close. I promise I won't try anything, but you look like you don't want to be here anymore. I'd suggest going for a walk but—" He snapped his mouth shut, maybe realizing he was babbling. "Sorry."

"No, it's fine." I thought about it for two seconds. The buzz of the other patrons grated on me. "Getting out of here sounds perfect. Tell me your address though, so I can warn my friends I might be ax-murdered tonight."

He laughed and winced at the same time. "I'm sorry, I shouldn't find that funny under the circumstances." He rattled off his address, and I typed it in, sending it to Thomas instead of Cleo because I could count on him not to send me twenty squeeing messages.

"It's fine," I said. I stood and shrugged into my jacket. "It's been really hard, but it's getting better. Oh, I didn't buy you a drink in return!"

He'd been about to turn to the door, but he looked back and smiled. "Next time."

On the doorstep of the pub, I lost my courage. We stood under a dripping awning, watching the rain. It had lessened, but we were still about to get soaked.

"I don't think I can do it." I hugged myself nervously. "Go home with you, I mean." I felt like an idiot and startled when he gently touched my arm.

"I understand. And it's completely up to you, obviously, but I do like you and I wouldn't mind seeing you again."

"Okay," I said, the relief so huge it came out in a deep breath. "Give me your number and I'll text you mine. And maybe . . . next Saturday? Or am I supposed to play it cool and not contact you for three days and then check in?"

He laughed softly as he pulled a business card out of his wallet. His hair had started to dry, and it curled around his ears. "Next Saturday would be great. I am on call though, so I might have to leave early. Same time, same place?" He jerked his thumb at the Irish pub behind us.

I shrugged. "Sure, why not?"

Peter bit his lip. For a split second I thought he was going to lean in and kiss me, but instead he held out his hand and I took it. It was warm this time. I was right. Rough with the gentle scrape of calluses.

"See you next week," he murmured, and he was gone. My phone buzzed.

You're going home with this guy after the first date? Jesus, Ollie. Be careful.

Like I thought, no squeeing from Thomas. I spotted my tram across the street and hurried over to catch it, getting soaked regardless. I didn't try to think about too much on my way home, and after a hot shower, I fell into bed.

I liked Peter. I didn't want to. But I did, and the thought stabbed me with fresh grief. I was betraying Sam just by thinking like this. The realization turned my stomach. I rolled over and hugged a pillow tight to my chest. Squeezing my eyes closed, I willed sleep to come so I could stop thinking entirely.

Around midnight I was still awake, and my phone buzzed again.

You still good?

I squinted at the sharp light until my eyes adjusted somewhat. It touched me that Thomas was checking in. I felt like a total tool for not telling him I'd changed my mind.

Am home. Didn't go with him.

A second later my phone rang. "Hello?" I croaked.

"You okay?" Thomas sounded a lot more awake than I did.

"Yeah, man. I'm sorry I forgot to text you back. I was telling him about Sam and we were going to go to his place to talk about it, but I changed my mind. He was fine with it. He's nice."

Silence. Then, "You like him?"

My chest hurt. "Maybe. I don't know . . ."

"What?"

"If I'm ready."

"It's okay if you're not, Ollie. But at least you tried. And next time it'll be a little bit easier. There's no time stamp on this, you know? You can make your own decisions about when you're up for dating."

I wanted to tell him I knew all that, but it was nice to hear. "No one else can tell you what to do. I think . . . I think you're doing great, actually. You've been so strong." My eyes began to droop. Thomas had a nice voice. Deep and soft. I could fall asleep listening to him talk.

"Hmm."

"Ollie?"

I woke up a little bit. "Yeah?"

"I'm glad you didn't go home with him."

I didn't know what to say to that. "Thanks for checking in, Thomas."

"Of course, man. Anytime."

"Night, Tommy."

Another silence, then very softly, "Night Oliver."

I fell asleep.

That week it seemed like someone was screwing with time. The hours at work flew by like a blur, while the minutes at home ticked one painful second at a time. Cleo called, as did my mom, and I talked to them but I didn't want to see anyone.

I contacted Sam's old lawyer during a slow hour at work to make an appointment about the house. My stomach contracted when he sounded far less optimistic than I thought he would. His caution made me realize I'd been assuming the will would hold up and I wouldn't really have to deal with any of this. Sam used to handle these unpleasant things. I'd done more than just rely on him.

In the evenings I drifted around the house, trying to imagine fitting all our things into a different place, and the idea was so wrong it made me nauseous.

The only time I felt somewhat normal was when I was texting with Peter, and that in itself became an unwelcome response. I wasn't ready for this. Every butterfly that fluttered to the surface when his name popped up on my phone gave me heartburn, and I squashed it down.

But I couldn't deny it. My entire week consisted of tunnel vision toward Saturday. I wanted to see him again and I didn't. I wanted to know I was wanted, and at the same time I didn't want to need anyone ever again. I was scared to death, but deep inside me a flicker of excitement couldn't be buried. It was like a tiny flame, and every sweet text from Peter fanned it until I didn't have the heart to starve it of oxygen.

I bought another outfit on Saturday and made sure I wasn't half an hour early this time. He was already there when I walked in. His smile lit the room when he noticed me. He rose to his feet and strode up to me easy as breathing. Like we'd done it our entire lives, he pecked me on the lips. Just like that. Realization swiftly dawned, and he clasped a hand over his mouth.

"Shit," he whispered. "I don't know why I did that. It felt so natural. I'm sorry."

"It's fine," I said as I took off my coat, even though a shiver ran up my spine. "Go with the flow."

He smiled down at me, and his right cheek dimpled. "You look really handsome."

"Thanks." My face flushed, and I fidgeted with my coat. "So do you."

He held my chair out for me, and I squirmed, half-uneasy, half-pleased. We talked all evening. It held none of the awkwardness from last time. When he kissed me good-bye, I lingered a moment, breathed him in, and discovered that I liked the generic soap on him. Just his skin and a generic scent and it didn't put me off at all, even if I sent a quick apology to Sam.

We made plans. I saw him again a week later on a crisp winter day. We walked through an empty, sleepy zoo. He held me tight when he kissed me good-bye, and I opened up and let him in.

I saw him again the Saturday after that. This time I texted Cleo to let her know I was going home with him. I didn't know why I chose her rather than Thomas, but she refrained from sending me a hundred replies, which was a win as far as I was concerned.

Peter's house was nice. He was really sweet. His pets seemed old and weren't very interested in meeting me, apart from a large tabby cat with one ear missing. He had to lock her up in the kitchen because she wouldn't stop rubbing herself all over me.

We kissed on the couch, and I liked it. We kissed on the way to the bedroom, and I quivered with anticipation. He was lovely and considerate and checked in with me at every stage. When he breached my body and held me close, I craved his touch so much I thought I'd start crying. I didn't. He murmured softly in my ear the whole time, praising me, making me feel wanted and loved until I shook in his arms. He rocked me to an orgasm that completely blindsided me. I'd forgotten what it felt like, and I thought my heart would burst.

When he was asleep hours later, I slipped out of bed and into his bathroom and cried and cried and cried. I felt terrible about it, but I sneaked into my clothes and left a note on his kitchen table. I crept out of his house like a thief in the early morning.

The first tram would come in half an hour. I sat and saw the sun rise over Antwerp, early tourists making their way into town. I imagined Peter's sweet face when he woke up and found the bed cold beside him, and cringed with guilt.

> Peter,
> I had a great time. I really did. I loved spending time with you, and if things were different, I could really have seen this going somewhere. But I'm not ready and I am so sorry for leaving like this.
> I hope you can forgive me.
> Ollie

He deserved better. I just didn't have it in me to give it in that moment.

I called Cleo a few hours later. She'd come off a night shift, but had a day shift the next day, so I knew she'd want to stay awake.

"Want to come over for breakfast?" I asked her. "I'll make eggs Benedict. Bring Imran." I wasn't much of a cook, but eggs Benedict were my specialty.

"Dude, I will even get out of my pajamas for that. And Imran's not home yet, but I'll let him know to come to your house." She hung up without another word. After some hesitation, I texted Thomas to come over too.

I knew Cleo would arrive first, so when she tumbled in on a cloud of soft snow, I gave her a hug and burst out, "I slept with him."

"Oh my God!" She danced up and down on one foot as she tried to extract herself from her boots. "Oh my God, I don't believe it! How was it? Was he any good? I want all the details. But give me coffee first."

"Cleo, I am not giving you any details." I led her into the kitchen, poured coffee, then said, "But it was good. Really good. I cried like a baby while he slept, and sneaked out of his house."

The wide grin fell off her face. "Oh, honey." She came around the counter and hugged me. "Do you want to see him again?"

I shook my head. "He's lovely. And maybe in another six months or so it would've been better, but I can't. I'm not ready." I thought of Peter touching me and then how Sam and I had always made love, and my stomach turned.

"That's fine." She patted my hair. "Now you know. And you had sex with someone other than Sam, so you also know it's not the end of the world."

"You're right. I feel bad about how I left it with him, though."

The doorbell rang, so I hurried into the hall to let Thomas in. He was wearing a ridiculously fluffy hat with earflaps and somehow still managed to look like a lumberjack rather than a Fraggle.

"Hey." He gave me a wide, toothy smile as he filled my doorway and pushed his way through. "Thanks for the invite." He hugged me, and squinted at me. "You look tired. You okay?"

"Ollie slept with Peter and then cried his eyeballs out, but yay progress!"

I groaned. "Seriously, Cleo? I told you that in confidence."

"We're all friends here, and Thomas cares about you. Don't you, Thomas?"

I glanced at him, embarrassed. He was frowning at me, no trace left of that beaming smile. "You slept with him?" he asked.

"Yeah. Last night. It was . . . a one-time thing. I'm not . . . I don't want to talk about it."

His jaw flexed. "Did he hurt you?"

"God, no! It was good." My face went so hot aliens could probably have detected it from outer space. "It's too soon, okay? Can we leave my sex life alone now, please?" Thomas stood frozen in the hallway, and I took that as acquiescence. "I need to start on the eggs."

I'd managed to ruin the atmosphere somehow, and felt bad all over again.

"Listen," Cleo said. "If you feel guilty about leaving him in the middle of the night, text him and apologize. I'm sure he'll understand."

"You don't owe him any kind of explanation," Thomas said mulishly, which surprised me.

"Is that what you do with your one-night stands?" I asked.

His eyes lifted to meet mine. The wounded look in them almost made me flinch back.

Cleo gasped. "That's not very nice, Oliver."

"No," I agreed. "I don't know why I said that. I'm sorry."

He shrugged but stared out of the window. "It's fine. You need to do what seems right to you, obviously. I meant that if you don't want to text him, you don't have to. You don't owe him anything."

I nodded. While the eggs poached, I pulled my phone out of my pocket. There were two messages from Peter.

You don't have to reply to this. I understand and I'm sorry. I really liked you and I would've wanted to see you again, but you have a grieving process to go through. If I helped in any way, I'm happy.

If you should want to see me again at any point in the future, you know where I am.

"That him?" Cleo asked. I nodded. "Can I see?" I gave her my phone. "Aww." Her voice sounded thick. "He sounds like a really nice guy. I'm sorry it didn't work out for you."

"Me too," I murmured. Thomas stared at the message but said nothing.

Imran appeared when the eggs were done. He burst through the door in an overtired flurry and kept us all captivated with gruesome tales from his job until Peter was almost forgotten.

I caught Thomas watching me every once in a while, and his concern touched me. I smiled at him, and after a second he returned it softly, if a little sadly. Before I could dissect the meaning behind it, Cleo said, "Don't forget! Christmas party next week! Where is your tree, Ollie?"

"I was going to set it up today."

"We'll help!" she declared. Imran and Thomas groaned but lumbered to their feet.

"Good breakfast, my friend," Imran said as he passed me and followed Cleo into the basement, where I kept my fake tree and all the ornaments. I'd buy a real one next week for the office at the front of the house, but I liked the huge fake one in the living room.

"I'll help you do the dishes," Thomas said, and he did, in a mostly companionable silence.

CHAPTER
EIGHT

Stan Doorn, the lawyer who'd processed the transfer of the house into Sam's name when his grandmother died, looked very grave when I went to see him early on the twenty-third. He shook my hand and ushered me into his quiet office. I sat down in a creaky leather chair and tried to get my thumping heart under control.

"How are you doing, Oliver?" he asked. I'd seen him at the funeral and briefly afterward to go over Sam's will. He always struck me as a severe but kind man.

"I'm doing okay," I said, and he nodded slowly.

"I've read through Sam's as well as his grandmother's will. I'm going to tell you straight away, it would've been better if Sam's will had been put together by me or another lawyer, instead of doing it himself." He pressed his lips together and gazed at me thoughtfully for a second. "I can imagine he hadn't considered he'd really need it this soon."

My throat began to burn, and I nodded again. "So they can fight it?" I asked.

"They can," Stan said. "And they will. If it will do them any good, I have no idea. But it will be a painful process. They can fight it in two ways." He held up a thick finger. "Either they contest the authenticity of it—" he paused for a second, held up another finger as he peered at me over his reading glasses "—or they contest his mental health at the time he wrote the will."

I made an outraged noise. "They'll lose on both counts," I said.

"Maybe. Maybe not. It will all depend on the judge. The house had been in their family for a very long time, you weren't married yet, and some judges aren't all that positive toward same-sex relationships even in this day and age." I opened my mouth to complain again, but he held up his hand. "What it comes down to is this: they can fight it and they will. Whether they win or not becomes almost an afterthought. What you need to decide is how willing you are to drag this out. It will cost a lot of time, emotional commitment, and money, no matter what happens. And at the end of it you might still lose. Is the house worth it? Because if not, I can negotiate a deal where you get fifty percent of the proceeds. Maybe more because you are willing to work with them."

Anger burned through my veins. The house was ours. Sam had wanted me to have it. All his parents wanted it for was money. They didn't care about the memories that haunted every single room like docile, friendly ghosts. I couldn't reconcile any of this with the people I'd known and loved my whole life. Especially Simon, who was fast becoming a stranger, after I'd seen him as a second father for so long.

Stan was watching me intently. "I'll think about it," I told him wearily.

"You can take your time. Nothing is going to happen during the holidays, so there is no rush." He pursed his lips, then went on. "Another option is that you offer to buy them out."

"I don't have that kind of money."

"You could get a loan if you wanted. Again, it all depends on how badly you want the house."

"Okay, I'll think about it," I repeated, and rose to my feet. I shook his hand and left, mind reeling. I had a lot to go over, and I decided to let it all percolate as I shopped for presents.

It turned out to be impossible to find something suitable for Thomas. I'd toyed with the idea of giving him a book, but how terribly impersonal would that be? Especially since I had no clue what he liked to read. I trailed the menswear shops and went through colognes, picked up and discarded art prints, moved on to a winery and almost bought a bottle of wine, only to remember we'd be drinking copious amounts of alcohol all night so what would be the point of that?

It was nearly three o'clock on the twenty-third and everyone would be arriving at my doorstep in four hours. I still had to clean the house, shower, and start the cooking. Everyone would bring a dish or two, but the ham was my responsibility.

In near desperation, I almost picked up a dumb set of whiskey stones, even though I'd never seen Thomas drink whiskey. My eye fell on a desk protector. It was a large world map. I remembered a late evening—or early morning—one of the few where Thomas hadn't pulled a one-night stand and we'd all ended up in Sam's and my living room. Sobering up but drunk on tiredness, Thomas had been sitting next to me. His head had lolled onto my shoulder, and in a soft voice he'd confessed he'd always wanted to travel, but he never seemed to find anyone he wanted to travel with. Or the ones he did, didn't want to travel with him.

At the time it'd seemed like nothing, but now it felt like a terribly intimate confession. I picked up the map. It didn't look like much, and I almost put it down again before I noticed it came with a little tool. The idea was to scratch off a brown layer for each country visited, to reveal a colorful world beneath.

It was perfect.

I had it wrapped up and hurried home so I could get on with the rest of my day. At six thirty I shoved the ham in the oven and rushed upstairs to shower, sending a group text saying the door was open and to let themselves in, in case I wasn't down yet.

I dressed with care but for comfort. I thought about applying some of Sam's products to my hair, but remembered that had never worked before. Though I'd had my hair cut, it still wouldn't work now.

"First Christmas without you, Sam," I said. I pulled a T-shirt from his drawer, but it smelled only of me now. "I guess I should start packing these up, huh?"

There was no reply. I listened in the stairwell for a second but heard no movement downstairs. I was still alone. In a moment's indecision, I stared at the steps that would lead me to the attic. It felt good. Right. I climbed up.

Somewhere below me, a door opened. "Only me!"

I opened the door to Sam's art room, calling back, "Up here, Thomas."

I walked inside and stood in the familiar room. I hadn't been up here in so long. Dust motes drifted in the last of the December light.

"Ollie? Oh."

Thomas appeared in the doorway, looking windswept and handsome. His hair was pulled back in a bun low on his neck. His eyelashes were so dark, it looked like he was wearing eyeliner.

"Hey," I said.

He took a careful step closer. "What's this?"

"It was supposed to be Sam's wedding present for me."

"Oh, Ollie." Thomas squeezed my shoulder. "Have you never looked at it?"

"No."

"Do you want me to go?"

I thought about that for a moment. The ache in my chest wasn't suffocating me. In a way it felt sweet. "No," I said. "I'd like you to stay, if you want."

He nodded. "Okay."

I walked to the easel and gently pulled the sheet off the canvas. Because I was so close to it, I didn't immediately register what it was, but Thomas did.

"Oh my God!"

Alarmed, I looked at him. He had his hands in his hair. His eyes flicked from me to the painting, and back to my . . . groin? He spun on his heel and faced the other direction. I took three steps back and echoed his words weakly.

"Oh my God."

Sam had painted us in the middle of having sex. I was on my knees, facing the viewer, arms stretched back to hold on to Sam, who was fucking me from behind. I had an erection that would've held a flag up. *I surrender.*

It was stunning, but, "Fuck."

I began to laugh and glanced over my shoulder. Thomas risked a look too. When he saw I wasn't upset, he gingerly turned around again.

"Damn, Ollie. Is that thing true to size?"

"Oh my God." I laughed harder, and Thomas sniggered along.

"That's an amazing painting. It really is. But maybe you should leave it up here."

"Yeah, that might not—"

"Hi! We're here!"

We stared at each other, wide-eyed, swore at the same time, and scrambled over to the painting. We fumbled with the sheet, giggling like naughty schoolboys, and covered it up before stumbling out of the room and down the stairs.

"What are you guys up to?" Cleo asked.

"If you drank all the champagne already, I'm going to be pissed," Imran said.

Thomas and I looked at each other, started laughing again, and didn't stop until Cleo began to get mad for not being included in the joke.

"It's nothing," I said. "We're being silly."

"Yeah," Thomas said. "Nothing's up, Cleo." He caught my eye, and that set us off again.

"Fine, don't tell me." She stomped to the fridge and put the dessert away.

I tried to feel bad but couldn't. I didn't know what it would've been like discovering that painting by myself, but it had been okay with Thomas there. Mildly embarrassing, but surprisingly okay.

We drank and then we ate and then we drank some more after we exchanged our secret Santas. The gifts themselves were rarely anything special, but it was a fun tradition that brought a touch of normalcy when Sam's glaring absence threatened to overwhelm the evening. Thomas stared at his map for a long time before he gave me a strangely solemn thank-you. I thought I'd made a mistake buying it, but throughout the whole evening he kept touching it, tracing lines all over the countries.

Cleo had brought a huge chocolate and vanilla ice cream log topped with pistachio nuts, and even though I'd eaten so much already that I had to pop the button on my pants, I ate two helpings of that too.

Sometime after midnight, we retreated to the living room and sprawled all over the sectional. I turned on the TV but left it on mute. Imran raised his glass unsteadily and said, "To Sam. We still miss him, and we always will." The house seemed to breathe in agreement, warm and fragrant with Christmas scents. I thought of all the holidays I'd spent with Sam wrapped around me and how happy we'd been here.

"To Sam," we echoed and drank. I remembered the painting upstairs and the urge to giggle bubbled up my throat. I felt Thomas's eyes on me, but when I looked at him, he was staring at the flashing TV screen. He did have a small smirk on his face though.

"By the way, is it okay if we crash here?" Cleo asked. Her head lolled to the side, and she blinked at me blearily. "I really don't want to call a cab right now."

"Sure," I said. "Like I said, you can all crash if you want to. You should stay too, Thomas. I have at least two spare bedrooms made up, so take your pick."

He sank down on his side of the sectional a little more, and his feet ended up in Imran's lap. "I think I might stay here," he said. "This couch is comfortable."

I knew that. I'd slept here plenty of times with Sam, sometimes because we'd been exhausted and had fallen asleep before we could drag ourselves upstairs, and sometimes because . . . well. It was a comfortable couch.

A flicker of awareness passed between Imran and Cleo. I didn't immediately understand what it was, but suddenly he dumped Thomas's feet off of his lap, stood, and dragged her up.

"Night, boys," she told us, blowing us each a kiss.

Thomas mumbled something incoherently and snuggled deeper into the couch. I watched them, tracked their footsteps, and oh God, they picked the bedroom right above our heads.

"Um," I said. "I don't know if you're going to want to sleep here."

"What?" Thomas's eyelids were already half-closed, and he blinked sleepily. I flopped to the side a little more so I landed near his head.

"They're going to—" And yep, there it was. Creaking bedsprings.

"Fuck no!" Thomas gave a disbelieving guffaw and grabbed a pillow and stuffed his head underneath it. I did the same. I lay so our faces were close, our feet at opposite ends of the sectional. "It's okay," he whispered loudly. "He doesn't last long when he's drunk."

I peeked from behind my cushion. "How the hell do you know that?"

"Remember when they were, uh, on a break?" When Thomas had slept with Cleo, in other words. "Well, after that we talked. The three of us. To see if we could work things out and remain friends. We all got drunk and Imran and Cleo started to do it *right there on my couch!* I escaped to my bed. He didn't last long, thank goodness."

I sobered up a little. "When was this?"

"Not long after the trip to Bouillon." Thomas flattened his hand on the couch. His fingertips nearly touched the heel of my hand. "We didn't want to bother you, Ollie, so don't feel left out. And I think it's something we needed to work out ourselves. It nearly ruined our friendship, and we kind of realized we couldn't do that to you."

"Hey," I said, sitting up. I reached for a half-empty bottle of champagne, took a lukewarm swig, and passed it to Thomas. "I don't want your pity. Any of you. If you didn't get along anymore, I could still be friends with you separately." I wasn't sure why it rubbed me the wrong way that they'd gotten together and decided they had to work this out for my sake, but it did. Even if the thought of our friendships shattering gave me hives, I wasn't the child of a divorcing couple, for God's sake. We drained the bottle while we tried to ignore the squeaking above us.

"Would you though?" He sat up too, and for the first time since I'd known him, this brick of a man looked small. "Would you stay friends or would we have . . . gone our own ways?"

"Of course I'd have stayed friends with you," I said, confused. I opened my mouth to say something else, but a loud groan erupted above us and we dove back under our pillows. "We could sneak up to the top floor," I whispered. "We won't hear them there."

"But the painting," Thomas said. He lifted my shield a little, and we were staring at each other in the semidarkness of our sanctuary. He laughed softly, and his breath whuffed against my face. I felt sleepy and comfortable. His eyes were dark pools of safety I could lose myself in.

"You've seen me naked now." An embarrassing drunken giggle escaped me, and I covered my mouth. Thomas lifted his finger and traced the back of my hand.

"And it was glorious," he said. I laughed. My hand fell away. His eyes locked on to mine. I didn't know who reached for whom, but our mouths came together, warm and comfortable and a little off-center.

My bottom lip stuck between his. I felt the moist press of his tongue. He laughed again, even as his eyes drooped, and then I was asleep.

I woke up with a pounding headache and with breath that could've come straight from the mouths of Cerberus. I groaned and stretched as I tried to peel my eyelids open. Sunlight spilled through the half-drawn curtains, but it was murky so I figured it was still pretty early. Someone had put a blanket over me. The couch beside me was empty. Had Thomas gone up to bed after all?

A small noise made me sit up. He was standing in the doorway, freshly showered and newly dressed. "I didn't mean to wake you," he said. "You can go back to sleep. It's early."

I frowned at him, pushed the bird's nest out of my eyes, and stood on wobbly legs. "What about you?"

"I'm . . ." I realized he wasn't looking at me. "I need to go."

"Thomas?" His eyes flicked to mine and away again. "Are you okay?"

"Yeah, I'm fine." He finally looked at me, and there was . . . guilt? What the hell? "Go back to sleep, Ollie. I made coffee. It's brewing now. It'll still be fresh when you wake up again. I'll—I'll text you." And then he was gone.

Stunned, I sat in my living room for a while until I realized I really needed to pee, and trudged up to my bathroom. Creeping by Cleo and Imran's room, I was relieved to hear nothing but snores.

My hair was an absolute mess. I had pillow lines in the shape of a flower on my face. I brushed my teeth and stared at my reflection, tried to imagine Sam standing behind me, and couldn't. I spit in the sink, wiped my mouth, and thought, *Oh*.

Thomas and I had kissed. Last night. I met my own eyes in the mirror and attempted to work out how I felt about that. Mostly confused about Thomas's reaction, because *that* was why he'd run off. It'd been a harmless kiss. And I'd liked it. But he obviously . . . hadn't.

I told Cleo about it while Imran showered. The longer I talked, the tighter her mouth pulled into a thin line.

"If Imran were here right now, he'd tell me it wasn't any of my business, but Jesus, Oliver. Je-sus."

Mind boggled, I sat back in my kitchen chair. "What?"

She blew out a breath that puffed up her cheeks, closed her eyes, and pinched her nose. All I had to do was wait, because I knew her, and I knew she'd talk eventually. Her eyes flew open. She grabbed my hands and gave them a rough shake.

"I love you," she said. "You know I do."

"Of course. I l—"

"But you can be remarkably dumb, Ollie. *Remarkably* dumb."

"What? Cleo!"

Her jaw flexed, and she squeezed my hands. "Be quiet, because I'm going to make a big mistake and my conscience is about to take over. Thomas has been in love with you from the minute you brought him to that first dinner almost four years ago. He thought you two were going on a date, you asshole. And instead he walked in to see you canoodling with Sam. Who was, by the way, as perfect a specimen of manhood as I've ever seen. You broke Thomas's heart."

"Cleo . . ." I laughed, but my stomach twisted. "That's not true. It can't be."

"We all knew, Ollie! Even Sam knew! You were the only one too dumb to see it."

"Cleo!" She jumped guiltily in her chair, and Imran strode in, eyes dark with anger. "That wasn't your secret to tell. I don't *believe* you."

"They kissed," she snapped. "And as usual Ollie has no idea why Thomas might be upset." She turned back to me. I'd never seen her this annoyed. "You know all those people he keeps sleeping with? It's because he knows he's not going to fall in love with anyone else."

"Cleo, that's enough!" Imran yelled. "Just because you're in love with him—"

"I'm not!" She sprang to her feet and balled her tiny fists on her thighs. "But you're never going to believe me, are you? You're never going to forgive me!"

She stormed into the living room, and I got to my feet.

"I'll go," Imran said. He didn't look mad anymore. Just sad. "But you might want to talk to Thomas."

"So she's . . . It's true? All these years?"

Imran shook his head. "She's right. You are clueless. Yes, Ollie. All these years."

I sat back down, tried not to listen to Imran and Cleo argue, but it was hard. Their voices rose and then they stilled, and they were quiet for a long time. Eventually I heard my front door fall into its lock. I wondered if there was anything of my circle of friends left. The thought made me want to weep.

I had a bit of a problem with crawling into my shell when things got uncomfortable. I went to see my mom for Christmas, and the days ticked past and no one called. I didn't call them either. Some distance seemed to be a good idea at the time, but New Year's Eve happened and still there was no word from anyone. I spent the evening with my mom, worrying about everyone else, and called Sam's parents at her urging.

I didn't particularly want to talk to them, and Simon felt the same, apparently.

"How are you doing, Oliver?" Martine asked after an awkward silence when Simon passed the phone on to her without saying a word.

"Okay," I said. "I'm just calling to see how you are. And to say happy New Year."

"Oh. Thank you," Martine said softly. "I'm doing all right. It's hard, without Sam."

"It is." Another tense silence fell.

"Oliver, I . . ." She trailed off, and I wondered if Simon was listening in, keeping her from speaking her mind. I felt sorry for the woman, but it only steeled my resolve. What they were doing was wrong, and I wouldn't let them get away with it. The house belonged to me now. It was my home, and I wanted to stay here. "Happy New Year," she eventually said. "I have to go now."

"Okay, b—" I began, but the line went dead.

The silence from my friends continued to reign. To escape the anxiety that brought me, I wandered Antwerp's cobbled streets. The ancient buildings leaned protectively over me as I breathed in the atmosphere. I loved imagining the old Antwerp, at the height of the Baroque period, with Peter Paul Rubens, the Treaty of Antwerp, the rise of commerce in the city. I walked the Great Market, watched for a while the fountain depicting Brabo throwing Antigoon's hand—our own version of David and Goliath—stood in the cathedral's shade, and wished Sam were here.

I didn't ache for him like I had. It wasn't the missing of a vital body part. It was simply the need to talk to someone who understood me as well as I understood him, who wouldn't judge me for my mistakes, for being oblivious about Thomas's feelings. I missed being known.

The weekend before I had to go back to work, I got into my car and drove to Thomas's house. A tiny but quaint home in Bazel, an equally quaint village perched on a riverbed. The Wissekerke Castle grounds were open to the public, and he could see the entry gate from his living room. I liked where he lived. It was so open and free and soothing.

I found his car parked in front of the house. The trunk was open, stuffed to the brim with bags. He came out carrying a suitcase, and my heart just about stopped.

"Thomas," I breathed. If I'd worn pearls, I'd have been clutching them. He'd cut his hair.

He jerked, startled, and actually took a step back when he saw me. "Ollie? What are you doing here?"

I couldn't do anything but stare at him. "You . . . you cut your hair."

The wind tugged it across his forehead, where it had been cut to eyebrow length in a chopped, modern style. It tapered down, leaving his neck pale and bare.

"I—" He brought his hand up self-consciously and ran his fingers through his locks in a way that showed he wasn't used to the new length yet. It immediately flopped down again. He tried to smile. "I thought it was time for something new."

His face was clean-shaven and smooth. Handsome.

"Are you . . ." *okay*, I wanted to ask, but what came out was, "going somewhere?"

"Uh, yeah." His smile turned real. "I've been looking at that map you gave me. And I thought it was time to finally do some of that traveling, you know? I took time off work."

I swallowed hard. "How long?"

His dark eyes fixed on me, and like a visceral shock, the memory of his mouth on mine came back to me. "Three months."

"I— Wow. Where are you going?"

"Driving to the south of France to start with. I want to see Italy and take a ferry to Greece. Drive to Turkey, and maybe store my car for a while and hop on a plane to Egypt."

"That sounds amazing," I said, but my heart wasn't in it. "Are you leaving right now?"

He shook his head. "Monday morning. A friend is coming to stay at my house while I'm gone, so I'm putting some stuff in storage."

"You could've stored it at my house. I have enough room."

Thomas shrugged. "I didn't want to bother you with it."

"Right." I stuffed my hands into my pockets, trying to look like that didn't sting. "I'm going to miss you. But I hope you have a great time."

"Thanks." He put the suitcase in the trunk of his car. "Do you want to take a walk around the castle? It's a nice enough day."

"Sure."

He nodded and locked his front door, then gave me a hesitant smile before we set off through the large stone archway that led to the castle grounds. We walked by the lake, up the hill by a braying donkey in its rolling field, and down between the trees, following the path until we found a lonely bench. In silent agreement, we sat down, looking out at the lake below us.

"Why did you come to see me?" he asked softly.

"I thought maybe we should talk."

He looked at me steadily, and I found it hard to keep his gaze. "We don't have to, you know. I understand."

"Well, that makes one of us," I said. "Because I have no clue what's going on. Cleo told me—" I faltered.

"What?"

I said nothing and he nudged me.

"It's okay. You can tell me. What did she say?"

"That you've been in love with me for years," I managed to croak, blood rising to my cheeks.

He smiled serenely at the sky. "I'm surprised she kept it a secret for this long. I never wanted you to know or feel awkward about it. But yes, she's right."

"I don't know what to say."

He gently squeezed my shoulder. "You don't have to say anything. It's not on you. It never was. It was my problem and mine alone. I never expected anything of you, Ollie. Especially after . . . after Sam died."

I didn't know if it was the right thing to do or not, but I wanted to touch him somehow, so I took his hand and held it. "I'm sorry," I said.

"For what?" His fingers tightened on mine. My hands were cold, and the heat of his felt so good I never wanted to let go. "We've been good friends. Great friends, even. I don't want that to change."

"But you're leaving." I was mortified when my voice broke on the last word.

"Ah, Ollie." He gently worked his hand loose and hugged me close. I wondered if I should be the one comforting him. "I'm not leaving you. I'm taking a little bit of the dream you offered when you gave me that map. And we'll talk, won't we? Whenever we can. I don't want this to change anything."

"Me neither," I whispered. I pressed my face into his shoulder for a moment and then sat up and looked at him. He was so young with his hair short, so much more vulnerable. I reached out and ran my hands through it. He closed his eyes. "I was pretty drunk that night. But I really liked that kiss."

His eyes flew open. "You don't have to be nice to me. I've been beating myself up about it all week."

"I'm not. I'm telling the truth." My heart began to race, and I realized I wanted to kiss him again. It would be an incredibly selfish thing to do though, because I had no idea what I could offer him, if this was me responding only to being wanted. It hung in the air between us. The tension crackled. I could tell he knew what I was thinking. His eyes darkened to pools of liquid heat, and a jolt of desire I hadn't experienced since I was with Sam awakened me from the inside out.

"I liked it too," he whispered. He cupped my face in his big hands and pressed his forehead to mine. "So much. But I can't keep doing this to myself."

I made a breathy sound. He kissed my temple, my eyelids. I tilted my chin, still not really knowing what I wanted, apart from him here, close. He hesitated, then let me go, and it felt like I was falling.

"I should finish packing up."

Unable to speak, I nodded. We stood in silence and walked the rickety iron suspension bridge that crossed the narrow part of the lake. When we reached his house again, I was cold to the bone. I had no idea what to say to him, so I hugged him tight instead. His arms wrapped around me like a warm security blanket.

"I'll miss you," he murmured into my hair.

"I'll miss you too. Be safe. And call me."

He nodded and took a step back, his eyes dark and unfathomable. "Bye, Ollie," he said and walked into his house.

Suddenly I wanted to rush after him, beg him not to go, because I feared he'd come back a different person. But I didn't have the right to do that, wasn't in a place where I could, so I got in my car and drove home.

CHAPTER
NINE

"**I**s he still pining?"

"I'm not pining." I drew a heart in the condensation ring of my beer. Oh my God, I was pining. I sat up. "It's all this Valentine's rubbish, okay? It's been going on since the beginning of January. Christmas decorations go down, and suddenly wild hearts appear everywhere. I'm sick of it."

"Aw, honey. You've never been alone for Valentine's, have you?"

"No." I propped my cheek up with my fist and continued drawing in the condensation.

"So, what, are you . . . in love with Thomas now?" Imran eyed me warily, like I might bite his nose off. For a second I wanted to, but I just sighed. My stomach felt tight with confusion. I couldn't seem to find any peace, torn one minute between missing Thomas and feeling guilty about it the next.

I hadn't heard from Sam's parents either, and every time I thought about Thomas and how much I wanted him near, I wondered if I even deserved to keep the house. And yet every morning I woke up, and every evening I came home from work, the place felt a little more mine. Sam was still there, in the furniture and the walls and the empty spaces in between. But his presence was an afterthought now, part of the building, like the touch of the architect who'd built it.

"I don't know. I guess I miss him, and whenever we talk on the phone, it's for hours and I feel happy."

"Sounds like love to me," Cleo mumbled. Imran elbowed her, and she sniggered. They'd been getting along a lot better since their little fallout at my house.

"Not necessarily," Imran said. "It's easy to mistake a deep friendship for romantic love, especially when it's one-sided to begin with. You might be responding to his feelings rather than generating feelings of your own."

I gritted my teeth. "I'm aware of that, thank you. And you're not helping."

"So what are you going to do?"

I lifted my pint and drained half of it. "Fuck knows. He's in Greece. Being bathed and fed olives while young, nubile, athletic Greeks wave banana leaves at him. Have you seen him recently? He looks like a god. With pecs and abs. And skin like honey. Ah, hell." I drained the rest of my beer as Cleo thumbed through her phone.

She shoved it under my nose. "Like this, you mean?" I knew the picture she was going to show me before I saw it. I followed him on Instagram too. It was in front of a cute blue church on the rocky island of Rhodes. He perched shirtless on a motorbike. His grin was white in his brown face. I seethed with jealousy at the person holding that damn camera.

"I think this may go beyond friendship," Imran said as he gave me a wide-eyed look. I pulled myself together.

"I honestly don't know. Some days I feel like I don't want to be with anyone at all because I'd be cheating on Sam."

"You know Sam would've wanted—"

"Yes, Cleo," I said tersely. "I've heard it all before. That doesn't change the fact that this is how it feels."

"You're right," she said, like I was a petulant child who needed calming. "So how often do you talk?"

"Oh, I don't know. Once . . . four, five times a week?"

"Five times a *week*?" Imran and Cleo shared a look.

"Yeah, whatever," I mumbled and played with my empty beer bottle. Thomas was my best friend. I couldn't risk losing him to a probably misconceived notion of romance. Besides, he was too far away to get romantic with, so why was I even worrying about this? A teenager walked past with a red heart balloon, and I wanted to pop it with a toothpick. Ten toothpicks.

He called me that night, because I was a giant liar and we talked every day. I'd snuggled into my pajamas like I always did, ready for him on the couch with the TV on mute and a mug of rose hip tea cradled in my hands.

"Hey, Ollie," he said.

"Hey, how's it going? You still on Rhodes?"

"Yes. I'll be leaving tomorrow for the mainland, and then it's up toward Istanbul."

"Man, that sounds so exciting. Tell me everything you did today." And he did. I closed my eyes, only for a moment, so I could bask in the warmth of his voice. I'd gotten used to ending my days with him murmuring in my ear. I wondered how I'd get on when he returned. He'd been gone for three weeks and already I couldn't imagine not talking to him every day.

Maybe he'll be here, actually murmuring in your ear, when he gets back, a little voice in my head told me. It made me sad because it made me remember Sam, how I'd loved him my whole life, and here I was not even a year later, thinking of loving someone else.

"Ollie, you still there?"

"Yes, I'm listening."

"Good, because I have to tell you something."

I sat up a little bit. "Yeah? What is it? You okay?"

"Yes, I'm . . . I'm great actually. I, uh, met someone."

In my head, all the gears ground to a screeching halt.

"His name is Stephen Dane. He's American. He's traveling too, for a whole year, can you imagine? He's, um, going to tag along with me for a while."

"Oh." My mouth felt dry as dust. "That's great, Thomas. So . . . he's nice?"

"Yeah, I like him a lot. He finished an international business degree so he's taking some time off before starting the job hunt."

"That sounds . . . amazing." I couldn't reboot my brain, so I mumbled nonsensical things as he went on about the places he'd visited with Stephen. It sounded like they'd been hanging out for days. Why had he not told me sooner? I didn't want to ask. It wasn't my place.

I didn't remember how we ended the conversation, but after that Stephen was in nearly all the pictures. He was disgustingly gorgeous in that wholesome American way. Broad shoulders, white teeth, close-cropped hair, and a jaw Michelangelo would've wanted to sculpt. I hated him. And maybe I wasn't very good at hiding it, because Thomas called less, and I didn't call him either.

The weeks crept by a minute at a time. Valentine's came and went, and so did Thomas's return date. Cleo told me he'd ditched his car somewhere and he was staying in Prague for a few weeks because Stephen loved it there so much.

I knew they both returned to Belgium at some point, but I saw neither of them. Instead I gritted my teeth and went to work, went to see my mom. I went for drinks with Cleo, consulted with my lawyer about the house, generally walked through life in a numb haze—and then there it was. The anniversary of Sam's death.

I hadn't planned anything in particular. It was a normal Monday afternoon in June, with weak sunlight and the threat of rain. I didn't expect anyone to take time off, but I sent a mass text to whoever I thought might care that I'd be at his grave at two, and that anyone who wanted to join me for a coffee afterward was welcome.

Because I wanted to clean up the headstone, I arrived at one so I could remove moss stains and trim the grass a little bit. He'd been cremated and his parents had dusted his ashes in their backyard where he'd played as a boy, so I knew he wasn't even remotely there. And still I felt him with me, like a warm presence at my back.

"Hey," I murmured as I pulled a daffodil from the grass. "Is it good where you are now? Is it warm and light, and do you get to stay up late and eat to your heart's content and never gain a pound?" I sat on my heels and smiled. "Or in your case, do they have the latest Hugo Boss suits, and do you get to drink the best cocktails without ever having a hangover?"

No response, obviously. But the warmth was there and the peaceful feeling in my stomach didn't leave.

"I'm so sorry," I whispered and tugged the gloves from my hands. "I'm so, so sorry this happened to you. It wasn't fair, and I shouldn't have . . . I should've stayed at the gallery with you. I tell myself that all the time. I know it makes no difference, that it does you no good now. But I want you to know I'll always be sorry for that. Part of me will always wonder what it would've been like to grow old with you. To be married to you. I think that hurts the most. That I never got to be your husband. I miss you." I touched the smooth marble of the gravestone. "I think I always will. It doesn't hurt as much anymore as it did in the beginning, so I guess that means I'm ... moving on. I listened to your voice mail this morning, and it didn't make me cry anymore. I think I'm finally ready to delete it. I'll forget what your voice sounds like, and that makes me sad. But I think I'm supposed to forget, aren't I? That it's okay to? I'm twenty-seven. I can't hang on to you like a crutch forever."

The wind stirred my hair.

"I love you, Samuel," I whispered. I tucked the gloves back into the small canvas bag I'd brought, arranged a bouquet of roses next to his name, and climbed to my feet.

I wanted to get rid of the bag before the others arrived. I had turned around to make my way down the path when I saw Thomas standing there. Tall and handsome and carefully smiling. I laughed. Laughed and threw myself at him. He caught me and hugged me and I finally cried.

"It's okay," he murmured. "It's okay." He held me for a long time. I closed my eyes and listened to the easy rhythm of his heart. I was so happy to see him, I couldn't stop smiling, and he gently rocked me side to side.

When I finally straightened, I noticed other people slowly walking up the path. I took a step back and quickly dried my face.

"You look great," I told him. "I didn't know you were coming."

"I wouldn't miss this," he said. "I wanted to be here for you, and for Sam. Are you doing okay? Is it ... very bad?"

"No. It's not so bad. I'm sad for him, but I'm doing all right."

"Good. I'm really glad to hear it. Do you ..." He ducked his head and blushed. My heartbeat picked up speed. "Do you want to meet Stephen? He's here too. I told him about Sam, and he wanted to come. I hope you don't mind."

And just like that my stomach sank to my feet, but I tried to keep my brave face on. If I failed, I hoped he'd ascribe it to the crying I'd been doing.

"Sure. I'd love to meet him."

Stephen was as American as he looked in the photographs, and the worst thing was, he was really nice.

He hugged me nearly as hard as Thomas had. "I'm sorry for your loss," he drawled, and oh *God*, was that a Texas accent? Was he a *cowboy*? "Thomas told me so much about you. I feel like I know you."

"Um, well." I awkwardly patted his back until he let me go. "It's nice to meet you. And thank you."

He nodded, and his baby blues shimmered in the June sun.

"Come meet the others," Thomas said. I watched them go. Stephen even had a swagger, like he'd just stepped off a horse. I waited to see what emotions would bubble to the surface, but all I could think was, *I hope you're happy, Thomas.* I'd have to tell him that later.

Now I just had to deal with being overwhelmed by all the people showing up. Cleo and Imran were there, of course. My mom, Sam's parents. Beyond that were Sam's boss, some of his coworkers I'd met what felt like a lifetime ago, my own boss, distant friends. I couldn't believe it.

We stood around his grave, and everyone had something nice to say. A few of the stories were so funny we laughed too loudly, and I was worried security would come and throw us out of the cemetery. Instead other mourners came to stand close and listen, and they too smiled, like they could find hope in this picture. Like there was a future after loss. Life. Love.

It took so long there was no time for most people to join us for coffee, so instead the usual gang, plus Stephen and my mom, came back to my house. I saw Martine and Simon have a tense discussion by their car, until Simon shook his head sharply and yanked the driver's side door open. Martine, looking over her shoulder at me, quickly climbed in too.

I did feel a vague sort of sadness, because I realized the death of a lover was something you carried with you for life, but it became a bearable sort of weight after some time. Whereas the death of a child was a burden that never lightened, an ache that never eased, a loss that was beyond healing.

I hadn't expected that many visitors, but it was okay. I made do. They mostly consumed lots of coffee, and I spent my time praying no one would come up with the brilliant idea of taking a look at Sam's art room. I hadn't touched that picture since Thomas and I haphazardly covered it up again.

"I can't believe it's been a year."

I jolted and looked up at Thomas. Automatically my eyes searched out Stephen, and I spotted him stuck between Imran and Cleo on the couch. They both looked a bit lovestruck, to be honest.

"You might lose your cowboy," I said, nodding in their direction. Thomas smiled so softly at Stephen's back, it made me ache. That faraway look had been mine for so long, only I hadn't known what it meant. "Are you happy, Thomas?"

The smile widened a little. "Yeah. I think I am."

I swallowed past the lump in my throat and sounded almost completely normal when I said, "Good. I'm glad."

His dark gaze zeroed in on me, but I didn't meet his eyes. "Are you?" he whispered.

It felt like a whole lot depended on my reply, but the day had drained me and I had nothing left to give. And really, it wouldn't have been fair to answer it any other way than, "Yes, of course I am. I want you to be happy." Like a coward, I added, "More coffee?" He didn't say anything for a long moment, then shook his head once. "Well, I'm going to—" I lifted my mug and tried a smile on for size. It didn't exactly fit right, but it would have to do.

As I walked into the kitchen, it felt like something was tugging me back. Then it gave with a sharp snap. I turned around and saw Thomas leaning over Stephen, giving him a chaste kiss on the lips. Cleo's eyes caught mine, and I looked away.

At nine I had the house to myself again, a strange quiet settling over the old building. It was too big for me, but the idea of giving it up made my heart hurt. Where would I go? What could I possibly find that would be better than this? Maybe I should get a roommate, a student, like I'd once upon a time suggested to Samuel, but the thought didn't appeal to me anymore.

Maybe I should do some traveling too. I had a nice little sum saved up. I could do with seeing some of the world. Maybe I'd travel to Texas and come home with my very own stud. They did seem to grow on trees over there.

I fell asleep on the couch, very much like I'd done with Thomas that fateful evening. Only now there was no one to kiss me good-night.

I dreamed of kisses though. Lots and lots of kisses, dealt out by two mouths. It was Sam and Thomas, and we were all naked, and my mind was about to blow when Stephen joined too. I jolted awake, a second away from shooting my load in my pants. I hadn't had a damn wet dream since I was sixteen years old! Half stumbling, I cursed my way up to the bathroom and took a shower to deal with my erection before falling stark-naked into bed. I needed to get laid.

Maybe I should call Peter.

CHAPTER
TEN

I didn't call Peter, but things almost did return to normal. We found a new bar to hang out in on Saturday nights, and we met up every week. I didn't dance on tables anymore like Cleo still did, but I did learn a new appreciation for how Thomas must've felt being surrounded by two deliriously happy couples all those years. His urge to sleep around suddenly made a lot of sense.

And yet, I didn't. I got propositioned a few times, but I always demurred. It didn't escape my notice that Thomas tensed whenever I did give in to some harmless flirting, but I wasn't bigheaded enough to think he was jealous. He cared, that was all.

At least this business with Stephen always being there did answer one question: I loved Thomas. There was nothing I could do about it, so I didn't, but there it was.

I went through life with a semblance of, if not happiness, at least contentment. It was more than what I thought I'd ever have a year ago, and I could live with it. Work was going well. I was healthy. I considered adopting a dog, but maybe I'd go on holiday somewhere first. I could take my entire six weeks again and plan that trip to Texas. Or maybe not just Texas, but see some of the USA. Because why not? I had no one to think of but myself. I made tentative plans, bought a Lonely Planet guide on the States, dog-eared the pages of places I wanted to see, and carried on with my life.

One Thursday morning I received a call from Stan, asking if I could come and see him as soon as possible. I made an appointment for the same day after work and left early once I became too nervous to sit around any longer.

He ushered me into his office as soon as I arrived. "How set on keeping the house are you?" he asked me bluntly.

I didn't even hesitate. "It's mine," I said. "It was ours. Sam wanted me to have it. It's my home. I don't want to leave." Panic squeezed my insides when I realized the reality of the situation was I seriously could lose it. I needed the house. I felt like it was the only thing keeping me tethered to earth.

He pursed his lips. "In that case, we have a proposal, and I strongly urge you to take it. If you refuse, they'll be taking it to court, and the assigned judge—" he sucked air in through his teeth "—let's just say you'll want to avoid him at all costs."

"What's the proposal?" I asked, mouth dry.

"My guess is they're having money troubles. They want you to buy them out. You pay them half of what the house is worth and it's all yours. I think I can reduce that to forty-five, maybe forty percent, because they're desperate and that works in our favor. However, if they're desperate enough and we push them too hard, they'll want to go the whole way. They'll know the judge is likely to rule in their favor. The only reason they're doing this is because this whole thing is becoming too expensive and they need money now."

I'd never had to pay a mortgage before, and an old house like that was a money suck regardless. Heating bills, repairs, it all fell to me now. If I had to pay off even half of a huge place like that, it'd break my bank account. And the thought of having to pay because Sam's dad was an asshole—pay for something that was rightfully mine—made me see red. "I can't believe they can do this."

"I know. And if we had any other judge, I'd say fight them to the end. With this one . . . it's a huge risk to take."

"I don't know if I can get a mortgage for even half the house."

Stan nodded. "Think about it, contact some banks about loans, but don't wait too long. I need an answer soon so I can plan a strategy." He put his palms flat on the desk and leaned a little closer. "If you want to fight this, I'll go there with you. But in the end all that matters is that you get what you want. And paying a mortgage might be the only way to do it."

I left his office in a daze, wondering, not for the first time, if this was all worth it. After all, it was just a house, no matter how much of a relief it sometimes was to pull that door closed behind me and shut out the world. I could feel the same about any other house. Couldn't I?

For a while I did nothing but wallow in indecision. More than anything, I wanted to talk to Thomas about this, but I couldn't bring myself to call him. I only saw him when everyone else was around, and I kept quiet about my troubles.

And then Thomas and Stephen broke up and things turned really awkward. It almost seemed like he was mad at me. He didn't come to our Saturday outing for two weeks in a row. Cleo said he almost never answered his phone anymore, and when I called him, all I got was voice mail, like I'd been blocked.

So I drove out there again, on a sunny summer day at the very end of July.

Thomas's car was parked in front of his door, so I knew he was home, but as I rang and rang the doorbell, no one answered.

I opened his letter box and peered through it. On the floor was a stack of mail that was days, if not weeks old. A chill of fear raced down my spine. Oh God, no.

"Thomas?" I yelled. "Thomas, it's me, Ollie! If you're in there, please come and open the door. Thomas!" Nothing. I dithered on the doorstep for a second, then opened the letter box again. "Thomas? I'm going to call an ambulance, okay? If you're hurt and you can hear me, help is coming!"

I heard a noise, a bang. A door creaked and then footsteps stumbled down the stairs. I saw something move, and the door snapped open so hard I nearly ripped the lip of the letter box off. I straightened and gasped. "Oh my God, what happened?"

His eyes were bloodshot and swollen. He looked sick, his pupils tiny. He was wrapped in a bathrobe, and even from where I stood on the doorstep, I could smell the body odor on him. Body odor and liquor.

"Are you hungover?"

"What do you want, Oliver?"

I gaped at him. He hadn't shaved in goodness knew how long. "What do I want? We're fucking worried about you! Your dad called Cleo, Thomas. Your dad! And here you are getting your fucking drink on? Now you're asking *me* what I want? I thought you were hurt. I thought you were dead, you asshole!"

His gaze softened for a moment, in a way that was so familiar, so dear to me now. The corners of his eyes went up a little, crinkled at the edges with his laugh lines. His sooty lashes lifted and cast shadows on his sharp cheekbones. And just like that the softness was gone. "Well, as you can see, I'm fine. So you can call everyone and tell them to leave me alone."

He was about to slam the door in my face, and I stopped it with my palm, which was a bad idea. It jarred my wrist something fierce, but I was too angry to care.

"Oh, no, you don't. I'm coming in and I am shoving you in the shower. You stink. I'm going to pour away all your liquor and make you breakfast. You're going to call your dad and apologize in person. You think he hasn't been worried sick? I expected better from you, Thomas."

He hung his head, and instantly I felt like a total dick. I took his arm. The bathrobe was ridiculously fluffy, like a warm hug, but oh God, the smell. "Come on," I told him gently. "Into the shower with you."

And he came with me, meek as a lamb. I glanced into the small living room to the right of his ridiculously steep stairway and saw nothing but darkness and vague shapes of messiness. Up the steps we went, into his only bathroom, where dirty laundry had been left lying on the floor. I turned on the shower to heat, set him down on the closed toilet lid, squirted some toothpaste on his toothbrush and handed it over. Without a word, he accepted it and began to brush. I lifted his feet and took off his socks. He didn't look at me, barely seemed to notice I was there, and again my stomach lurched with worry. Was he on something? Was he drugged up?

"Come on, spit in the sink and rinse your mouth."

He was so far gone, I didn't trust him not to step into the shower with his robe on. So I took it off him and managed valiantly to keep my eyes above nipple level.

"Don't forget to wash your hair," I told him, and handed him a loofah and his bottle of bodywash. He met my eyes for a second. He tried to smile at me, but his mouth quivered. "You'll be okay," I said. "It hurts now, I know. But it will be okay." He nodded and put some soap on his loofah, so I was confident he could take it from there.

I stepped out of the bathroom and fished my phone out of my pocket. "Cleo?" I said when she answered. I went into his bedroom, held my breath until I could yank open the curtains and the windows, then looked around, stunned. "I'm at Thomas's."

"Oh my God, is he okay?"

"I honestly don't know. He's definitely hungover, maybe still drunk, but he's acting weird. I'm scared he might've taken drugs or something."

"Weird how?" she asked, all businesslike, and I knew she'd snapped into nurse mode. "Is he shaking? Convulsing? Vomiting or losing consciousness?"

"What? No! He's taking a shower right now. But he's really spaced out. And his pupils were tiny. First he was really mad at me, and a little later he was all agreeable and quiet."

Silence, then she softly said, "He probably didn't do drugs. He's probably sad, Ollie. Because what you're telling me is exactly what you were like when Sam first died."

"But nobody died," I said stupidly. I remembered what I had just said to Thomas: *It hurts now, I know. But it will be okay.* Some part of me had recognized his grief for what it was, even if I hadn't consciously realized it.

"No, but that doesn't mean he didn't just lose someone."

"Okay," I said. "If there are no drugs involved, I can deal with it." The shower turned off, and I began my hunt for clean clothes—easier said than done. His suits and shirts were strewn all over the place, so at least I had hope he'd been going to work and wasn't out of a job. Yet.

"Do you need me to come over?" Cleo asked.

"Not now. Maybe later. I'll let you know."

"Okay. And Ollie?"

"Yeah?"

"Take care of him, all right? He's hurting and he'll be vulnerable."

"Yeah, sure, of course."

I hung up, found a clean pair of boxers, some sweatpants, and a T-shirt. Not knowing what I'd find there, I turned back to the bathroom.

Thomas was staring at himself in the mirror. His towel hung off a pair of narrow hips, bones jutting out sharply on either side of a lovely six-pack. He'd lost some weight—not drastically so, but enough to make his muscles stand out even more. His reflection met my eyes.

"I'm sorry," he whispered. "I never meant for you to see me like this."

"I think you've seen me worse," I said, holding out the clothes. He took them but didn't put them on. I really wanted him to cover up because any second now my gaze was going to drift again, and he'd catch it.

"Yes, but you lost someone."

I thought of what Cleo had said. "So did you. Come on." I picked the T-shirt off the pile and pulled it over his head. His face was very close when he emerged.

"Not in the way you think," he murmured and turned away to stick his arms through the sleeves. When he picked up the boxers, I spun around and left the bathroom.

His small living room was in a right state. He might not've done hard drugs, but he'd done everything else under the sun. Tequila, wine, beer, vodka. I didn't gather a single whiskey bottle, so at least I'd been right not to buy those whiskey blocks.

He came downstairs as I was pouring the last of it down the drain—not that there'd been much left to drain away.

"You don't have to do that," he said, his cheeks flushed with what must've been embarrassment. "You've done more than enough for me already."

I set the bottle of tequila next to the other empties, took his hands in mine, and really looked at him. "If it weren't for the people taking care of me day in, day out after Sam died, I wouldn't be here, Thomas. Let me give something back, okay? You're hurting. I want to be here for you."

His bottom lip quivered, and he broke our eye contact. I let him. "I made coffee. Want some?"

He sat down at his small, round, wooden kitchen table and nodded. I found mugs and sugar, but no milk since it'd gone bad. In fact, his fridge was pathetically bare. I'd have to go back on that breakfast I'd promised.

I left him alone with his thoughts for a bit, opened the curtains in the living room, tidied up the throws and pillows and laundry that had been left there too, and made my way upstairs, where I gathered more laundry and put in a load. I stripped his bed, then realized I didn't want to invade his privacy any more than I already had and left it at that. I'd help him remake the bed later, if he wanted me to.

He had his head down on the table when I came back to the kitchen, and I ran my fingers through his hair. He'd kept it short, and I mourned a little bit. I'd never gotten to tug his long hair, and I found I wanted to. So I massaged his scalp instead, his hair damp and soft under my fingers, and he let out a helpless noise.

"Feels good," he mumbled, rolling his forehead back and forth on his arms.

I crouched down beside him and kept carding my fingers through his hair. "One of the worst things after Sam died," I said, "was being absolutely touch-starved. It was like going cold turkey off the best drug. I'd always had him there beside me, and I'd never had to do without someone to hold me. In my darkest hours, I thought it'd kill me."

He lifted his head, and I let my hand fall away, smoothing it over his nape, down his muscular back. "What did you do?"

I smiled ruefully. "I hugged his pillow."

"Oh, Ollie," he whispered. "I didn't know. I would've hugged the crap out of you."

That made me laugh. "I know," I said. "And it's okay. It got better. It will get better for you too."

"I don't think so," he whispered, and I frowned at him.

"Why not?"

Thomas kept his eyes on the table, and he traced his fingers along a wooden vein, back and forth. "He left because he said I still love you, Ollie. He said he couldn't be with someone and not come first. Even when I'm trying to be over you, I can't be. I don't think I ever will be."

No point in lying. My heart sprang to life and began to beat at a canter, but I tried not to let it show. Like Cleo said, he was vulnerable and hurting.

I put my hand on the back of his neck and pulled lightly. He came to me like it was instinct. Just sank onto the ground until I sat back on my heels and held his entire weight against me. I'd never seen anyone so broken-down before. I wondered if he'd regret letting me see him this way later on. This strong, beautiful man on his knees with me. It was hard to comprehend.

"It's okay," I whispered. "It's all going to be fine. You'll see." It was a promise. And I intended to keep it.

I could feel when he began to tense a little later, embarrassment settling in. His shoulders curled away from me first, and he wouldn't look at me, so I ignored the awkwardness, rose to my feet, and pulled him up.

"I'm starving," I said. "Do you think we can go grab some sandwiches at Bruno's and go eat them in the park?" He still wouldn't look at me, but I didn't mind.

"Yeah, that sounds good."

I didn't ask him again if he was okay. I chattered about everything and nothing, from Cleo and Imran being good together again to shenanigans at work, to the point that I forgot I was trying to distract him and told him of my plans of taking some time off and going to the US. We were sitting on the same bench as last time, with the view of the castle and the iron suspension bridge below.

His head snapped up. "You're leaving?"

"What? No, not really. It was, you know, a vague dream." One that wouldn't happen if I had to pay for the house. I didn't tell him about that.

"But you've been planning it."

"Somewhat." I sighed and put my baguette on the paper bag in my lap. "Imran and Cleo were working things out, and you and Stephen were so happy. I felt like a fifth wheel. I wanted to do something for myself."

He raised a sardonic eyebrow. "I know how that feels."

"Yeah, I can see that now. Shame you already took all that time off work. We could've gone to the US together."

His eyes narrowed, and his dark gaze penetrated me. I felt my face go pink and returned my attention to the baguette. It should've been very tasty, but I wouldn't have noticed if it were filled with tofu.

"You and me," he slowly said. "On vacation together."

I tried to shrug nonchalantly. "Sure. Why not?" Pretending to bask in the sweet sunshine, I tried not to let his scrutiny thrill me.

"Yeah," he said after a while. "That would've been nice. So you still going?"

"Maybe at some point, but not right now."

"Why not?"

I realized, money issues aside, I still didn't want to go. Not alone anyway. "Because you broke up with Stephen. I want to be here for you." I lowered my voice. "With you."

He stared at me. His mouth turned up at the corners in a shy smile. He dropped his gaze to the barely touched sandwich in his hands. "Shit, Ollie." So much for returning us to normalcy. His smile fell away. "I wish you hadn't seen me like that this morning. I feel bad about that."

I gripped my sandwich tightly because if I hugged him now, I didn't think I'd want to stop there. "You've seen me cry, haven't you?" I asked quietly. "You've seen me at my lowest. Do you think less of me?"

He stared at me, wide-eyed, and set his lunch aside so he could slip a hand around the back of my neck. "God, Oliver, of course not. I could never. You're the strongest person I know."

"Then why would I think less of you? You're human. It was a very human reaction. I'm sorry you were alone for as long as you've been. I wish I'd come sooner, before you drank all that booze. I wish I'd been there for you. But I'm here now. I want to be here now."

He searched my face, dark eyes lifting to mine. Eventually he nodded and drew me into a hug.

"I'm glad you came," he softly said. I pressed my nose behind his ear, breathed him in.

CHAPTER
ELEVEN

The next few days I spent more time on the phone with banks than doing any actual work, and tried not to get too upset when the first two turned me down flat. I'd been in my job a long time and earned good money, but I was still just a single income, and even forty-five percent of the house's worth would slap me upside the head with a twenty-five-year mortgage and a monthly payment I could barely afford. Especially since banks had tightened their rules and required borrowers to have a certain amount of money available after payment of the mortgage.

I kept these money woes to myself, although I didn't entirely know why. Maybe they embarrassed me, or maybe I needed to feel like I could solve something on my own.

"So tell me what's going on between the two of you. I want to know everything." Cleo was sitting on my backside, using her tiny fists to work a kink out of my shoulders that had been there for five days and wouldn't budge.

"Argh," I mumbled into my couch cushion.

"Well?"

"I've been on the receiving end of one of your massages, Cleo," Imran said, "and believe me when I tell you that simultaneously talking and dying is not possible."

She squeaked in outrage and dug her knuckles in extra hard.

"I hate you," I groaned at Imran. He smirked at me, turned a page of my Lonely Planet book, and pretended to read.

"Where is he anyway? I haven't heard from him in days."

"That makes two of us," I said. "Oh my God, Cleo, enough! I'd rather have limited movement in my shoulder than lose it altogether."

With a last poke, she jumped off me. "Men," she sniffed. "Babies, all of you."

I groaned in agreement because that was all I could do as I levered myself upright.

"Yeah, but seriously," Imran said, putting the book aside. "What happened? Did you guys fight? He didn't come out again on Saturday."

A hot summer wind wafted through the house, billowing my curtains behind the open windows. I tried to remember sitting here like this with Sam, and while I could, it felt distant, like a snapshot rather than a memory. He was fading, and here I was, moping over someone else. I missed the way Sam looked at me. I missed feeling like I meant everything to him. Knowing that no matter how shitty my day was, or how many bad decisions I made, he'd be there at the end of it, saying it would all be okay. He knew me better than I knew myself, but at the same time I couldn't remember what his laugh sounded like.

Ah, love.

Cleo gave me her worried face. "What happened, Ollie?"

"Just what I told you on the phone. He broke up with Stephen. We had lunch, talked a little bit and then I went home with some vague promise of seeing each other soon."

"Did you tell him how you felt?"

"Jesus, Cleo!" I burst out, just as Imran said, "Of course he didn't."

She gave us an indignant look, and I shifted deeper into the couch, fighting the urge to hide behind a pillow. "What? Why not?"

"Because he just broke up with someone! I can't sweep in and go, 'Oh great, my turn now!'"

Imran waved his hand at me in a *See? Exactly* kind of move.

"Ye-es," Cleo said, like we were being particularly slow. "But he broke up with a guy he was only with because he thought he couldn't have you."

Suddenly I felt exhausted. I buried my head in my hands. What was I doing? Sam had only been dead for a year. These three people were the most important ones in my life. Could I really risk fucking all that up for something that might fizzle and burn out before it even had a chance to catch a spark?

"This is crazy, Cleo," I said. "I don't think I can do this."

"Do what, honey?" She stroked my hair and patted my back. "Fall in love again? Because I think it's too late for that."

Oh God. "What if I'm not ready?"

"It's not something you can chose," Imran said, gentler than I was used to from him. "It happens. And it's messy and almost always at the wrong time, but are you really willing to let this go? Because you're . . . afraid?"

And that was the problem, wasn't it? Torn between two fears.

"I don't even know if he still wants me."

Cleo burst out in a loud laugh. "Oh, he wants you, Ollie. And it's going to be *glorious*."

I froze. "He didn't."

She giggled. Imran looked uncomfortably amused.

"He *didn't*!" I repeated, scandalized.

"Aw, don't blame him. He was drunk and maudlin and missing you. But I have to say . . ." She gave my groin a meaningful glance. "I wouldn't mind taking a look at this piece of art myself."

"Cleo!" Imran said, laughing.

"I meant the painting," she told him, then ogled me with a deliberately lecherous look.

"Ew, ew, ew. You are like my sister. I'm not showing you the painting."

"One day," she said, "I'm going to sneak up there and see for myself how, and I quote, 'breathtakingly beautiful' you are, Ollie."

I grabbed the pillow and whacked her with it. "Shut up," I mumbled, to their apparent hilarity.

I couldn't call my job monotonous, but I did drag myself through the next week like a drone. I tried not to miss Thomas and did anyway. I tried to remember Sam, and while I could, and found solace in the memories and photographs, he felt further away from me than ever.

At the same time I realized the emptiness of the house didn't haunt me any longer. When Sam died, I'd been confronted with my greatest fear. It had taken a while, but being alone finally didn't scare the crap out of me anymore. Beyond anything else, I knew I wanted to keep this house, needed it. Everyone my age had a mortgage, and I was lucky I'd lived rent free for this long, really. This place had been Sam's and mine, and I would make sure it always stayed that way, no matter what happened next. In the end, money was only money, while this place was . . . home.

Sam wouldn't have rolled over at the first sign of trouble, and I didn't plan to either.

One night I dreamed about him. I couldn't quite see his face, and his voice was muffled as if we were having a long-distance phone call. I missed Sam in an abstract way. I missed Thomas in a painful way.

At last I found a bank that would give me my loan, even though it meant tightening my belt just about everywhere else for . . . the rest of my life, most likely.

I emailed Stan.

Thomas texted me on Thursday. *You want to go for a drink tomorrow?*

Sure! I replied. *What time and where?*

I'll pick you up at seven.

Huh. That was unusual but definitely not unwelcome if it would save me a tram ride.

Sounds great.

I slipped into a pair of jeans Sam had always loved on me, combined them with a short-sleeved slate-gray button-down, and slapped some cologne on my neck. My hair was getting too long again, so I tried to tame it a little and left it to flop around my ears. At seven my doorbell rang. I was surprised Thomas hadn't honked like he usually did, but maybe he'd found easy parking.

"Hey!" I yanked the door open and smiled too brightly, but fuck it—I was so happy to see him. "Oh wow, you look great."

"Um, thanks." He stuffed his hands in a pair of really tight jeans. They hugged his thighs lovingly, and I envied them a little. I also wanted to gnaw on the biceps straining the sleeves of his button-down.

"How have you been? We haven't heard from you in a while. Do Cleo and Imran know where we're meeting up? Oh, Imran has a late shift tonight, doesn't he? Well, maybe he'll join us after." I closed the door and looked up at him. His mouth was parted as if he'd been about to say something, but he just stood there, looking at me. "What—"

My phone rang, and I glanced at the screen and froze. "Oh, it's Sam's mom. Do you mind if I take it?"

He seemed to shake himself from whatever was keeping him tongue-tied. "Of course not. Go ahead. I'm parked right here." He clicked his key, and his car unlocked about three spaces down from where we stood.

"Okay." I brought the phone to my ear, my heartbeat fluttering with nerves. Were they going to try to talk me into giving in? Was I even allowed to talk them about it? I had no idea. I answered cautiously. "Hello?"

"Oliver? It's Martine."

"Yes, I know. Is everything okay?" Despite the whole situation, I hoped nothing was wrong. I didn't wish them any more tragedy in their lives.

"Yes. Well, that is to say . . ." She sighed softly. "Simon doesn't know I'm calling."

"Oh." I leaned against Thomas's car and wrapped one arm around my middle. "What's this about, Martine? If it's about the house—"

"It's not. The thing is, the trial starts in two weeks. For Sam's killer. I . . . We won't be able to go. It's too much. But I wish someone would be there. For Sam, so someone's present for him."

"And you want me to go," I said.

Martine didn't answer for a long time, then whispered, "Yes, Ollie. I wanted to ask you if you could go."

I ground my teeth together. "You have some nerve asking me for favors," I said quietly, unable to contain my anger. Part of me felt bad because I didn't think she was the catalyst in the house situation, but I couldn't help it. "That house is mine. Sam wanted it that way. You are going directly against his wishes and making my life unnecessarily difficult."

"I know," Martine said, crying. "It's not—"

"But I'll go," I interrupted her, not wanting to hear it. "I'll go for Sam." I left the *and not for you* unsaid, but I thought she heard it regardless.

"I have to go," she suddenly said. "I'll email you the details." And just like that the line went dead.

I was shaking by the time I managed to open the passenger door. Thomas smiled up at me, but his face fell when I sank into the seat.

"What is it? Ollie?"

Slowly I turned to stare at Thomas. "The trial for Sam's killer starts in two weeks. Sam's mom wants me to be there."

His hands made the steering wheel creak. "And what do you want?" he asked.

"I . . . I don't know. I never thought about it." The killer had been caught thanks to CCTV footage during my month of near-unconsciousness following Sam's death. I hadn't given it much thought beyond, *Good.* I stuffed my hands between my thighs. The seams of my jeans dug into my skin. "It's not something I normally would've done. I mean, what good will it do? It's not going to change anything. But it's for Sam. So I said I would go. And I think I will, but . . ." The idea scared me so much my palms were already sweating.

His jaw flexed, and he stared resolutely ahead. "I'll come with you." He pushed the gear stick into first.

"Thank you," I said after a while, and he threw me a half smile.

We drove in silence until Thomas found a good spot in the center of town. "Are you hungry?" he asked. "I haven't eaten yet."

"Yeah, sure. Do you want to get pitas? I haven't had pitas in forever."

He gave me a pained look. "That's a lot of garlic."

"Eh." I shrugged. "I don't mind if you don't." Thomas buried his face in his hands. "What?" I asked, laughing a little confusedly. "What is it? What did I do now? We don't have to eat pitas, Thomas. It was just an idea."

He sat up so fast I startled, and his eyes were dark and fiery. "This is a date, okay, Ollie? A *date*. Cleo won't be coming. In fact she helped me get dressed and then she went home and she's expecting me to text her after we have all the hot sex, because that's what she thought was going to happen. So no, if it's okay with you, I don't want to eat pitas."

"I . . ." I was squashed against the passenger window. I shuffled back into the seat. The heat in Thomas's eyes dwindled, and his mouth pinched together. He ran a hand through his carefully styled hair, messing it up. The way he was dressed, the pickup at my door . . .

I should've known. "Shit," I breathed. "Oh man. I had no idea. I fucked up. Did I fuck up? I fucked up, didn't I?"

He blew out a hot breath and stared at the street, where traffic crawled by. "No, Ollie." He reached for my knee and squeezed it, letting go quickly. "You didn't fuck up. I did. I should've called you and asked you out properly and actually mentioned the word *date*. Not just texted you and asked you to go for a drink like we always do. Let's"—he reached for the keys still stuck in the ignition—"forget it and go home."

"No!" I sprang at him and yanked the keys out of his grip. "No. We can do this. Let me . . . get my head around this. Okay. See over there? Andre's. I've heard of that place, but I've never been there. I am getting out of the car, and I'll grab us a table. You wait five minutes and join me. We can pretend that's when our date starts. Okay?" My heart hammered, then flopped around like a fish on dry land when Thomas slowly began to smile.

"Yeah," he said. "Okay. That sounds good."

I handed him the keys. "Five minutes," I said, grinning stupidly. "You and me. On a date."

He laughed under his breath and glanced away with a blush on his cheeks. I hurried out of the car before I made a complete idiot of myself. When I crossed the street and glanced over my shoulder, he wasn't looking at me. He frowned briefly at his phone before pressing it to his ear. I didn't think anything of it, but when he followed me into the restaurant not five, but twenty minutes later, he was white as a sheet.

"Thomas?" I rose to my feet and took a step toward him. "Are you okay? What's wrong?" A waiter had been approaching our table, but he took one look at Thomas's face, spun on his heel, and walked away. "Hey, come sit. You look like you're going to pass out."

"I can't . . . I can't stay."

"Oh. Is it your dad? Did something happen? If you need to go, I can take a tram. It's no problem."

He shook his head. "It's not that."

To my absolute shock, he was shaking. "Come on," I said. "Let's get out of here. This is no place to talk." I shuffled Thomas out of the restaurant. "Well, that was the shortest date in the history of all dates," I tried to joke.

He turned his soulful eyes down to me. "I can't date you," he whispered.

My heart began a slow thud I didn't like at all. "Well, that's . . . a pity, but we can work it out. It's all fine. Um, why don't you tell me what changed your mind over the past twenty minutes?"

He tried to unlock the car, but his fingers shook so hard he dropped his keys. I began to get really worried.

"Okay, buddy," I softly said as I put a hand on his shoulder. "Why don't you let me drive, and we'll talk at my house. Unless there's somewhere you need to be?"

"No, your house is fine." He didn't say anything else as he climbed into the passenger seat, and he remained quiet on the short ride home. Every once in a while I caught him squeezing his eyes closed, like his brain had conjured up something he couldn't stand remembering.

I managed to park pretty close to my house and let him inside. "Are you hungry?" I asked him in the hallway. He shook his head. "Coffee? Beer?"

"A beer would be nice."

"Make yourself comfortable in the living room. I'll be right there."

I grabbed two Hoegaardens and hurried back to find him sitting on the edge of the couch, his head in his hands. "Thanks," he said hoarsely when I nudged him with the beer.

"You've got me really worried now. What's going on, Thomas?" I sat down on the coffee table so I could look him straight in the eye.

"Remember that girl in the Nine Barrels last year? The . . . the night Sam died?"

"Yes," I said and a chill ran down my spine. "Of course."

"I didn't meet her that night. I slept with her on and off for about six months. We both knew it was casual. Apparently something went wrong with a condom. I'm . . . She had a baby."

I gaped at him. "Oh my God." He was a *dad*? "And it's definitely . . . yours?" I cringed as I asked it, but he gave me a wry smile.

"She says so. She says she didn't sleep with anyone but me during that time, and I believe her."

"Okay." I wanted to tell him to think about paternity tests and whatnot, but that wasn't my place. Besides, he'd probably thought about that too. "Why didn't she let you know while she was pregnant?"

"She thought she could handle it alone."

I didn't say the obvious. "Well . . . that's unexpected, sure. And it's a shock. But I mean . . . you have a good wage, a steady job. You're an amazing person. Does she want you to be involved?" Naively, or maybe even stupidly, I warmed to the idea. "It'd be kind of cool, wouldn't it? The baby would be with you like, what? Every other weekend? Or does she want a fifty-fifty split? Or does she only want money? Because you can fight that. Or not, whatever you want, obviously." I frowned and my heart chilled a little. Did she want him with the baby permanently? As in a relationship? Did Thomas want that too? "But why can't we date? I'm going to be insulted if you're assuming I don't want to be in a relationship with you just because you might come with a little extra."

He laughed, a desolate sound. "Oh, Ollie." He put his hand on my knee and held on. "It wouldn't be like having a little playmate every other weekend. Liesbeth is suffering from severe postpartum depression. She's been trying to fight it herself, but she has no family and all the party friends she had basically dropped her like a stone. She was still in college and had to put it on hold. I wish . . . I wish she'd reached out sooner."

I felt bad for my selfish thoughts. "Jesus, Thomas, what happened?"

"She was having some unhealthy ideas, so she went to see a psychologist. He recommends she go to this new clinic in Bruges, an inpatient place where she'd stay for sixty days. If I don't take the baby, he'll go to foster care during that time. Probably longer."

"Oh, Thomas." And he wouldn't let that happen. Of course he wouldn't.

"But what do I know about caring for a baby, Ollie?" He looked so out of his depth that I wanted to hug him. "And even when she's out after two months, she'll be the one with every other weekend parenting time. I'd still have him eighty percent of the time. I don't know what to do. I don't have any family either, apart from my dad. And he might stop by every once in a while, but it's not like he can babysit every time I go to work."

"You'll take him to day care. And you have me," I said. "You have us, your friends. We'll all help you."

"But you've seen my place. It's tiny! And definitely not babyproof. I have terrible, loud neighbors, and one with a scary dog. I can't raise a child there. Oh my God. Oh my God, what am I going to do?" He set his beer down and covered his face. I rubbed his shoulders, the nape of his neck.

"You come live with me," I said, even as I saw the glimpse of a possible future with him blink out. But that was irrelevant. It had been a blip. It could've been forgotten in no time. He had other, more important things on his mind now. "I have enough space, and you'll be closer to work. You won't be alone with a scary new baby, and my mom will want to help out too."

Thomas stared at me with his big, brown, teddy-bear eyes. "Ollie, I can't take you up on that."

"Yes, you can. And you will. I'm lonely in this house, and it's far too big for me. There's plenty of room for both of us and a baby."

His eyes were shining. "I'm so sorry. I really wanted—"

I gripped his hands and kissed his knuckles. "I know. And it's fine. Maybe it's for the best. Who knows? We might've ruined our friendship."

"If a relationship didn't do it, a screaming baby will."

"Don't be silly. I love babies."

CHAPTER
TWELVE

Oh my God, I did not love babies.

A week later Thomas stood on my doorstep, holding a tiny bundle of yellow fluffiness. Only within the fluffiness lay a creature with the lungs of Aretha Franklin. I heard him screaming before Thomas rang the doorbell, and we were unable to say hello as he wailed his unhappiness.

We'd moved in some of Thomas's essentials the day after he received the "Surprise! You're a dad!" news, and we'd agreed to leave the rest of his house until we'd given this thing a trial. I really did hope he'd stay. I hadn't been lying when I said I was lonely.

I'd never really understood the difference. *Alone* and *lonely* had seemed like two lanes on the same road when I had Sam's constant company, but I realized now they were different paths altogether. I didn't mind being alone anymore. That was a transient state between one filled moment and the next. But loneliness was a presence, a hovering shadow that made my nights darker, my dreams restless, and my days a little empty.

"I thought you said you loved babies," he told me, raising his voice to be heard. I was pretty sure his frightened-rabbit expression very much resembled mine.

"Uh, I love them in cute clothes as accessories in magazines?" I said, and that got a wan smile out of his tired face.

"*Ohhhhh,*" my mom cooed behind us. I gave Thomas a resigned look. She bustled down the hallway and fluttered her hands like a beauty queen near tears. "Where is he? Give him here." She stretched her arms out. I'd never seen Thomas that relieved. He awkwardly passed the bundle on.

"I asked her to stay awhile," I told him as my mom made embarrassing noises over the baby. He instantly stopped crying. "I hope that's okay?"

"Okay?" Thomas said, shaking his head like he was trying to dislodge the echoes of the baby's cries. "You're brilliant."

I opened my mouth to say something, caught sight of my mom, and closed it again. After a second I asked, "Are you crying?"

"No," she sniffed. "Yes. Okay? I never thought I'd have grandbabies. Look how precious he is. What's his name?"

"Mom, he's not actually your grandb—" Thomas elbowed me, so I shut up.

"His name is Milo."

"Oh, I love that. Will he have your last name?"

"Yes." Thomas's cheeks stained a dull red. "Liesbeth gave him my last name."

Mom smiled. "Milo de Ridder. It's so nice to meet you. I bet you're hungry huh, little sweetheart?" Without missing a beat she took the diaper bag off Thomas and disappeared into the living room. Easy, like she'd done it all before.

"I love your mother," Thomas whispered, and I laughed.

"Come on, let's get you settled in. Then you should probably take a nap. You look like death. Do you have any more stuff in your car?"

"What do you think?"

"Okay, fine, let's go get it."

We dragged his bags into the house and listened, but the house was silent. I assumed that meant happy baby.

"I picked him up last night. I didn't get any sleep at all. How do people do this?" He gave me a horrified look. "And more than once. Voluntarily."

"I'm sure it's not that bad," I said soothingly and led him up the marble stairs. We'd given Milo the room at the end of the hallway to the left on the first floor. Mom would sleep in the room opposite, Thomas would have the room beside Milo's, and my room was on the right side of the stairs. *Farthest away from any crying*, I thought, but had the grace not to mention it to anyone.

"I really appreciate this," Thomas said when I showed him his room. "I don't know how to repay you."

"Don't worry about it." I dumped one of his bags on the bed. All the others had some kind of zoo animal on them, so I guessed they weren't his.

His face crinkled. "But I do worry about it. I can't accept this from you and not do anything in return."

"Thomas, if the situation were reversed, would you leave me stranded?"

"No, of course not. But you'd insist on paying half the bills and groceries and whatever."

I rolled my eyes and took a bag with a smiling giraffe off of him. "We can sort that out later." He was gritting his teeth, so I offered him my sweetest smile. "Let's wait until the bills come, and then decide. For now, relax and enjoy your baby, dude." I froze in the hallway. "Oh my God, you have a baby."

He still had that wide-eyed terrified appearance to him, but a slight, wondrous smile tugged at his mouth. "Yeah. I'm a dad."

I laughed and dragged him toward Milo's room. "Here, what do you think?" I threw open the door and stepped aside.

"Oh wow."

My mother had found my small rocking crib in her garage, and she'd given it a good scrub. It was old but sturdy, and pretty in off-white with a fresh blue sheet. "She says it won't last him much beyond six months. Less if he's a big baby, but for now—"

"It's perfect." He looked around the rest of the room: the cleared dresser at waist height, perfect for diaper changes; the sea life decals I'd stuck to the walls to distract Milo from what I was sure would be unpleasant things to do with diaper cream. The newly made queen bed with soft linens. Mom had even found a comfortably cushioned rocking chair, goodness knew where.

"The bed's in case you want to stay in this room," I told him a little sheepishly. "I can imagine you won't want to leave him alone all night at first."

"No." Thomas turned around, and I saw a flicker of that confidence I liked so much return in his gaze. He was a big guy, with broad shoulders and strong hands. I hated seeing him down. It was good to notice the real Thomas returning. All he said was,

"Thank you," and for some reason it made me want to jump his bones. Which, with my own baby crib in the room, was all kinds of wrong.

"All right." Mom burst in, and we both startled. "Time for you two to do some bonding. Take off your shirt."

"What?" I squeaked.

She tutted at me. "Not you. Thomas and Milo. Babies are very tactile, and he needs to learn the scent of his daddy. I gave him a bottle and changed his diaper, and he's about a second away from dozing off. So take off your shirt, lie down, and you can snuggle with your son."

"Okay," Thomas said, looking wide-eyed but determined. "But what if I fall asleep? Won't I roll over and squash him?"

"You'll sleep very lightly if you do doze off. If it makes you feel better, Oliver or I can keep you company."

Thomas threw me a look I interpreted as "Please don't leave me half-naked in a bedroom with your mom."

I sighed, resigned, as Thomas unbuttoned his shirt. If having bad thoughts with a crib in the room was wrong, having vague boner-like feelings with a baby nearby would send me straight to hell.

"I'll go get my laptop."

I had no idea babies could snore. At first I thought it was Thomas, and I thought it was really endearing. Then I realized it was Milo, and just wanted to laugh. Milo made these tiny noises that ended with a little snort, and once I felt sure Thomas wasn't about to open his eyes again, I looked my fill.

He'd unbuttoned his shirt but kept it on, and Milo had one side of it clutched in his little fist. The baby had a full, pouty mouth, pink like the pads on kitten paws, and he kept making small sucking motions like he was dreaming of his next drink.

"You and me both, dude," I mumbled under my breath. I tried to concentrate on a work project I was setting up, I really did, but there was a hunk of a man in my guest bedroom, with his shirt half-off and a baby sleeping on his chest. My eyes crossed so often from the effort not to look away from my screen that I gave myself a headache.

Thomas's hair hung over his forehead. One thick strand of it tickled his nose and lifted a little whenever he breathed out. My fingers itched, I wanted so badly to get up and move it aside for him.

A date . . . less than a week ago I'd nearly had a date with him. My breath caught in my chest. *What do you think of that, huh, Sammy? A date with Thomas.* Even if the whole thing had been cut short. I'd never thought it would come to that. *Can you imagine us together, Sam? Weird, right?*

My heart gave a little lurch, like it expected to jump back to life after lying dormant for so long. Thomas was hot as fuck, so no problem in that department, and I'd always really liked him. But wasn't that a problem? We'd been friends for so long. Could I imagine being with him? Kissing him? Slipping that soft white shirt off his muscular arms and working my way along his pecs, the downy hair on his chest tickling my mouth as I— Oh God. I shifted in my seat. No problem there either.

But love? Could I do it? Was it even an option if I had to ask myself that question? I looked away when my eyes began to burn. How could I sit here in Sam's house and feel that way about someone else?

He'd want you to, a little voice told me, but I shook it away as if it were a gossamer spiderweb. Behind me the sun crept past the window, the city noises dull through the triple glazing. So when the wail broke the silence, it was extra startling.

"Jesus!" Thomas went rigid in the bed, from fast asleep to three hundred percent awake in less than a second. I could see his frantic heartbeat thundering in his neck. I jumped up from the rocking chair, shoving my laptop aside, and lifted a crying Milo from his chest.

"It's okay," I said. "He's okay, and so are you."

Thomas blinked and sat up. "Well, that sent my blood pressure through the roof. How long did we sleep?"

"Close to two hours." I looked at him. The bags under his eyes were even deeper than before. "Why don't you grab another hour's sleep? Mom and I can keep this little fella entertained, can't we?" *Oh God, what am I saying?* I cradled Milo awkwardly, head so small it fit in one hand, rump in the other. I held him away from me like I was presenting Simba to his subjects in *The Lion King*.

"We'll be—" with a really disturbing amount of noise, Milo filled his diaper, and just like that he stopped crying "—fine. Well, at least we know what woke him up. Was it all those onions Granny Louise fed you?" I held him even farther away from me, and Thomas laughed softly as he snuggled back into bed. "Yeah, laugh it up," I said as I moved toward the door, because Granny Louise needed to do something about this pile of poop. "Tonight he's all yours." And with that sobering thought, I left him to it.

I found Mom heating a bottle in something I probably would've tried boiling eggs in.

"He has a present for you," I said as I wrinkled my nose and held Milo out.

"Oh great, I'll help you change his diaper and you can give him his bottle."

"*Me*?" I gave her a horrified look and put Milo on my shoulder so he wouldn't hear me putting his business out there. "But he *pooped*," I whispered.

"Yes, babies do that. Come along."

She'd cleared a corner of the table that stood at the other end of the living room. It used to function as our dining room, but I never used it anyway and had set up a changing station there. It was made out of two thick towels and a bunch of diapers and bottles and wipes.

"We should probably get him some better stuff."

"This will do for now," she said. "He has a better changing pad upstairs, and soon enough that'll be the only one you need. All right, put him down."

Milo had somehow managed to grab a lock of my hair and held on to it with the strength of a tiny ninja, so I counted it a win when I only lost half a dozen hairs. I glanced at my mother.

"Go on."

I thought she could do with enjoying herself a little less, but pried the snap buttons of Milo's onesie open. I didn't realize how hard I was concentrating until he kicked out and caught me right on the chin. "Ow! Okay, buddy, I'm working as fast as I can. How about you do some talking and keep us entertained, huh? Can you say, 'Hi, Uncle Ollie'?"

Beside me, Mom snorted and shoved me gently. "Get on with it, because he's about two minutes away from a meltdown. He's hungry."

"How can you tell?" I managed to push the onesie up and started in on the diaper. Oh God. With as little contact as possible, I pried the Velcro loose.

"See those sucking motions he's making? That means you're running out of time fast."

"Okay." I folded the diaper down, looked, and made a weird *berk* noise. "Oh, that's nasty. Milo, you're going to have to have words with Granny Louise about those onions."

"Aw." My mother pressed her hands to her bosom. "You really think he'll call me Granny?"

I shrugged. "Who knows? But seriously, Mom. The smell. Do something." I was about to gag, and she finally took pity.

"Oh, step out of the way, but the next one is yours. You use the scented wipes for number twos, and you can use the others for number ones."

I only then noticed the two different brands. "Why?"

"Because the unscented ones are better for the environment."

"Milo's mom thought of everything," I said as my mother dealt with the diaper as if she did it every day. Maybe it was one of those skills that, once acquired, never went away.

I took the moment to look around my living room. Mom had pushed the coffee table against the wall, and on my soft rug lay a colorful little mat with two arches over it. Toys and plastic mirrors dangled down. A little bouncy chair sat beside it. There was a trunk of soft toys by the TV. On my table sat a basket with fresh onesies and other things I couldn't identify. It didn't look like Sam's home anymore. I pressed my hand against the tightness in my chest and resisted the urge to sweep it all into a bag and return the house to its usual, tidy shape.

"Just because she has postpartum depression doesn't mean that she doesn't love her child, Oliver. It's very serious, but she will get better, and she will want her child back." She closed Milo's onesie. "So you shouldn't get too attached." She lifted Milo and smiled at him. I didn't think it was me we needed to worry about. "I bet you're hungry, huh, little boo?"

On cue he started crying, and she handed him over to me. "Go sit. I'll bring the bottle."

"But—" I began, uselessly. She was already gone. "Well. It's you and me and—" I glanced at the couch where a fat stuffed toy waited "—a yellow pig with a belly button." Milo cried harder, and I awkwardly sat, trying to curl him up into my arms in the way I'd seen other people do with babies. The noise he made grated on my nerves. Like Thomas said, it was the kind of sound that made my blood pressure rise. I tried to keep calm and took a steadying breath. "Shush, little fella, you're going to wake Daddy. Uh." My eyeballs nearly fell out of my head when Milo began to nuzzle my shirt, right where my nipple was. "Dude. You're not going to find anything there. No, that's just wrong. Stop it."

"Babies do that, Oliver. It's instinct. Here's his bottle. Now you make sure the nipple is always full of formula. If he swallows air, his tummy will hurt. When he's halfway done, gently pry the bottle loose, put him over your shoulder, and pat his back until he burps. You might want to put this towel underneath first."

"Okay. You hungry, little man?" He lifted his tiny fists and waved them around. I took that as enthusiastic agreement and put the bottle to his plump little lips. Immediately he latched on and began to suck. Gosh, his eyes were blue.

"See? Piece of cake," Mom said, and she patted my shoulder. I squinted at her. Did she look a little misty-eyed?

"Hey, wait! Where are you going?" I asked as she began to move away.

"I'm going to take a nap," she said, and left me *all alone*.

CHAPTER
THIRTEEN

I t was a good thing I remembered the towel, because he burped up what looked like half his bottle. "Aw." I gently patted his back as he squirmed. "Are you going to go hungry now? Do you want some more?" I put him in the crook of my elbow again, folded up the towel, and tossed it as far away from me as I could, because holy crap, how could milk that had gone down a second ago already smell so sour?

He happily drank the rest of his bottle. When it neared the point the nipple would fill up with air, I took it away.

"Was that satisfactory for you? Because if not, I'll write to the formula company. After all, milk is such a dull flavor. Maybe we can ask them to add some strawberries, huh?" He blew me formula-flavored bubbles, and I made a face. "Or mint."

At a loss for what to do, I carried him and the bottle into the kitchen, somehow managed to rinse it one-handed—I figured new parents had to do a lot of things one-handed—and went back into the living room.

"I probably shouldn't put you on your belly," I told him.

"Brrr," he said.

"No, no. Don't argue. I can be a fun uncle, but I can be strict too. We don't want to lose all that precious formula again, now do we?"

Milo stared at me and waved his fist.

"I knew you'd come around. How about the bouncy chair? Shall we try that? I spotted some riveting literature in that box of toys over there. What do you think?" I had a scary premonition of this being my future instead of Saturday nights on the town and doing my own thing. I tried not to hyperventilate.

I put Milo down, and he kicked his arms and legs. And that was why Thomas found me cross-legged on the floor, reading *Polly Puppy* to a six-week-old baby.

"Nice sound effects," he said, and my face went fiery hot.

"Well, they're dogs. They're going to bark." I rolled onto my stomach and looked at him. "You look better. Did you sleep okay?"

"I did." He sank onto the floor beside me, in such a graceful way, it shouldn't have been possible for a man his size. He took my hand in his and looked at me with those sincere brown eyes. "Thanks for that."

"Aw, *pssh*," I said, waving my free hand, feeling flustered. "Milo and I are buds, aren't we? We have an understanding." Milo scrunched up his face and gave a dopey smile. "See that? That's either an 'I just tooted' or 'I just tinkled' smile. I'm learning."

Thomas squeezed my fingers lightly. "You're really good with him."

"You didn't see me nearly pass out over the diaper from hell." Gently working my hand loose, I sat up too, with Milo in the bouncy chair between us. "What are you going to do about work?"

He sighed and ran his hand through his hair. Milo waved his fist at him, and Thomas gave him a pinkie finger, which Milo promptly gnawed on. "I called them yesterday. It'd take a while to apply for parental leave, but they agreed to let me work part-time for the next six months. They weren't happy about it, especially since I took such a long time off a few months ago. I have a friend who runs a day care, but he only has one spot available a week. It's not enough. I'll have to look into some of the bigger childcare places. It's not ideal, but ideal would be Milo having a normal mom and dad, wouldn't it?"

"He does have a normal mom and dad, Thomas. It'll take some time to work out the details, that's all. And I bet my mom will be happy to watch him while you and I are at work."

"I can't expect that from her," he said.

"You're not. I'm positive she'll want to. She loves Milo to bits already. She's thrilled. She always knew she wouldn't get any grandchildren from me."

Thomas gave me an odd look. "You don't want kids?"

I shrugged, not wanting to get into the subject of Sam and his allergy to kids and pets right then.

Thomas sighed. "I'll ask your mom. But I insist on paying her."

I lifted my hands. "That'll be between the two of you."

Milo kicked his arms and legs and started to complain a little. "He wants you to hold him," I said.

Thomas raised an eyebrow at me. "How do you know that?"

I shrugged, almost said, *Because that's what I'd like right now*, but kept my mouth shut. "Why don't we go for a little walk in the garden?" I asked. "I bet Milo would like to see some birdies, wouldn't you?"

Thomas unclasped the straps and awkwardly lifted Milo from the bouncy chair. "I don't even know how to hold him," he whispered, and I patted his back.

"You'll get there."

The house had the kind of deep, mature yard only found in these parts of the city. The reason why we had so much space was thanks to the hospital down the street. We had to put up with ambulances leaving at all hours of the day and night, but to be honest, I didn't even hear them anymore. The yard was worth it regardless. A slice of heaven walled in by six-foot brick walls, with old oaks and big weeping willows, and flower patches I hadn't bothered with the last two summers. Maybe I should. It was my slice of heaven, and I wanted to take care of it.

Milo stared at everything with big, blue eyes as the wind rustled the leaves around us.

"I'll go get a blanket," I told Thomas. "I'll be right back."

I ran inside, grabbed a throw from the couch, and hurried outside. Thomas was pointing at a little red robin, talking softly to his son.

Holy crap, he had a son. And they were going to live with me in Sam's house. In *my* house. I'd been ready for a tiny step toward maybe having a relationship again. Was I ready to play family? Without the benefits?

He hadn't heard me approach, so I took a moment to watch them together, this handsome man with a small baby on his arm. My heart hurt a little bit. Sam hadn't been a father figure. And because children weren't something Sam wanted, I'd automatically assumed I didn't want any either.

But seeing Thomas there, blowing gentle bubbles on the palm of Milo's hand, awakened something within me that burned hotter than any kind of desire I'd experienced before. Milo smiled wide, and

Thomas laughed, wondrously. The problem wasn't going to be having them here. The problem would be living with them and keeping my heart out of the equation.

"Here," I said, carrying over the blanket. "I'll put it down in the shade. I bet Milo would love to look at the leaves and the clouds." I straightened the corners and rose.

Thomas grabbed my arm when I turned away. "Stay."

"But you probably want some bonding time. I don't need to—"

He ducked his head so he could look straight into my eyes. "Stay," he murmured again. And who was I to say no to that?

As I was bringing the blanket out, I'd had this idyllic image in mind of the three of us lying on it, baby Milo giggling as we pointed out shapes in the clouds. In reality he started fussing after fifteen minutes, and for the next forty-five, Thomas and I took turns wandering around the garden. Apparently Milo wasn't on board with my romantic notions but wanted to be carried around until our arms threatened to fall off.

When even my magic bounce didn't stop his fussing anymore, we made our way inside, ready to tackle the mysteries of diaper changing—in other words, wake my mother. We found her already in the kitchen, doing that morning's dishes.

"You two change his diaper," she said when I cheerfully tried to hand her Milo. She rudely ignored me. "And then come dry the dishes."

Thomas shrugged at me, so we went into the living room instead.

"Liesbeth showed me yesterday," he told me as he grinned. "So I'll talk you through it."

"Oh, I see how this goes." I gingerly sniffed Milo's behind, then promptly promised myself never to do that again. At least I didn't get a whiff of the pits of Mordor this time. "Fine. But the next *numero deux* is all yours."

Thomas laughed as I undid the onesie and pushed it out of the way. Carefully I eased the Velcro loose and tugged the wet diaper out from under him. "This thing weighs a ton," I said as I handed it to Thomas. "At least we know his equipment works." He gave me a droll look. "Okay. Wipes." I plucked a wipe from the box, used it so gently

I probably shouldn't have bothered, then didn't know what to do with the wipe.

"Next time keep the diaper under him until you're done with that, and you can wrap the wipe inside."

"Okay, Mister Experienced, how about you do it next time?" Milo cooed like he thought that was funny, and I smiled at him. "Yeah, you and I, we understand each other, don't we? Yes, we do. Yes, we do, you cutie poo." Oh my God, why was I using my *I spotted a cute dog* voice? I plucked a diaper from the box, studied it to make sure I didn't put it on backward, and glanced over my shoulder when my mother walked in.

"How's it going?" she asked.

"Great," I said, and as I bent down to put the diaper on, Milo peed in my face.

Thomas at least managed to look contrite as he handed me a towel—after laughing so hard, he cried. My mom had no such scruples. She kept laughing all through finishing the job of changing Milo, then burst into laughter again every time she looked at me as I helped her with the dishes.

"I'm going to go home for a bit," she said when we were done. "But I'll be back tonight so you boys aren't here by yourself. Milo will need another bottle in an hour or so."

Thomas made a noise that sounded mildly panicked as he held Milo in his arms.

"Hey, Mom, before you go, Thomas needs to talk to you." He gave me the stink eye as I fled the room, but it served him right for laughing at me.

I went up into my bedroom and felt a soft peace descend on me as I closed the door. It was good to be alone for a minute. I took my time showering and changing my clothes. After, I sat down on my bed and glanced around the bedroom that had once belonged to two people so in love, they'd never considered a *what if*. The picture on the nightstand called to me, and I lifted it. Sam smiled at the camera. He had his arms around me from behind. It was a meaningless shot, really. No big day, no big deal, but it brought out everything that had attracted me to him from the very beginning. His gorgeous smile, his sophisticated face, his kind, warm eyes.

"There's a baby in our house, Sam," I whispered. "An actual, crying, wailing, pooping, peeing baby." I laughed disbelievingly. "You'd have hated it. *Hated* it. But I have to tell you something. I love it. He's only been here for a day, and I love him already. If you were still here . . . I don't know. I think I might've wanted a child of my own someday. But you would never have wanted that, would you?"

I quietly began to cry and wiped angrily at my tears, not understanding where they came from this time. I was so confused by my own feelings. I just wanted to talk to him one last time. He'd know the answer even when I didn't quite know the question.

I put the frame down again. It didn't matter. Sam wasn't here, but Thomas and Milo were. My tears dried and my heart ached in a good way as I left the peace in my bedroom behind. Thomas and Milo were on the couch.

Without thinking, I walked up behind them and pressed a kiss to Thomas's hair. He looked up, startled, and I made an *O* face at him when I realized what I'd done.

"Um," I said. "I don't know why I did that."

He flushed a gorgeous pink. "That's okay," he said hoarsely. "I don't mind." He patted Milo on the back. "He won't burp. He wouldn't burp last night either, and then he cried for an hour."

"Give him here," I said and took Milo from his arms. I held him against my shoulder and walked around the living room until he let out a little burp. "Do you think he'll sleep when he's done?"

Thomas took Milo back to give him the rest of his bottle. "I think so, yes." He held my gaze, and I realized I really liked the way he looked at me.

"I'll make us some lunch. And maybe afterward we can go for a walk." I'd seen something folded up that looked like a stroller. How hard could it be to put that thing together?

"That sounds nice," Thomas said, and I left them to it.

Knowing I'd have guests, I had stocked up the fridge. I decided to show off a little. I couldn't cook much, but I made a mean salad.

I opened a can of tuna, drained and rinsed chickpeas, chopped iceberg and arugula, quartered grape tomatoes and olives, and then coated the chickpeas in the oil from the tuna. After I tossed it all together, I cut up a fresh French baguette, put some Brie on a platter, and tugged a bottle of sparkling water out of the fridge. The country-style kitchen had a big, white-oak table, and I set it with cheerful orange-and-white placemats, the nice cutlery I'd bought when Sam and I moved in, and wineglasses, because why not. We would drink water in style.

Just as I put the salad, bread, and cheese on the table, my phone buzzed. It was an email from Stan.

Oliver,

I believe it's important to move ahead at this point in time. If you have had the chance to think things through, please let me know what you have decided, and I will set the ball rolling as quickly as possible.

Once I receive the go-ahead, I can find out what will be required to buy them out. I still have high hopes for a figure below fifty percent.

Regards,

Stan

Thomas walked in, closing the door softly behind him, so I quickly typed out my short answer and stuffed my phone away.

"Is he asleep?" I asked. Suddenly I had a weird feeling—not déjà vu exactly, but something similar, like a premonition. Or maybe it was wishful thinking, because I could get used to Thomas coming down the stairs with a baby monitor in his hand so we could enjoy a moment of quiet together.

He set the monitor on the counter. "Yes, Milo was out before I even put him to bed."

"Take a seat, you must be hungry."

"Starving." He pulled a wooden chair out and sat. "This looks great, Ollie."

"Thanks." I piled some salad onto his plate and moved the bread basket closer as he poured us each some water. "How does it feel now? To have, you know, a son."

Thomas laughed softly. "I still don't quite believe it. I woke up from that nap wondering what I was doing in your guest room, and then saw that crib. It all came back to me. *God*." He put his fork down and covered his face. "I'm a dad."

"Yeah. I can't quite believe it either."

We ate in companionable silence, either too tired or too shocked by the whole circumstance to really say much. Milo was still asleep by the time we'd tidied up the kitchen, so we brought the monitor with us and sat on the patio outside.

"What will happen with his mom?" I asked.

"She can have no visitors for two weeks, and then they will evaluate how she's doing. If she's well enough, we can go see her once or twice a week, depending."

"And then what? Do you think you're going to try to be parents? Together, I mean?"

"No." He let his head fall back on the chair and looked at me. "I'm not going to do that to her or Milo. I don't love her, and she doesn't love me. It'd be a disaster. But I hope she'll let me be part of his life down the line. And how crazy is that? A week ago, that sounded like my worst nightmare, and now . . ."

"It was a shock last week. And you'll be part of his life. She can't shut you out."

"I don't think she'll want to, but yeah. If it came down to that." He widened his eyes at me, and I thought I could fly in the infinite depth of them. "Jesus. I'm a dad."

I had the feeling he'd be saying that a lot over the next few weeks.

Milo woke about an hour later, crying for we had no idea what. It wasn't time for food, we changed his diaper, we took him into the yard, we read him stories, and on he cried.

"Let's try a bath," I said, at wit's end. My last nerve was being shredded like someone needed it for nerve zest. "The master bath is probably better."

"Whatever," Thomas said, a slight bite to his tone I tried not to take personally. "As long as it stops."

We put towels on the floor and undressed him as the bath ran. As soon as he was naked, Milo seemed a lot happier. "Maybe he was hot." Thomas rose to adjust the temperature of the water.

When it was full enough, Thomas leaned over the edge into the tub, Milo lying in the crook of his elbow, and gently lowered him. I leaned aside and watched as Thomas scooped water over Milo. Father and son stared at each other, dark brown eyes into blue. They were absolutely absorbed, unaware of me watching. Milo stretched out his arms, and Thomas smiled.

"He's gorgeous, isn't he?" Thomas asked as he glanced at where I stood, clutching the towel because I was afraid my chest cavity might open up to let my heart flop out. As if to say, *Here, I'm done with it. You can have it. Please don't trample on it too hard on your way out.*

"He is," I croaked.

CHAPTER
FOURTEEN

That night we put Milo to bed together. Again I thought maybe I'd be intruding, but again Thomas pulled me into the room and included me. I sat on the bed as he gave Milo a bottle and rocked him to sleep in the chair. Feeling a little bit awkward but mostly overwhelmed with this . . . want. And it wasn't just a physical desire. It ran deep like a vein of crystallized minerals in a mass of rock. I wanted to curl up on the couch with him after the day we'd had, and either wrap his arms around me or put his feet in my lap and rub them.

When he finally eased Milo into his crib, I turned on the monitor, Thomas grabbed the second part he'd need to hear Milo, and we crept out of the room.

"How long will he sleep for?" I whispered.

"Four to six hours if I'm lucky."

"And he'll need another bottle then?"

"Yes."

I nodded and stuffed my hands in my pockets. *Ask him, damn it.* "Do you want to—" I began, just as he said, "So I guess I should grab some sleep."

"Oh, yeah. Of course." I looked down.

"What were you going to ask, Ollie?" Thomas said, so softly I had to look up again.

"Oh, nothing that can't wait. Night, Thomas."

His fingers curled around my elbow, and suddenly he was very close.

"I don't think it can wait." He ran his hand through my hair, cupped my jaw, and thumbed my cheekbone before gently resting his hand at the back of my neck. I was caught in his gaze as I stared up at him, his face in shadow in the semidarkness of the hallway. He was so gorgeous, I thought my knees might give out. When he spoke again, I couldn't look away from his full mouth. "I've always thought you were pretty amazing," he murmured. "But today you just about blew my mind."

"Likewise," I managed.

"What were you going to ask?"

"If . . . if you wanted to go downstairs and watch some TV." I swallowed hard and bit my lip. "And maybe cuddle."

He broke into a slow smile. "Is that all?" He moved infinitesimally closer. He had faint freckles on his nose, a very small scar running through his left eyebrow that I'd never noticed before. Something inside me gave way.

"No," I said and gripped his T-shirt. "No, it's not."

His hand tightened on the back of my neck and we shared—right there in front of the room where his child slept, in this house where I had dreamed of a future with Sam—a real first kiss I would never forget. We slipped together like lock and key. My mouth fit to his so perfectly, it was as if we'd been kissing our whole lives.

Without a second thought I opened up for him, and his arms tightened around me. All I could think was *yes* as, for a few blissful seconds, my body and mind let go of the grief. Sam was with me, for the briefest of moments, and then his warmth was gone. I didn't need it anymore.

Thomas moaned softly as I shifted, pushing closer. That little sound nearly undid me, because I heard what it meant for him too. I felt how his large body trembled, and the happiness in me grew so huge I could hardly stand it.

When the kiss ended, he pressed his forehead to mine and petted my hair, running his fingers through the strands as if he'd wanted to do that for a long time.

"Wow, Ollie," he whispered, laughing softly. "That was really . . ."

"Yeah," I said, my mouth throbbing a little. "I would definitely be in favor of moving this to the couch and doing more of it. TV can be on or off, I don't actually care."

He gave me a look like he thought maybe the couch bit was optional too, and the carpet right here would do fine, thank you, but he angled his body in such a way that I immediately understood it wasn't going to happen. He stroked my arms at the same time, so I tried not to feel rejected. He sighed.

"I really want to, Ollie. But for one thing—" he nodded at the baby monitor he'd dropped and I hadn't even noticed "—and for another, I kind of want to take this slow right now. There's too much . . ." He shook his head. "I've wanted this for too long," he whispered. "I can't fuck this up."

"Aw, Thomas." I cupped his cheeks and kissed him lightly on the mouth. "You're not going to fuck this up. But slow is good. You have enough change going on in your life right now."

"Okay." He pulled me against him and hugged me. "I meant it though. You're amazing."

I closed my eyes and smiled against his chest even as I reminded myself that letting my hands drift down to cop a little feel of his nice, pert ass would ruin the moment.

We parted in the hallway, and he went into his bedroom while I went down to wait for Mom.

She got back around ten and sat beside me on the couch. From the way she said nothing for a long time, I knew she actually had a lot to say, and I could sort of guess what direction her thoughts were taking.

Just as I couldn't stand the silence anymore, she said, "If you do this, you can't go into it without considering all the consequences. Not when there's a child involved. You haven't been in a relationship since Sam, and it might hurt in the beginning. So if you decide to go for it . . . make sure you know this is really what you want." She took my hand in hers and squeezed it.

"He's great though, isn't he?" I asked.

When I looked at her, she had tears in her eyes, but they only made her smile shine even more. "Oh, sweetheart, you've got it bad," she said, and laughed. "Go to bed, because tomorrow will be another long day."

"Did Thomas ask you about the babysitting?"

"Yes, he did. And of course I'll do it." She kissed my temple and rose to her feet. "Night Oliver."

"Night, Mom."

Exhaustion seeped into my bones as I brushed my teeth and changed clothes. I sneaked between the covers, too tired to even do something about the hard-on I was carrying around.

Sometime during the night I did think I heard the baby crying, but I slipped right back into sleep until morning.

Milo woke up everyone at once early that Sunday morning. While I'd barely heard him during the night, that siren wail at 6 a.m. was unavoidable. I pulled on a pair of sweatpants and ratty T-shirt to make coffee for whoever was on diaper duty—because it wouldn't be me—and bumped into a bleary-eyed Thomas who was wearing nothing but a pair of sweatpants and a tiny baby pressed to his naked chest. If I had ovaries, I'd have been instantly pregnant.

"Oh, for heaven's sake," Mom said. I hadn't even noticed her standing there. "Thomas, I'll get Milo changed. You grab a shower and put a shirt on before Oliver spontaneously combusts."

My face went so hot I thought it might actually catch fire. I mumbled something about coffee as I hurried down the stairs. Mom followed at a more sedate pace. She wrestled Milo into a new diaper and change of clothes as if he weren't screaming the house down. My left eyelid kept twitching, and for the first time since I'd lived in the house, I worried about the neighbors.

"You hold him while I make his bottle," Mom said, then pushed a crying Milo into my arms.

"Okay, little man," I said, wishing Thomas would hurry the hell up. "It's okay. Your bottle will be here soon." I shushed him in any way I could think of—singing, bouncing, making silly facing, putting him down, picking him up—but he was inconsolable. By the time the bottle was ready, I'd lost part of the hearing in my left ear.

Since I was holding Milo and his mouth was wide open anyway, I decided to pop the bottle right in there. His mouth closed, his eyes flew open, and his cheeks began to work like a hungry chipmunk's.

"Hey," Thomas said a minute later, looking freshly scrubbed and completely scrumptious. He glanced toward the kitchen and dropped a quick kiss on my mouth. "I tried to hurry."

"It's fine. He's happy now." I looked down at Milo. "And don't worry about my mom. She figured it out last night."

Thomas gave me a wide-eyed look as he sat down beside me. His hand went to my leg, and he stroked me lightly. "How?"

I shrugged. "She knows me too well."

"What did she say?"

"To be careful. It's not just you and me now."

"No," Thomas said, his gaze drifting to Milo, who was happily scarfing his formula down. "It's not."

"She also wants me to be happy," I said. "So there's that."

He gave me a sweet smile. I put my head on his shoulder when he scooted closer. Tentatively he put his arm around me. "Will it be weird, you think?"

"You and me? It didn't feel weird last night."

He made a small noise, then turned his face to nose my hair. "No," he whispered. "It really didn't."

I wanted to stay like that forever, but I needed to burp Milo, and he needed entertaining, and by the time he went down for his morning nap, I was still in my sweatpants and ready for a nap of my own. Mom had made breakfast, and I told them to help themselves while I quickly showered.

Sunday had always been *us* time, and over the past year it had been *me* time, and yet once I had showered, changed, and turned human again, I didn't mind it one bit that my house was filled with people. Mom was sitting on the couch while Thomas lay on the floor, with Milo in tummy time on the colorful little blanket.

"Go on," Thomas was saying. "You can do it!"

Milo lifted his head, tried to look around until it began to wobble, stuck out his tongue, and put his head down again. Mom and Thomas applauded, and I looked at them like they were aliens.

"What a strong boy," Mom cooed. "Yes, you are. Such a strong little boy."

I bent down and said to Milo, "Now they're cheering for you carrying the weight of your own head. Next thing you know, bringing home straight As won't even get you a congratulations."

"That was one time!" Mom cried, and I laughed and danced out of the way as she tried to pinch my arm. "I had a lot on my mind."

I pressed my hand to my chest. "Scarred," I told her. "Scarred for life."

"Go get your breakfast, you," she huffed.

I caught Thomas smiling at me and fled before Mom saw me being all moony-eyed at him. She'd never let me live it down.

The rest of Sunday was relaxing and hectic at once. We went through bursts of madness when everything had to happen at once and we were all scrambling to entertain the little fella. Then suddenly we had to have an absolutely quiet house as he slept.

In the afternoon we finally tried out the stroller as Mom made another trip home.

"So are you back to work tomorrow?" I asked Thomas.

"Just for the morning," he said. "Tuesday and Wednesday I have to go in all day, and I have Thursday afternoon and Friday off. I'm on call for the weekend though. The on-calls are planned ages in advance, and I couldn't get out of that."

"It's fine. Mom and I will be here."

Thomas took one hand off the stroller and slipped it into mine. "Thank you."

"Sure." I took a deep, slow breath. I knew that Sam's death hadn't been a hate crime, but I still felt exposed for some reason. I'd never cared about who saw me out and proud before, so it didn't make sense to be jumpy now. I pushed it aside. It was fine. I squeezed Thomas's hand and kept walking.

"What about you?" he asked. "Working all week?"

"Not on Wednesday afternoon. The trial starts."

"Oh no, Ollie." Thomas stopped the stroller and peered down. Milo was taking in his new surroundings with big eyes. Reassured, Thomas looked back at me. "I completely forgot. I'm so sorry. I promised I'd go with you and now . . ."

Everyone had forgotten, including me. I tried to ignore the hollow anxiety gnawing at my gut.

"That was before the sudden-baby moment. I understand, Thomas. Seriously, don't feel bad about it." I knew I couldn't come first, and I'd have to be okay with that or we'd have no future.

I turned away, but Thomas tugged at my arm. He looked into my eyes for a long moment and winced a little. "But I do. I'm really sorry

I forgot." He rubbed his thumbs over my cheekbones, and I swallowed hard. "I don't want you to go through that alone."

"You'll be there when I get home, won't you?" I asked. Thomas said nothing, just put his arms around me, and I buried my face against his chest. He smelled so good, so familiar, I couldn't even pinpoint exactly *what* he smelled of. He was . . . Thomas.

"Of course I will be," he said.

Milo made an impatient noise, and we resumed our walk.

"If he wakes up more than once tonight, I can change him," I told Thomas. "You have to work too tomorrow. We should split the awake time."

"You don't have to do that. And besides, as long as he only wakes up once, I can deal with it."

"I'm going to leave my door open regardless," I said, and flushed when I realized that sounded like an invitation. Thomas didn't bat an eye though, so we clearly weren't in that stage of our budding relationship yet.

Secretly, I hoped it wouldn't take too long.

It took forever. By Wednesday we still hadn't had the chance to do more than kiss each other quickly and surreptitiously on the mouth. For supposedly sleeping fourteen hours a day, babies were awake a hell of a lot. Between work, baby, more work, more baby, a quiet minute here and there with Thomas, and my mom keeping us company, I suddenly found myself sitting in the stuffy courthouse before I felt ready for it. I'd barely slept the night before, thanks to Milo waking up four times for unfathomable reasons, and I didn't feel too confident about being there.

Because the whole thing had been caught on CCTV, I hadn't had to do more than sign a statement, but I did *not* look forward to being in the same room as the killer for however long. For some reason, I'd imagined the place would be packed, but apart from me there were a few journalist types and other bored-looking people who could have been waiting their turn for all the interest they showed.

The guy's name was Kurt Boons, alleged meth addict, and the minute he walked in, I went tense all over. My knee began to bounce, my heart slammed, and my clothes became glued to my skin with cold, nauseous sweat. I sat there for an hour and a half, unable to hear a thing the judge said because of the blood roaring in my ears.

Kurt had trouble sitting still. I could only see his back, but he was fidgeting restlessly the whole time. A few times his lawyer leaned across and said something to him, and then Kurt would remain motionless for a little while, but before long he'd start up again.

I wondered what he was thinking. I wondered if he regretted taking a life. If he even remembered. I wondered if he ever thought of the consequences, the gaping hole the murder he committed had left behind.

I couldn't take it anymore. I rushed out. Someone tried to stop me at the door, but I tore myself free and reached the bathroom just before I lost my lunch.

I'm sorry, Sam, I thought. *I can't do this.*

Who did it benefit anyway? Not Sam, that was for sure. I didn't want to exact any revenge on this guy. It wouldn't bring Sam back. They caught the killer. Hopefully whatever punishment he received would prevent him from causing this amount of grief to anyone else. That was all I cared about.

I washed my face and patted it dry with paper towels, ready to go home. For a split second I wished I were going back to an empty house, if only for an hour or so, to soothe this thumping headache.

As I aimed for the door, my phone buzzed in my pocket. Another email from Stan. My heart fluttered anxiously in my throat as I opened it up.

Oliver,
They declined our offers of forty and forty-five percent. Are you still ready and able to go ahead with the buy-out at fifty?
Regards,
Stan

I closed my eyes and leaned against the wall, too defeated to stand on my own. What would Sam say if he knew what my relationship with his parents had become? Shouldn't I have tried harder to remain on good terms with them?

For a split second I wanted to email Stan back, tell him to let them have it. I was exhausted. But I thought of Milo and Thomas in that beautiful house, how maybe, just maybe, the three of us could turn it into the home of a warm, loving family someday, as it was meant to be. I knew I couldn't let go yet.

I'll pay the fifty percent, I emailed back, then gathered my strength and went outside.

The courthouse was a gorgeous building on the south side of Antwerp, and I adored the design. It always reminded me a little of the Sydney Opera House, although in this case the sharp peaks represented sails as a nod toward the international harbor. Regardless, when I stepped outside, it felt like I was escaping the bowels of the darkest dungeon.

I could've taken a tram home, but the day was bright and warm, so I walked instead. It did me good to be alone with nothing but my own thoughts, and when I finally opened my front door, the house was quiet.

I found Mom in the backyard, reading a book.

"Oh, hello. How did it go?" She took one look at my face and stood up to hug me hard. "Tell me you don't have to go back. Don't go back, Oliver. This isn't helping anyone."

"No, I pretty much came to that conclusion myself. I don't even know if this was the only day in court. I don't care. I'm done with it. And I'll tell Sam's parents that if I have to."

"It wasn't fair of them to ask you to go."

I sighed and gave Mom another one-armed hug. "They're afraid people are going to forget Sam."

She *tsked*. "Like you ever would. Just because you're falling in love with someone else—" A wail interrupted her, thank God.

"Oh, hey, they're back!" I said and sprang away from her to hurry into the house.

Thomas's hair was in disarray, and he had tight tension lines around his mouth as Milo screamed and screamed in his stroller. I quickly bent down to unstrap him and lifted him into my arms.

"Walkies before dinnertime, bad," Thomas said, and I laughed even as my headache sharpened a little. Turning around, I handed Milo to Mom. I peeked up at Thomas, stood on the tips of my toes, and kissed his cheek. His eyes went wide. Behind me Mom laughed softly, and I heard her retreat.

"Well, hi," Thomas said and began to draw me closer, but I pulled back.

"Um," I said, covering my mouth. "I should probably brush my teeth first. I, uh, barfed at the courthouse today."

"Oh, Ollie." Thomas's dark irises seemed to turn liquid with empathy. "Are you okay? I'm so sorry. Do you have to go back?"

"No, I'm done with it now. No more."

He pulled me into a hug so tight I could feel my ribs creak. I held him just as hard.

"Why don't you go brush your teeth," he murmured, his eyes on my mouth. "And then—"

And then Milo began crying louder. I laughed and patted his arm. "I'll help you feed him and play with him, until we're so exhausted we'll fall asleep on the couch again. With all the sex we're not having, it's like we're married." I grinned but Thomas didn't smile back.

"I'm sorry," he whispered. "I know this is a huge inconvenience. I want . . ." He looked at me in a way that made me wish I could pay my mom to babysit for a week so I could take him somewhere private and let him do all the things his eyes promised me.

"Be right back!" I squeaked and sprinted upstairs to hide in the bathroom for a while.

Mom was changing Milo when I came down, so I went into the kitchen to help Thomas with the bottle. We were getting the hang of it, but there was still a lot of peering at the schedule and carefully measuring the formula and double-checking all the settings on the bottle warmer.

"Does this get easier at all?" Thomas asked me as he mixed the powder and water.

"I think whenever you get used to something, things change with babies," I told him.

"It'll get easier once he starts on solid foods," Mom said. She was wearing an orange rubber necklace, and Milo was happily mouthing on it.

"And when's that?" I asked, touching one of the rubber beads. They felt kind of nice and springy, and my mind went to bad, bad places.

"When he's about six months."

Thomas stopped what he was doing. "That's when his mom might want him back permanently," he said.

Mom sighed softly, I took over the bottle making, and Thomas reached for Milo. "There's no reason to believe she's not going to want you in his life."

"Yeah, but it won't be all the time."

"No," I said, "but what if it's every other week? Wouldn't that be nice? You could spend half your time with him and half your time doing, uh, other things." Mom gave me a disbelieving look, and Thomas seemed to have trouble not laughing. At least he didn't seem sad anymore. "I mean, whatever, have time to yourself and stuff." I rolled my eyes. "God."

"We know exactly what you meant," Mom said, and Thomas finally began to laugh.

"Yeah, yeah," I grumbled. "Go to the living room, you two. I'll have this bottle out in no time."

CHAPTER
FIFTEEN

Friday morning my alarm went off exactly one hour after I'd finally fallen asleep. Milo hadn't woken up more than usual, but I'd had a hell of a time going back to sleep every time he did. I was in an awful mood when I rushed through my shower and hurried downstairs.

"Coffee?" Thomas asked when I passed him in the hallway.

"You'll have to make your own. I'm late," I snapped, and he gave me a startled look.

"I know. I made it, and I was offering you some," he told me, stung. "I know this is difficult. We're taking advantage of your kindness. Maybe it's time we start to reconsider—"

"No," I said desperately. "Please don't reconsider anything. I want you here, and Milo too, I just . . . I'm a bit tired, okay? I—" My phone buzzed. "Shit, I have to go. They need me in Brussels today. Don't—" I held up my hands as I walked backward toward the door. "Don't leave," I whispered. I couldn't read his face in the dimness of the hallway, but I was out of time. The door closed behind me with a finality that scared me.

I had to work late because of course I did, and couldn't make it home until it was time for Milo's last bottle of the day. I found myself rushing through the door and into the living room.

"Is he in bed yet?" I needed to talk to Thomas, apologize for being so rude that morning, but I wanted to see Milo before he was in bed, so I could say good night too.

"Nope." Thomas looked up from where they were playing on the rug in the living room. He smiled at me, but I couldn't tell for sure if I was forgiven. "He rolled over today! I'm pretty sure it was accidental, but still."

I bent down. "That's awesome. Who's awesome?" I lifted Milo's right hand and gave him a tiny high five. "Yes, you are." I leaned across Thomas, hesitated, then kissed him lightly. "I'll change him," I said, just as Mom walked through the door. I gave Thomas a hand up.

"And I'll make his bottle." He grinned a little knowingly, gave me a one-armed hug, and we turned to see my mother staring at us, looking mildly watery-eyed.

"Well," she said, sniffing. "I think I'll go home for the weekend. Call me if you need anything. Thomas, I'll be back early Monday morning so you can get ready for work."

"Wait!" I said, panicking as she disappeared into the hallway. She stopped with one foot on the marble staircase. "You're leaving? For the whole weekend?"

"Sweetheart, you guys are doing great. You can handle a weekend by yourselves." She pressed a kiss to my forehead and had one for Milo too. I thought back to that morning and didn't think I was doing great at all. "I'm so proud of you, Oliver. Here." She put the teething necklace around my neck. With that she disappeared up the stairs.

I hurried into the kitchen.

"She's really leaving," I told Thomas as he mixed formula. "For *two whole days*."

Thomas smiled down at me. "I know you're not half as panicky as you're pretending to be. We got this. Together." He held me tight, kissed Milo's head, then turned to me and gave me a long, deep smooch that made my knees weak. "And," he said, "it'll be just you and me tonight if we manage to stay awake."

"Oh," I breathed.

He sobered a little. "I think we need to talk about how we're going to move forward, though. I feel uncomfortable living here without contributing anything, and I know it's causing friction between us." He rubbed his palm over his jeans. "And the beginning of a relationship shouldn't be like that, should it?" Thomas didn't meet my eyes, and he had a faint flush on his cheeks.

"Do you . . . want to stop?" I asked, hating how small my voice sounded.

"No," he murmured miserably. "I don't. But I'm not quite sure how to make it work either."

"Okay, well, after we put Milo to bed, we can talk. Is that okay?" I tried to sound calm and confident, but the anxiety that seemed to be ever present lately flared up wildly. I smiled at Milo. "Come on, Milo. Let's get you changed and fed." I was relieved when Thomas followed us upstairs.

We woke up in the guest bed a few hours later, Milo still soundly asleep in his crib.

"How did we get here?" Thomas asked groggily. "I don't even remember lying down."

He looked sleep-ruffled and warm, and I reached for him without thinking. His T-shirt felt so soft against my palm when I ran a hand over his chest, up his shoulder, to his neck. The daze in his eyes disappeared instantly, and he rolled over, half trapping me under him. Without a word he kissed me, his tongue slipping smoothly into my mouth, and I opened for him. He licked my tongue, nibbled my lips, ran his mouth along my jaw, until my toes were curling against the mattress and fire flared hotly in my belly.

"Thomas," I whispered. "Can we move this into another bedroom?"

He lifted his head. Doubt clouded his eyes. "I feel like . . . we should talk first. The last few days have been so hectic. I want you. And I think you want me too, but—"

"Can't that be enough for now? It's not like we're going to have time for a three-course meal with dessert on top, if you know what I mean." I knew we needed to talk, but God, just for a little while I needed to feel good, everything else that clogged my mind be damned.

Thomas let his head thud down onto the pillow. "I really want that three-course meal," he mumbled into the fabric, and I snorted, which turned into a moan when he shifted a little so I could feel his erection. "Okay, come on."

He stood and tugged me up from the bed. By the light of Milo's turtle nightlight, we watched over him for a minute, hand in hand, and I realized then that when the time came for Thomas to go home and take Milo with him, it would break my heart.

We went into his room, since it was closer to Milo's room than mine, and took the monitor with us. I drew the curtains, turned on the bedside lamp, and felt incredibly awkward.

"I don't know what to do now," I told him.

He took a step toward me. "Can I hold you?" he asked.

"God, yes." I walked into his arms, and he enfolded me, spreading warmth and safety and a slow burn of something oh-so-sweet through my veins. I buried my face against his chest, and he nuzzled my hair until I lifted my chin. He kissed me again. I slipped my hands under his shirt, a hint to see what he'd do, and immediately he stepped back and lifted his arms. I had to stand on my tiptoes to tug it off him, he was so tall, and I tossed it aside so I could bury my fingers in his downy, dark fur. It crinkled against my palms. His breath shuddered out of his mouth when my thumbs brushed his nipples.

"Can I take yours off too?"

I nodded and let my arms fall to the side. Somehow I managed to still be stuck in my work shirt. He undid it slowly, one button at a time. When he was about halfway, he kissed my temple. I closed my eyes. He kissed my eyelids, my cheekbones, my jaw. He worked his way down my neck, spread my shirt, and kissed the divot between my clavicles. He kissed my breastbone, dropped to his knees, pressed his mouth to my stomach, and hugged me hard, resting his cheek against my belly.

I carded my fingers through his hair and waited. The moment felt loaded and my sinuses began to burn. I blinked so I wouldn't cry, but my heart beat fast with overwhelming emotions.

"Thomas?" I asked.

He shook his head, pulled me down, stripped me of my shirt, and kissed me thoroughly.

"There's a bed right therrr— Never mind," I gushed when my back hit the thick carpet.

He spread my legs and lay down between them. We kissed until my face stung with stubble burn. I was so turned on by the time his hand began to inch toward my belly button, I could've waved a peace flag from my dick. And I was also babbling. It'd been so long since I had sex that I'd actually forgotten that was a thing I did.

"Oh God," I heard myself say. "Yes, please keep going in that direction. Oh jeez, why is your hair so soft, it's not fair, I really want to lick you all over."

Thomas laughed against my neck, his breath cooling the path he'd been licking. And seriously, my dick was trapped between my stomach and my waistband now. I needed his fingers . . . one . . . inch . . . lower . . . and then . . . Milo began to cry.

"*Gnnnnnoooooo,*" I groaned pathetically. Thomas thudded his head against my shoulder three times before he rose to his feet. I spread my arms and legs wide and played dead.

"Oh, man," he said. "Look at you. I want to—"

Milo cried louder.

I sat up and winced when my pants pinched my cock. "You change his diaper," I said, resigned. "And I'll grab two ice packs for blue balls."

Thomas hauled me up. "You're really something," he murmured, and kissed me one last time.

On the upside, I did get my cuddle on the couch afterward. It was only midnight, and we had to be up again in about four to six hours, depending on when Milo decided we'd slept long enough, the little brat. I felt bad for my unkind thoughts toward the teacup human, but my balls really hurt.

"I don't think this is going to be easy," Thomas said against my hair. I rubbed the forearm he had wrapped around my chest, playing with the direction of his hairs.

"No, you're right. Maybe we should ask my mom to babysit overnight one weekend, and we could go back to your place."

Thomas bit my earlobe, and I yelped. "I meant this thing between us. You're taking on a lot more than a potential new boyfriend."

"A potential—" I sat up. "I know this part is new, but we've known each other for a long time, and the way I feel about you goes way beyond potential. And I was sort of hoping you felt the same."

He threaded his fingers with mine as he smiled slightly. "I do," he said. "I always have. And if it were just me, I'd jump into this with both feet. But it's not just me anymore. Do you really want a boyfriend with a kid? And what if it doesn't work out? Milo will become attached to you. He already has a mom and dad who aren't living together. I don't want him to lose you too."

"Why would he lose me?" I asked him.

"If we broke up—"

I squashed the annoyance that threatened to bubble up and took a calming breath. Blue balls and tiredness really did a number on my mood. "Okay. I know you're being responsible. But I'm not exactly known for my slutty ways." I bit my lip when Thomas reared back a little, looking stunned. "Shit, I didn't mean it like that. I mean, why talk about breaking up already?"

"Because." He blew out a deep breath and wouldn't quite meet my eyes. "I know how I feel. It hasn't changed over the years, no matter how I wanted it to. I know I've been sleeping around a lot but that was . . ." He shrugged, embarrassed. "When you asked me for a drink and I saw you sitting there with that sophisticated-looking guy, you were so obviously in love. I thought, 'Yeah, okay, I can get over this.' But I never did. And I don't—" His dark eyes found mine. "Sam's shoes are hard to fill. Why now, Oliver? After all these years, why now? What changed?"

Ah, the question I'd been dreading. I'd have to answer this one carefully—but truthfully. "I was with Sam at the time, and I *was* deliriously happy and in love, Thomas. I'm not going to deny it. Sam will always be part of me, somehow. If he were alive today, we'd still be together. But I also realized, having Milo here, that Sam never would've wanted this. And I do. I think if I had been single when you and I met, we'd have worked out too, and we would've been in this exact same position." I wrinkled my face. "With less blue balls, hopefully. And maybe with a baby we adopted and not one you actually physically conceived."

He laughed, and I took his hands in mine. I closed my eyes for this bit. "I've loved you as a friend and a person for years. I've been falling in love with you slowly over the last six months or so. When we talked every day while you were traveling, it was the highlight of my day. I couldn't wait for you to come home so I could figure out some way to have you whisper in my ear at night for real. And then you met Stephen."

"But you said you were glad I was with him."

I glanced up. Oh, my gorgeous man. I kissed him lightly on the mouth, because how could I not with him looking at me as if I were an ephemeral dream on the verge of dissolving? "I saw you being happy. I wanted you to be happy, even if it made me sad. So, yes, Thomas, I'm in love with you and I want this." I indicated the house, Milo, him, everything. "I want it all with you."

"What about payment? I don't want to live here rent-free, Ollie."

"Okay." I chewed on my lip. "Well, the truth is, I can't afford to let you live here rent-free anymore." Thomas startled a little, so I pushed on. "You know how Sam's parents are trying to get the house?"

"Yes. The assholes."

I smiled weakly. "If I fight them, there's a big chance I'll lose."

"What? You never said anything about that!"

"I know. Anyway, my best bet is to pay them for fifty percent of the house and get a mortgage."

Thomas whistled between his teeth. "For a house like this? That's gonna hurt."

"I know. I found one bank that'll give me the loan, but it will be tight regardless." Something I didn't like to admit, but there it was.

Thomas took my hand in his. "I'll pay what I can. It won't be half your monthly payments, I think, because I still have my own rent to pay, but I want to help."

"Thanks." It didn't sit right that I had to accept this, but I had no choice. Thomas squeezed my hand. I squeezed him back. I'd have to sit down and go through my finances tomorrow, and—

Thomas squeezed my hand again, so I looked at him.

He grinned. "Serious conversation over now?" His rakish smile made me feel giddy, and I laughed.

"Yeah, okay. Did you have something else in mind, maybe?"

He tackled me onto the couch and kissed me breathless. The weight of him grounded me, made me feel safe. I loved it. I loved feeling him like this.

"I don't know what will happen with Milo and Liesbeth," he whispered. "But I want this too."

"If you give me blue balls again, I may actually cry," I groaned when he dove back in. He laughed and peppered my face with kisses, but sat up in the end.

"We should probably go get some sleep."

"Ugh. Yeah, okay." I hesitated. "My room?"

I didn't have to explain the note of doubt in my voice. He gave me that warm look of his and asked, "You sure?"

You don't mind, do you, Sam?

"Yes," I said, taking his hand to guide him upstairs. "I'm sure."

He disappeared into his bathroom for a minute, and I got ready in mine. When I was done, I contemplated putting Sam's picture away, and that's how he found me.

He slipped his arms around me from behind and kissed my neck. "You can leave it," he murmured. "You don't have to put it away."

"Okay, but maybe—" He let go of me when I lifted the photograph and put it on my dresser instead. "There. C'mere."

I slipped into bed and held the covers out for him. He was wearing nothing but a pair of boxer briefs, and I wished I hadn't put on a T-shirt either. Our kisses were slow and sweet. We held each other as, in no time, we slipped into sleep.

When Milo wailed in my ear from the monitor, I opened my eyes with the thought that I missed the sound of my alarm clock. Thomas was already on his feet, but my whole body tingled with warmth, and I suspected he'd held me all night. I stretched, and my limbs quivered with pleasure. It'd been so long since I'd slept with the comfort of another man beside me. I'd missed it something fierce.

"I'll get his bottle started and make coffee," I said around a yawn.

Thomas leaned across the bed, kissed me morning breath and all, and smiled. "Morning, gorgeous," he murmured.

"Aw, stahp." I flattened my hair, but he ruffled it and left the room.

Milo was in a much better mood when he appeared in his daddy's arms. He blew a raspberry at me and took a swing at Thomas's nose.

"Oy," I said, wriggling my finger against his tummy. "I happen to like that nose, so don't you do any damage to it."

"I think that's the baby equivalent of a hug," Thomas said a bit smugly.

"Whatever gets you through the day, babe."

The rest of the weekend went by really well, not counting our little trip to Stijn's bakery where Milo had a blow-out diaper the minute we walked inside. Our chocolate croissants didn't appeal after that, but I told Thomas to wait for them to be wrapped up anyway, while I took Milo home and changed him.

We played in the yard with him, read books, pointed out birds, changed diapers, and cleaned spit-up from our hair, the couch, the floor, Milo's nostrils. We walked miles and miles and miles, because while the bouncy chair was good for five minutes, Milo's favorite thing was being held.

I couldn't blame him. We napped when he napped, and my favorite thing, too, was being held by Thomas while we dozed.

On Sunday night, Milo went to sleep at eight. Maybe he was as tired from the weekend as we were. We collapsed on the couch. I was about to reach for the remote to see if we could watch a movie, when Thomas's hand crept toward my leg.

"Oh, no," I said, crawling away from him. "Don't even think about it."

He withdrew his hand with a startled look. "Is . . . Are we okay? Did I do something wrong?"

"Every time you touch me, Milo wakes up and starts crying. I can't deal with more crying right now, so hands to yourself."

Thomas smirked. "I see." He folded his hands in his lap and faced the TV. I turned it on. And waited. He didn't try to touch me again.

Well, damn.

I glanced at him out of the corner of my eye. It could be a smile tugging at his mouth, or he could really be into *Midsomer Murders*. It was hard to tell. I tried to pay attention to the gazillion killings that always seemed to happen in a town of two hundred people, but I kept being drawn to Thomas. Was he seriously not going to make another move?

I let my hand creep toward him.

"Oh, no," he said. "Hands to yourself, Ollie. Stick to your own rules."

My hand kept on creeping. When I was nearly touching the fabric of his shorts, he grabbed my wrist and held it. He kneeled up on the couch and loomed over me as I sank deeper and deeper against the armrest. "What if he wakes up?" he asked as he pressed my hands above my head. I shifted so I could cradle his hips between my legs and we were stretched out with him on top of me.

"I take full responsibility," I whispered, and then he was kissing me like there was no tomorrow.

We'd made out quite a lot this weekend, but not like this. Not with his whole body against mine. I was aware of the hardness of him all over, but mostly where he pushed into my groin, hot and wanting.

"Thomas," I whispered, my voice coming out reedy. "If this gets cut short again, I'm going to have to wank in the shower. I'm really sorry, but I won't be able to stand it if—"

"I know, shh." He mouthed at my neck, flicked my earlobe with his tongue, and I squirmed and panted and made needy noises until I felt his hand between us, undoing first my shorts and then his. "Lift your hips a bit."

"Oh God," I breathed, and did as I was told. He let go of my hand, and I immediately petted his hair, his neck, his shoulders, and then, oh, glorious freedom. "Waitwaitwait."

Thomas froze. "What?"

"Lemme see. I wanna see." I lifted up his T-shirt and *Hmm, lovely*. "Oh yeah." He was big enough, but not huge, with a nice girth and a mushroom cap I wanted—

"You're making me self-conscious," he said. When I looked up, he really was blushing.

"Aw, baby." I filled my fist with the silky skin of his cock and squeezed, relishing how his eyes drooped shut and a small groan gushed from his mouth. "This is all yummy, nummy goodness."

He shoved my T-shirt out of the way and rubbed my belly, just above my pubic hair. I used to groom with Sam, but I hadn't bothered in a long time. Thomas didn't seem to mind. His palm tickled my pubes. He grabbed the base of my cock, and I thought fireworks might burst from my ears.

"Move your hand," he told me, and I let go. He sank down so we fit together nicely, wrapped his large paw around the both of us, and moved his hips in a slow, sensuous glide. Our foreskins rubbed together, and my ass clenched as I threw my head back. Thomas kissed my throat, gently lapped at my Adam's apple, and squeezed his hand around us.

"I am so not going to last," I told him, and he laughed against my jaw.

"Probably a good thing, since the baby will wake up soon."

The baby. It should've been a mood killer, but instead, a different kind of warmth unfurled in my belly. For now though, I pushed the thought aside, grabbed Thomas's ass, parted my knees wider, and wriggled closer.

"Jerk me off, Thomas," I whispered in his ear. "I need to come all over you."

He kissed me deeply, and I let him overwhelm me, body and soul. He smelled delicious, he felt even better, and he kissed like a god. It took no time at all for the muscles in my buttocks to tighten as the climax built in my groin. It wasn't going to be an earth-shattering orgasm—I wouldn't last long enough for that—and yet in that moment it was the sweetest thing I'd ever experienced.

"Thomas," I whispered, clinging to his shoulders. His head dropped to the crook of my neck and nodded. He let go of himself and concentrated on me, and I managed to bite down on his T-shirt in time to muffle the shout. The first spurt of come slicked his grip, and the sound his fist made around my cock was obscene, but I shuddered and hung on, unable to care.

Before I came down, I wriggled a hand between us, found his cock, and stroked him. "I want to blow you," I murmured in his ear.

"Oh God, no."

"What?"

"Ah fuck, I meant, *gnnn*, if you do that, I want it to last more than a second. Jesus, Ollie, can you—"

"Oh." I released the death grip on his dick and petted it a little in apology. "Sorry. I thought you meant—"

"I know." He lifted his head and looked at me. His irises had been almost completely swallowed by his pupils, and with his hair covering his forehead in thick, sweaty peaks, he was beyond edible. I moved my hand over his cock and rubbed my thumb over the head, under the foreskin, and watched a dark-red flush creep along his throat. His cheeks were mottled pink with arousal, and his thighs shook with the effort of holding himself up so I could stroke him. He was falling apart, and he was all mine.

I shifted to the side a little so Thomas could lie between me and the back of the couch. I leaned up on one elbow. I kissed him while I familiarized myself with what he liked and what he loved, until I could feel the tension in him ratchet up. I gave him what he needed. He buried his face against my shoulder and orgasmed quietly, come hitting his T-shirt and bare belly. As I watched him come down, my stomach clenched a little and I closed my eyes. *Oh, Sam.*

In that moment, I had to make a choice. I could let Sam come between us and ruin these precious minutes, or I could truly let him go. I opened my eyes and saw Thomas look at me like he knew what I was thinking. I didn't know if I was ready to make that choice, but life—and love—didn't wait for opportune times. Even wanting to be happy here with anyone but Sam fed the pit of guilt that gnawed at my stomach.

Thomas gently caressed my cheek, and I leaned into his touch. The idea of giving up on this, on the other hand, made me feel infinitely worse.

I pursed my lips, taking in the mess we'd made of ourselves. "So, you ready for round two?"

His eyes widened, and he laughed as he pulled me down for a kiss.

"Fuck," he murmured and pressed our foreheads together. "That was really—"

"Fast? Belated? Overdue?"

He chuckled. "Great. I was going to say great. And now I'm going to want to do it all the time, and—"

Right on cue, Milo began to cry.

# CHAPTER
SIXTEEN

I came home on Monday with a box full of fresh groceries to find the house oddly subdued. Mom was in the kitchen, preparing dinner, and I spotted Thomas and Milo doing laps around the yard. Every once in a while he'd point at something, then walk along.

Stan had emailed me again, and I had one eye on my phone as I yanked open the fridge to put the milk away first.

"I'll do that," she said.

I froze as Stan's words registered.

"Well, this is it."

"What is it?" Mom peered at my phone. "I can't read that without my glasses."

"Sam's parents agreed to me buying out the house."

"Oh, Oliver." My mom covered her mouth. Her eyes hardened. "I can't believe those people. How dare they go against their son's wishes like that!"

"Money and grief is a weird combination," I said, even as my stomach dropped to the floor. I hadn't allowed myself to think of it too much so far, but this meant I'd have to give up every single penny of my savings as down payment or the bank wouldn't grant me the loan. I'd have nothing in reserve.

Mom squeezed my arm. "What are you going to do? Are you sure the house is worth it?"

"It's my home," I whispered. "I can't stand the thought of giving it up."

She studied me carefully. "If you're just trying to hang on to Sam's memory . . ."

I shook my head. "It's more than that. I mean, yes, he's part of it, but not because I can't let go of him." I hadn't entirely yet, but I didn't tell her that. "It's a wonderful house. I don't want to live anywhere else. And if I sold it, with my fifty percent I'd never be able to afford anything even half as nice as this. I want to do whatever I can to keep it."

"Okay." Her face was drawn with worry. "Just don't overextend yourself."

"Thomas said he'd help," I told her, although the idea soured my stomach.

We both turned to the window and watched Milo and Thomas explore the garden. "That's a short-term solution, Ollie. And one you need to be careful with." I frowned at her, but she sighed. "You might want to talk to Thomas anyway. He seemed a little down this morning."

My heart skipped a beat. "What? Why?" Had I done something wrong the night before? No, we'd changed and fed Milo, and we'd gone straight to sleep in my bed. He'd kissed me awake that morning, right before Milo began to cry, and he'd been playful and happy when I left. It couldn't be about us. Could it?

"Go on." She nudged me out the door. I stepped onto the patio, hands damp with nervous sweat. It was still warm out, even though a dark rain cloud covered the western sky.

"Hey." I stuffed my hands in my pockets, and Thomas turned around. He looked tired but had a smile for me, and my heart settled a little when he gave me a chaste but lingering kiss. "Hey, little buddy," I said to Milo. He made a pouty face and stuck out his tongue. "That's how the cool kids say hello these days, huh?" I turned my attention back to Thomas. "What's up?"

He tilted his head from side to side and sighed. "Liesbeth called today. She wants to see Milo on Wednesday afternoon."

"Oh. And that's bad?"

"I don't know. What if she wants to get out of the clinic early? What if she wants to come home and take Milo?"

"Okay, deep breath." I put my hand on his shoulder, and he kissed my knuckles. "You're worrying too much about this. And I get that's what parents *do*, but this isn't you."

"I know," he said. "I know. My entire world has changed. For the better. I don't want to lose this. But maybe she's well enough now.

I mean, obviously I want his mom to be well. But what if she won't want me to keep Milo at all? God, he's hard work. He cries so much. I had no idea babies did that. On the other hand, to think that I won't see him every day . . ." His face twisted, and I put my arms around him, careful not to squash Milo. Thomas leaned his head against mine.

"It will be okay," I said. "You have legal rights. Even if she comes home early, you can get a lawyer and draw up a contract saying he's with you fifty percent of the time. You work part time now and—"

"I can't keep doing that forever, Ollie. I have to pay my rent and pay you. And my house is really not childproof. Who's going to babysit him once I'm back home? I can't stay here forever, can I? My dad? He loves me, but he loves his retirement more. And your mom can't drive to my place every day."

"No," I said, "but you could drop him off at her place on your way to work, if it came to that. You could slowly start looking for a place to live closer to town. Or . . ." I toed the grass with my shoe. "You could move in here. Permanently."

He took a small step back. "Ollie . . ."

"I know. Just think about it."

Thomas blew out a hot breath through his nose. I was startled to see he was actually angry. "I can't. I can't risk everything. You understand that, don't you? Give up my home and live here with Milo, and what if it doesn't work out?"

"Then we deal with that at the time. I'm not going to force you, obviously, but you could sublet your place to someone using short-term contracts. And I really hope you don't think I'd kick you out on the street if we broke up."

"No, of course not," he said. "I know you'd never do anything that could hurt Milo, but life happens." His voice gentled a little. "You of all people should know that. What if something went wrong? I know you wouldn't kick me out, but I'd have to look for somewhere else to live, and uproot Milo again. I . . . I can't do it. I'm sorry."

That stung. And it wasn't like I'd fought and won my own battle with guilt over Sam, this house, or loving someone else. At least I was ready to try. Maybe my expectations were unrealistic. Of course he would look out for Milo. I shouldn't be childish about this. Milo came first. My heart hurt nonetheless.

"It's only an idea. You can think about it," I said again and tried to smile.

He stopped me before I could walk away. "Ollie. It's more than just Milo."

"What?"

He ran his fingers through my hair and held me gently by the back of the neck. It sent a hot shiver down my spine whenever he did that. "I don't want us to step into this domestic routine of parenthood before we've had a chance to even explore the honeymoon phase. No beginning of a relationship should be about diapers and midnight feedings and being too exhausted for sex."

"So, what?" I demanded, my annoyance finally bleeding through. "You want to wait until he's off bottles? Out of diapers? Going to college? This is life, Thomas, as you so nicely pointed out earlier." He winced, but I pushed on. "And I want to share it with you. No relationship should end because someone got stabbed, either. I dealt with it. This isn't easy for me. Dealing with Milo . . ." I looked down. Milo was sucking on his fist. Soon he wouldn't be waiting so patiently for his bottle. "It's my pleasure. I love the little guy, and I hope someday I can prove to you just how true that is."

"I'm not doubting you."

That stopped me short. "Then what? You doubt yourself? I'm not expecting a marriage proposal here, but I thought we could at least—"

"This is scaring me to death," he whispered. He walked away from me a little, tugged at his hair, and turned back. "Two weeks ago I had nothing but my tiny house and my job. Suddenly I have a son and I have you. Before, I couldn't miss what I didn't have. But now . . . what if I lose you both?"

Everything crashed down on me. Sam's parents, the house, the guilt over falling for Thomas while Sam still lived so close to my heart. It wasn't fair. Not to Sam. And not to Thomas either. My heart thudded wildly, and I couldn't take it.

"You don't know the meaning of loss," I snapped. "You don't know what it means to drag yourself out of bed day after day, realizing the person you loved more than anything isn't here anymore. There were days when I screamed at the universe. There were days when I didn't want to get out of bed at all. Ever again. But I pushed myself out of that. I'm here now, and I'm taking a huge risk again, although I feel really torn about it sometimes. But at least I'm willing to try. For you."

"Are you sure it's for me, Ollie? Because it sounds like you're still in love with Sam. Maybe it's not me you want. Maybe it's someone to help you pay your mortgage."

I gasped. Thomas looked stricken, but while I stood there trying to make sense of what he'd said, he remained silent.

"Wow," I whispered.

"Ollie, I—"

"We're both tired," I interrupted, staring out into the garden. "We don't have to make any big decisions right now. You go to Liesbeth on Wednesday and see what she says. We can deal with everything else later."

Thomas nodded miserably and gently swayed side to side to soothe Milo. "Okay."

He bent down, and I turned away a little so the kiss landed on my cheek. His eyes flashed with hurt. I wanted to apologize but didn't.

He was afraid of losing what he had. If there was one sentiment I could understand, it was that one. I'd lost everything once, and I was on the verge of putting my heart on the line again. Now that the idea had taken form, I couldn't shake it. Resentment nibbled at me until the ache grew deeper. If I could risk it, then why couldn't he?

I went home early on Wednesday. No matter how much I kept the smile plastered on my face and reassured Thomas that all would be fine, in reality nerves made me consume twice my daily amount of coffee. I made phone calls and wrote emails to get the ball rolling on acquiring the mortgage, which didn't help my mood. Eventually I had enough.

My brain buzzed with caffeine overload the whole tram ride home, and I was pretty sure people were eyeing me suspiciously. I didn't care. I practically ran home from the tram stop and fell through the door, only to have Thomas shush me as I kicked off my shoes in the hallway. He tugged me into the living room and quietly shut the door.

"Milo went down for a nap."

"How did it go? Where's Mom? Did you eat? What did Liesbeth say?"

Thomas's eyes grew larger with each question. In the end he shut my mouth with his. Without breaking contact, he dragged me to the couch, pushed me down, and cushioned my fall with his arms.

"You taste . . . caffeinated," he said, and laughed. "Your mom went home when I got back from work, dinner is in the oven, and Milo is fine. Listen, about the other—"

I wasn't ready for that conversation, so I grabbed his button-up and tried to shake him, which wasn't easy from my position. "How. Did. It. Go?"

He grinned and kissed me again, so I figured it couldn't have gone too badly. For a moment I let him have his way with me, because, oh *God*, I really needed to get him all to myself for one night. Just one night. Was that really too much to— He dug his tongue into my ear, and I yelped.

"It went fine," he said, and pushed the hair out of my eyes so he could see me. "She cried a lot. But she was very happy to see Milo. She said we're taking good care of him, but—"

"But? Why is there a 'but'? There can't be a 'but'! We *are* taking good care of him."

"Ye-es," he said slowly, "but she wasn't too thrilled about us living here. With you."

"What?" I sat up so fast I nearly brained him. This was the last thing we needed. "Because I'm a guy? Did you tell her we're together? Is she having issues with me being—"

"Ollie, chill." He eased me down again and began to unbutton my shirt. "Not because you're gay, or a guy. Because she doesn't know you. She wants to meet you next time we go to see her."

"Oh." I tried to process that, but his fingertips were tickling my belly, sending little zings of pleasure downward. "There's going to be a next time?" I said weakly.

"Yes, she can see Milo once a week. And you can come too."

"Okay. That sounds . . . good." He tugged his shirt off and lay down on top of me.

Not-so-pleasant feelings were churning on the back burner. Fear of him pulling away when I was already in too deep. Guilt for lying here with him and not Sam, and liking it. Annoyance because I knew this could get cut short again any minute, and I realized that wasn't fair, but *God*. I just *wanted*. So I pushed it all aside and tried to be here with him—not my past, not the uncertain future.

I loved how his chest hair felt against my skin. I wriggled a little as I sighed happily. "You know," I said when his hand drifted downward and he cupped me through my slacks, "I thought I was done with handjobs on the couch when I turned twenty."

He kissed my jaw, my neck, lifted his head, and murmured, "Who said anything about handjobs?"

I gulped as he licked my left nipple. I gave a nervous laugh that turned into a moan when he sucked it into his mouth. With a sharp pop I felt in my balls, he let go.

"Unless that's what you want? I mean, I don't have to go down on you. I could—"

"No, no," I said. "Don't let me stop you. Who am I to stop you from doing what you—*ah Jesus*—want?" He'd unbuckled my pants and yanked them open. My cock slapped my belly when he pulled my boxers down.

He bit his lip. "Hmm, Ollie." His eyes were laughing at me, but in a kind way.

"What?" I snapped, almost desperately. "What now?"

"I have to admit, I've wanted to do this ever since I saw that painting." And then he grasped the base of my cock, pointed it at his face, and devoured me whole.

"Oh my God." I pushed the pads of my thumbs into my eyeballs and tried really hard not to shove my way down his throat. He applied some sweet, sweet suction, and moved his mouth up so slowly that it was pure, awful agony at its finest. I could feel the soft touch of his palate, the smooth roll of his tongue as he pushed it under my foreskin, a hint of teeth at the back of his mouth. I couldn't believe how good it felt. Sam had never been a fan of blowjobs—which had been fine with me. We'd enjoyed the main event too much to linger on the lack of mouth action. But this . . . "Thomas," I whispered far too soon. "Ah, I'm not going to last."

He let go of me, and I made a bereft sound. Instead of giving up, he gently licked my balls, worked a finger behind them, and tickled my taint. "How about now?" he asked, rubbing my perineum with his thumb.

I gritted my teeth. "Yep. Nope. Now I'm just going to come all over myself."

He laughed softly, and his breath cooled the spit on my balls. I shivered and groaned and clasped a hand over my mouth because he'd taken me down again. He was done playing and was going in for the kill. He sucked me on the way up, tongued me on the way down, squeezing the base of my cock with one hand as he kept his balance with the other. He went at it in a rhythm that made me sympathetic for his jaw. Only for a second though, because my balls drew up, my breath stuttered in my chest, my legs went rigid, and I shouted into the palm of my hand. He kept sucking me through my orgasm, swallowing until I had nothing left to give.

When he resurfaced and sat back on his heels, he looked so deliciously debauched that I did a crunch so I could reach for him and pull him down. As I kissed my own flavor away, I wriggled out of my pants, straightened my boxers, and pushed him up to sitting.

"Right," I said as I kneeled between his thighs. "I haven't done this in a long time, but—" I'd reached for his jeans, but he caught my wrists before I could touch his belt. "What?" I asked, suddenly self-conscious. "You don't want me to?" I eyed the large bulge in his pants.

"I do," he said. "But if blowjobs aren't something you usually do, then . . ."

I tilted my head to the side. I'd have put a hand on my hip if he weren't still holding my wrists. "Do I look like I don't want to?"

He smiled. "No. Wearing nothing but underwear and an unbuttoned shirt, you look like you want very much."

"I do." I lifted my chin and strained for him as I said, "I want an awful lot of things we don't have time for right now, just so you know." I kissed his slightly slack-jawed mouth smugly. "Now let go of my hands, handsome. And let me get reacquainted with the act of fellatio."

He groaned. "Please don't call it that."

"No? You prefer kneeling at the altar? Bob some knob? Gobble—"

"Stop talking, Ollie."

I grinned up at him. "Make me."

His eyes darkened, and a hot spark raced down my spine. With slow movements, he undid his belt, his button, his zipper. He pulled his jeans and boxers down. His cock sprang free. Was he going to— Oh yeah. He put his hand on the back of my neck and drew me forward. He was gentle about it, which I appreciated since it had been a long time, but there was no mistaking it. I let him push my face against his cock. I nuzzled him, inhaled him, licked him root to tip. He let go of my head and sank back into the couch with a deep, satisfied sigh.

I rubbed his thighs soothingly, a promise in a touch. *Let me take care of you.*

He gently swept my bangs aside, and take care of him I did.

On Friday I met with my lawyer, Sam's parents' lawyer, and Simon and Martine themselves. Martine kept throwing me watery glances, but Simon sat in stony silence, staring at the wall behind me like I wasn't even there. The whole thing went by so fast, it felt unreal. I wrote signature after signature, until I couldn't keep track of the documents anymore.

When it was done, I felt shivery, as if a fever lurked. I stood on the doorstep outside of the lawyer's office, hugging my arms around myself as rain came down hard, contemplating whether I should wait it out or make a run for it. Martine appeared behind me and faltered when she saw me.

"Oliver," she whispered. Her bottom lip trembled. She looked ten years older than the last time I'd seen her. "I'm sorry."

I wanted to say a million things. *Not as sorry as I am* was one of them. *Not as sorry as Sam would've been, if he'd known.* But Simon came out behind her, taking her arm in an iron grip and marching away like it wasn't raining at all, and I said nothing. I was sorry, but not for myself. Money was only money, after all, and I had a glorious, warm home to return to.

"What's up?" Thomas asked that night, startling me into closing my laptop quickly. Milo looked all nice and clean from his bath. Thomas eyed me curiously, raising his eyebrow.

"It's nothing," I said, ignoring his dubious look. I didn't want him to see how empty my bank account was. I didn't want him to feel obligated in any way. If he was staying, it was because he wanted to be with me and for no other reason. I'd make sure of that.

My phone rang. On autopilot, I pressed the Answer button and put it on speaker.

Cleo and Imran had been caught up in a coinciding double-duty nightshift, which didn't happen very often, but when it did, they tended to fall off the face of the earth. So I wasn't surprised Cleo didn't sound completely sane. "Ollie!" she practically shouted. "Tell me everything! How did the date go? Oh my God, I can't believe I haven't spoken to you in so long. Did you guys get on okay? Are you resurfacing from a black hole of sex and debauchery? Is that why we haven't heard from either of you?"

Thomas turned around slowly at the same time I looked up. He began walking Milo around the kitchen. Milo had no interest in going to sleep tonight.

"I thought you told her," I whispered to him urgently.

He shook his head, eyes wide. "I thought *you* told her."

Oh God.

"Um, Cleo there's something you should know."

"What?" She suddenly sounded dead serious. "What is it? Are you okay?"

"Yes. We're both okay. Uh, the thing is . . . Thomas had a baby."

Silence.

"And Thomas and the baby are—" I glanced at him, then back at the phone "—temporarily living with me until things settle down. It's a long story." Why was I so nervous about telling her this? And why was she not saying anything? "His name is Milo, and he's gorgeous. We were wondering if you and Imran would like to come and meet him?"

"Thomas had a baby?" she asked in a really small voice, and promptly started crying.

Thomas gave me a *what the hell?* look, and I shrugged. He leaned over the phone. "Cleo? You okay?"

"Yes," she said. "No."

There was a rustle, muffled voices, and Imran came on the line. "I can't get any sense out of her, guys," he said, sounding resigned. "What did you say to her?"

"Uh." I looked at Thomas. It was his turn.

"I had a baby," he said without preamble. "The mother is in treatment for PPD, so Milo and I are staying with Ollie."

I waited for the *for now*, but it didn't come.

"Oh, Jesus," Imran said, and he sounded annoyed.

"I have to say, this isn't the reaction I thought we'd get when we mentioned a baby," I tried to joke.

"No? Well, I guess Cleo never told you she had a miscarriage."

The phone went dead, and I stared at Thomas as my brain tried to process the words. "What the hell?" I asked him. "Why would he be such an asshole about that? Unless . . . Was it yours?"

Thomas rounded the island, holding one hand up in plea as he clutched Milo to his chest. "It can't have been," he said. "Oh my God, Ollie, you have to believe me. It can't have been."

"I—" I stared into his kind, warm eyes. Right then they were shiny with anguish. "I don't know what to think," I said. After the jab about me wanting him here so he could help pay my mortgage, I wasn't feeling exactly magnanimous. "I need a minute." I knew he'd slept around a lot. I *knew* that. And it had never bothered me. I knew he'd slept with Cleo, and that hadn't bothered me either. But this? My heart hurt. *God.* I couldn't do this. I wanted Sam. I nearly started crying there and then.

He opened his mouth, but closed it again and nodded. "If you leave, please let me know when you're coming back. If you want us to go, I can—"

I was about to reach for the door, but I turned to him, angry suddenly. "Don't insult me. I told you I wasn't going to kick you out of here no matter what. And I meant it. For the record, I'm also not using you to pay my bills." A low blow and I knew it. Softer, I said, "I need a minute, that's all." It didn't seem like too much to ask, but his dejected expression made me feel like a jerk regardless.

"I'll be here when you want to talk." He looked defeated when he turned to the living room. My heart shattered when Milo began to cry quietly. Had he felt the tension? Was he sensitive to fights already? I felt terrible.

For some reason my feet carried me up to the top floor. The painting sat under its cloth, and I carefully revealed it. Seeing my face in ecstasy like that was still a shock, and the whole thing made me squirm on the inside. How had Sam done that? Just from memory in the bedroom mirror? Had he taken a picture I wasn't aware of? Not that I minded. I only wondered. My eyes were closed in the painting, but Sam looked right at the viewer. Godlike, he was, even though I was sure he hadn't meant it like that. He'd been aware of his beauty, his presence, but never in an arrogant way. This look on his face was meant to say, *See? See how much he's all mine?*

And I had been. But I wasn't anymore.

Of course Thomas would've told me if he'd known about Cleo's baby. He was a good person through and through. And good people made mistakes too. I'd made my fair share, and he'd always forgiven me.

I sighed and covered my face. I hadn't signed up for this, but that didn't mean I didn't want it.

I'd taken Sam for granted in the best ways, and I'd lost him. But if I had the choice and knew what was coming, I'd do the same again. Sam had been worth every ounce of pain I'd felt over the past year.

But what about Thomas?

I tried to imagine never knowing what his kisses tasted like, what he looked like first thing in the morning, sleepy and soft. The way he gazed at me when he thought I wasn't watching. I let my hands fall away and rose to my feet.

I hurried downstairs and found him on the couch, Milo asleep on his shoulder. He looked too exhausted to even carry him to bed.

"Here," I whispered. "Let me. You put on the TV. I'll be right there."

"Ollie?"

"It's okay. I won't be long."

I very carefully changed Milo's diaper, and while he woke briefly, he snuggled back to sleep as soon as I put him in his crib. After turning on the baby monitor, I made my way into the kitchen, grabbed two beers, and joined Thomas on the couch.

He accepted the beer but wouldn't look at me.

"You okay?" I whispered. "I'm sorry about what I said."

He nodded and drank from his beer. "This isn't easy," Thomas said. "And I think we'd be really good together, Ollie. I do. But—" Oh no. My breath stuttered in my lungs. "When you said you needed a minute, I thought that was exactly what we both needed."

"What?"

He set his beer down and pulled one leg underneath him so he could face me. With gentle fingers, he began to play with my hair. "I think we both need some space. Some time to sort ourselves out. I don't want to end this." He picked up my hand and kissed my knuckles. "But this isn't turning into anything sustainable at the rate we're going. Ollie . . . I'm going to go home for a while with Milo. I understand if that means you don't want to continue this. I know financially you're in a tough spot, and I can lend you some—"

"I don't want your money," I said, wanting to sound angry and hurt. Instead I sounded resigned. "I'm sorry. I shouldn't have doubted you. Here I am asking you to have faith in me, and I didn't show you the same kind of respect. Maybe you're right. Maybe we need some space." I'd only ever been in one relationship, and Sam and I had never needed space. I knew what it generally meant when couples came to that conclusion. Tears prickled against my eyelids, but I managed to hold them back. "When do you want to leave?"

"Tomorrow, if that's okay with you."

"It's fine, Thomas," I said, and my heart ached. "I'll help you pack. But I do think we need to resolve this thing with Cleo and Imran somehow."

"Ask them to come over in the morning if you want." He sounded so tired. "The thing is . . . there is no way that baby was mine."

"What?" I sat up a little. "But you guys had sex, didn't you?"

"Yes, we did. But I never came."

"What?" I sat up even straighter. "But you did . . ." I had no clue how to put this delicately.

"Yes. With a condom. And I didn't have an orgasm. I sort of faked it when she came, and hurried into the bathroom and squirted some shower gel into the condom in case she saw it when she emptied the bin."

I tried not to laugh but a snort came out anyway.

"It's not funny," Thomas said, but he laughed too. "Oh my God, I'm ridiculous."

"Little bit." I put my head on his shoulder, and he put his arm around me. I couldn't decipher what this meant, if this was friendly affection or love, and I was too emotionally exhausted to try. "You have to tell Imran this. And Cleo. Or this is going to ruin more than our friendships."

"Shit."

I picked up my phone and sent Cleo and Imran the same text. *Come over tomorrow. We need to talk. All of us.*

CHAPTER
SEVENTEEN

I felt like some sort of reality TV armchair psychologist as I sat in my living room, Cleo and Imran on one side of the sectional and Thomas on the other. Milo was making cooing noises on the floor, completely fascinated with the plastic mirror dangling from his play mat.

Okay, Cleo why don't you tell the audience your side of the story?

I wanted to giggle. But didn't, thank God. "A beer, anyone?" I asked, my voice pitched a bit higher than usual.

"It's ten in the morning," Cleo said.

Meh . . . "Okay, well, coffee, then?"

"What are we doing here, Ollie?" Imran asked for the second time. "I have to go to work in an hour."

I frowned at him. He had always been blunt, but this? And the way he wouldn't look at anyone? "What's the matter with you?" I asked him. "Why are you being such a dick?"

"He's being a dick," Cleo said, "because he never believed me when I told him there was no way that baby was Thomas's." I noticed they were sitting next to each other but not touching at all.

Thomas made a startled noise and turned bright red. "You . . . knew?"

"Honey, I know the difference between spunk and shower gel."

I still wanted to laugh, but managed not to. "Okay, so now you know." I pretended to bring their heads together. "Now kiss and make up."

"He can't," Cleo said. "It was never about the baby, just like our previous fight wasn't really about me sleeping with Thomas." She turned to Imran. "I know you tried, but you can't, can you?" She began to cry. When Imran reached for her, she ran out of the room. I gave Thomas a baffled look, but he shrugged, clueless as well.

"What the hell?" I asked Imran. "What's going on?"

He sighed and rubbed a hand over his face. "She wants commitment," he said, and when he didn't go on, I made a *duh* face.

"Uh, well, you've been together for years. You got her pregnant. How is it ridiculous that she wants commitment?"

"All I ever do is work, Ollie. I'm not ready to be tied down into a routine at home too."

"Maybe you could've thought of that before she invested years of her life into a relationship with you," Thomas quietly said.

Imran sneered at him. "You're one to talk. Why the fuck did you have to sleep with her, huh?"

"Hey, that's not fair," I said and rose to my feet again. "You guys had broken up, she was feeling lonely, and one thing led to another."

"That's the oldest excuse I've ever heard," Imran snapped.

"You're saying you don't want to commit!" I yelled. "But at the same time you don't want her to see other people. And what? You can?"

"I never said that."

"You need to make up your fucking mind. She's a great person, and she deserves better."

"It scares the crap out of me, okay? The idea of marrying and having babies, and basically being a slave to work and home life forever."

"Sometimes you have to take a risk with the scary stuff to get to the good stuff," I said. "Sometimes you need to decide whether or not someone is worth the risk. And it's not fair to leave someone hanging while you take forever making up your mind." I didn't mean to, but I glanced at Thomas.

"What does that mean?" Thomas asked.

"I wasn't talking to you," I said, sharper than I meant to.

"Okay. I think I'll be upstairs packing."

Imran glanced between us, and Thomas rose to his feet. I wanted to stop him but didn't.

"What the fuck?" Imran asked.

"None of your business," I said tiredly. "Go talk to Cleo."

It was time for Milo's bottle, so I lifted him from his play mat and went into the kitchen. My heart ached like it hadn't in a long time, but it ached for Thomas, not Sam. At least Milo kept me distracted as I waited for his bottle to heat.

When I heard the front door slam, I had no idea who'd left, but I doubted Thomas would go without Milo. Unless he'd gone to park his car closer to the house.

Cleo appeared in the kitchen and took Milo off my hands to change him. The bottle was done by the time she came back. Milo had his hand tightly clenched in her hair.

"So what's it like? Living here with Thomas and . . . I can't believe it . . . his *son*?" she asked.

"It's . . ." I grinned at her. "It's exhausting. And frustrating. On so many levels, Cleo, oh my God. Half the time I don't know why Milo is crying, and the other half I'm suffering from blue balls." She wrinkled her nose, but I ignored her. "And it's perfect." I flopped down on the couch so I could put my chin in my hands and look at her. I sobered. "I mean, it's not anymore. I want Thomas to move in, and he's reluctant. I can understand why, but it hurts my feelings anyway. And at the same time I keep thinking this shouldn't be possible. To be this happy twice? I keep . . ."

I blew a breath through my nose, trying to put this heavy feeling in my chest into words. "I keep waiting for the other shoe to drop. Like . . . I'm afraid to give it my all because no one gets to have this twice, do they? I mean, I want it. I want him so much, Cleo. But how? How could I? It doesn't seem possible. We're going to take some time apart. He's packing right now."

"He's *leaving*?" She gaped at me.

"For now. We're not breaking up." I hoped.

"Aw, babe." She nudged my side with her small foot and shifted Milo so she could burp him. "Happiness isn't a finite thing. It's not a purse that runs out of happy coins. Happiness is . . . what you put into the world. You're such a good person, and you have such a huge heart. You'd find happiness in whatever you did or whomever you chose to be with. It's not something that overcomes you. You make Thomas happy, and so he makes you happy in return. Of course you were going to fall in love again. But maybe he's right. Moving in together after what you've been through, and with a baby in the picture—that's pretty intense. I'm convinced you guys will work it out. Give it time. You two are so good together."

"You think so?" I whispered.

She pressed her lips together, and I couldn't tell if she was going to smile or cry again. "Do you love him?"

I laughed a little giddily and rested my head on my arms before lifting it again. "Yes," I said. "I really do."

The smile she offered was brittle at the edges, and the levity of the moment drained away.

"What's going to happen now? With you and Imran."

She shrugged, but one tear dropped from her eyelashes, and my heart ached. "I don't know. I don't know if we can come back from this. We're going to talk when we get home."

I walked her to the door. As she stood on the steps, she whirled around and said, "Next weekend we're babysitting for you."

"What?"

"We both have the weekend off. Take your pick: Friday or Saturday. Go out for dinner, spend the night together. You guys deserve a break. And a real date."

I wasn't going to pass up an offer like that.

"I'll talk to Thomas and text you." I wasn't sure if he'd want to take her up on this.

"Do it. And text me photos of Milo too. What a cutie."

"Isn't he?" I asked proudly, like I had anything to do with it.

She reached out, and I hugged her.

"Take care of yourself, okay?" I whispered. "We're here for you."

"I'm so happy there's a we again, Ollie. So happy." She kissed my cheek, and then she was gone.

When Thomas came to find me, he was carrying three bags.

"Do you think you could give me a hand?" he asked.

I swallowed hard. "Of course."

He put his bags down and cupped my face in his palms. "This isn't the end, is it, Ollie?"

"I don't want it to be."

"Me neither. Maybe when we're back on our feet a little bit, we can talk about buying a smaller house together. Something that just belongs to us."

I reared back and inevitably pulled myself free from his grasp. "You want me to sell this house? After all I've done to try and keep it?"

He sighed, looking uncomfortable, but pushed on regardless. "I always wondered why you were so bent on keeping it, Ollie. You got yourself into some dire financial straits, and for what? Because you couldn't let go of Sam? I don't want to live in his shadow forever."

I stared at him. "Is that what you think? I— Okay, I've had some trouble letting go, but I don't think that's hard to understand. It's one thing to try and move on, which is what I'm doing, but you what? Want me to forget him?"

"No, of course I don't. I'd never want you to forget him. It's just . . . I don't know. I don't want to argue about this now."

"Why not? Let's just have it all in the open, Thomas. You're about to leave anyway. You think I'm not letting go of Sam, and you're what? A poor substitute?"

"I think," he said calmly, "we've come together in very unusual circumstances, and we need a breather to put everything in perspective."

"I don't need perspective," I said. "I know exactly what I want. You and Milo in this beautiful, once-in-a-lifetime house. And yes, sometimes Sam haunts me. Sometimes the past haunts me. If you're going to hold that against any potential partner, you're going to have a hard time finding someone. You know what I was thinking when I signed the contract with my lawyer, Thomas? What a gorgeous family home this would be. I wasn't thinking of turning this into a mausoleum for Sam. He's gone. He's dead. No one knows that better than I do."

Thomas chewed the inside of his cheek, and his eyes were damp. "I love you, Ollie," he whispered. "So much. That's part of the problem."

My throat felt scratchy and dry. "I don't understand."

"I know." Milo began to doze in my arms. "I should put him in the car seat so he can nap on the way home."

I nodded, feeling numb. "Do you have a bed for him?"

"A travel cot. It'll do for now."

"What . . . what happens next?"

Thomas stopped by the front door. "I heard Cleo say she'd babysit next week so we could go on a date. What do you think?"

One week without him? It seemed like eternity, but at least that meant he had hope.

"Sounds good," I said.

He gave me a wan smile and walked out of the door.

CHAPTER
EIGHTEEN

I took Wednesday off because my anxiety was playing havoc with my stomach. Thomas had called last night to ask if I still wanted to go see Liesbeth with Milo and him. Even though it had only been a few days, I already missed them both so much I would've agreed to a bout of hot-coal walking.

Thomas arrived right before lunchtime. I was thrilled to the tips of my toes that he used his own key to let himself in. He walked into the living room, smile growing bigger with every step when he saw me waiting for him, curled up on the couch. Leaning upside down over the couch, he gently kissed me. "Hi."

"Hi," I breathed back. He was wearing Milo in one of those slings against his chest, and the sight did gooey things to my insides.

"I missed you."

"Good. I missed you too." I couldn't take my eyes off him, and God. God. I wanted this. I wanted him back here. My house was lifeless without their light. "Hey, Milo." I wiggled my finger, and he grabbed it while giving me a serious look.

"You ready for this afternoon?"

Ready to meet the baby mama? Nope, no, not at all. "Sure."

Thomas's eyes danced. "It'll be fine. You'll see. She's nice."

"Not too nice, I hope," I grumbled. I'd said it as he turned away to the door, but apparently I'd underestimated his hearing. He stopped and came around the couch. He crouched, hands resting loosely on my knees. Milo waved a fist up and down, then stuck it in his mouth.

"Are you jealous?" he teased, poking my thigh.

I could feel my face go red all the way up to my hairline, and kept my eyes on Milo.

"Ollie?"

"Maybe," I mumbled and played with a fine little thread coming loose in the baby carrier.

"Aw, love." Thomas stroked my jaw. "You have no reason to be."

I nodded.

"You sure you're okay?"

I looked at Thomas, at this man with his kind eyes and easy smile, who made me feel safe and treasured in a way I never thought I'd have again. We'd gone through some tough times, but here he was, staring at me like I'd hung the moon.

"I'm fine," I said.

He kissed me and lingered a little, let his tongue touch my lip until I opened for him. He made a soft noise and tilted his head—and then Milo smacked his chest.

"He wants me all to himself," I said primly. "Don't you, little boo? Yes, you do. And I don't blame you. I'm fabulous."

Thomas laughed softly, and I grinned at him, pleased with myself.

"Do you want some lunch?" I asked.

He glanced at his watch. "Sure, we have an hour or so before we need to leave." He unstrapped Milo and handed him over to me. Didn't even think twice about it, like he trusted me to the core with his child. It moved something deep inside me, and my throat tightened. "I'll just take off my shoes," he said and disappeared into the hallway.

One of the things Thomas had left behind was Milo's bouncy chair. I dragged it into the kitchen so I could prepare lunch. I pulled a bunch of grapes from the fridge and rinsed them. "See these? These are grapes, and they're super yummy. Soon you'll get to eat some." I studied one grape and frowned at it. "We'll probably have to cut it into pieces at first. But won't that be fun? You're so lucky, getting to discover all these foods for the first time. These—" I reached into the fridge again "—are strawb—"

I caught Thomas leaning against the doorframe, watching me with a small grin on his face. "Don't stop," he said, waving at me. "I think I'm learning something here."

I stuck out my tongue at him, but damn, he looked delicious. I pretty much forgot what I'd been about to say. He was wearing knee-length shorts and a soft, red V-neck shirt that showed a hint of his chest hair. I wanted to lay him down and feed him strawberries and lick the flavor from his everything.

"*Guh*," Milo said, and I did a double take.

"He totally said 'grape,'" I told Thomas. I bent down and bumped Milo's fist. "You awesome, clever little dude."

Thomas came up behind me and hugged me tight. "He did not say 'grape.'"

"Yes, he did, you party pooper. Don't you listen to your dad," I told Milo. "You said 'grape.' I heard you."

I didn't know what to expect from the clinic. We drove for an hour to get there, and the entire ride over, Milo slept while I grew more and more anxious.

"What if she doesn't like me?" I burst out when we pulled into a parking space in front of a building that looked like any other hospital I'd ever been to. I clutched my hands in my lap.

Thomas killed the engine and turned in his seat, resting one arm on the wheel. "She's going to like you, Ollie. Who doesn't like you?"

"Uh. Plenty of people? I make a point of surrounding myself only with people who do like me, but at work I come across idiots all the time. And in high school, nobody liked me."

"Nobody likes anyone in high school. And you had Sam, so I'm sure it wasn't all bad."

I shrugged. "I guess."

"Aw, love." He cupped the back of my neck and pulled me close. "Liesbeth is going to like you. She's going to see how great you are with Milo, and she'll be put at ease. That's all we're doing here. She's worried about strangers taking care of her baby. You understand that, don't you?"

I looked over my shoulder, but Milo was tucked away in his rear-facing car seat and I couldn't see him. "I do understand," I said. "But you're not living with me anymore, so what's the point? Not that I don't want to be here, but—" I looked away.

Thomas squeezed my knee. "I'm sorry this is hurting you," he murmured. "It's hurting me too. But I don't know what else to do, Ollie."

I nodded and pressed my lips together. This wasn't the time or the place to talk about us. "Let's go meet your baby mama."

"Don't call her that. She won't like you if you call her that."

I glared at him, one hand on the car door handle, and he laughed, leaned across the console, and kissed my cheek.

"You're just too cute."

I huffed, secretly pleased, and got out of the car. Milo was still fast asleep, but at least he was in one of those easy carriers I could lift from its base.

Whatever I'd been expecting from the inside, it hadn't been a modern building that looked more like a stylish apartment complex than a clinic. Thomas signed us in, the nurse called Liesbeth to let her know we were on our way, and up the stairs we went.

The hallway was really quiet. Thomas walked with purpose, diaper bag slung over his shoulder, all the way to the room at the end. In the seat, Milo stirred a little but kept on sleeping. Thomas knocked on the last door to the right.

"Come in."

He opened the door and stepped aside so I could go in with Milo first. The girl I remembered from the most awful night of my life was sitting on a neat, queen-size bed, reading a magazine.

"Hi," she said, rising to her feet. She glanced at me briefly, but her eyes zeroed in on Milo almost immediately. "Oh, he's sleeping." She pressed her hands to her mouth. She had very small hands, I noticed, and thick, blonde hair that was almost wiry. Her blue eyes filled with tears. I set the carrier down. I felt a little pang in my chest, because she was awfully pretty, and she and Thomas would've made a really amazing couple.

Thomas came to stand beside me and put his arm around my waist as Liesbeth kneeled and gently stroked Milo's fingers.

"Hey, sweet boy." She looked up at us. "How long has he been asleep?"

"Nearly an hour and a half," Thomas said. "He'll wake up soon."

She nodded as her gaze slid toward me. I held out my hand, and she shook it.

"I'm Oliver," I said.

"I remember you." She let go of my hand. "From that night. I'm really sorry about what happened."

"Thank you." An awkward silence fell.

"Do you have coffee, Liesbeth? I could make some." Thomas gestured toward a little alcove to the right I hadn't noticed before. In it sat a dining nook with counter space to the side. She had a sink, microwave, minifridge, and coffee machine. Tiny, but functional.

"I'll do it," she said. "You guys take a seat."

On the other side of the bed were two chairs facing the window, so I picked up the car seat and carried Milo over. Liesbeth's view was of the grounds—invisible from the street—and I tugged her sheer curtain to the side to have a better look. Below us lay a park with a winding path that led across the lawn toward a pond with the typical weeping willow.

"This is pretty nice," I said to Thomas.

"Yes, it's not a bad place to be." He glanced at the kitchen. "Excuse me a minute."

"Sure." I sat down and waited while he went to talk to Liesbeth. The room wasn't big enough that I could avoid overhearing, but I kept my gaze fixed on the window anyway.

"How are you doing?" Thomas asked her.

"Not bad. I miss Milo a lot, but I can see now that I made the right choice coming here."

"Do you know what's going to happen when you can go home?"

The tap ran, so I missed some of her reply. ". . . for six months. Then he'll be with you for seventy-five percent of the time and twenty-five with me for another six months, and after that, fifty-fifty if that's good with you. Have you two decided if you'll be staying—"

"No," Thomas said quickly. "Not yet."

I bent down to look at Milo. His bottom lip stuck out like he was pouting over something in his sleep. It made me smile. His little socks were coming off his feet, but I didn't want to risk waking him yet by pulling them up. He scrunched his nose and made a kissy face.

"You're too adorable," I whispered. "I mean, how could you not be with parents like that? You'll be real clever too, like your dad. And I bet your mom kicks ass too. I thought maybe I wouldn't like her, but yeah, she seems really nice." I swallowed hard. "You're going to turn out just fine, little boo. No matter what." I straightened and found two pairs of eyes gazing down on me. "Uh."

"Here," Thomas said, handing me a cup. "Too sweet, just as you like it."

I felt my face go hot. "Thanks."

Liesbeth sat down cross-legged on the floor. Milo kicked his legs and opened his eyes. He yawned widely and with his entire face, in that way only babies can. And then his gaze fixed on his mother. I nearly burst into tears when he gave her the most beautiful smile.

The thing with babies is, sometimes they cry and cry, and no matter what you do, they won't stop. We arrived back at the house around four, and Milo had been crying since we got in the car.

"What's wrong with him?" I asked, turning around in my seat. All I saw was the back of his carrier. "Do you think he's missing his mom?"

"I think he's too young to realize what's going on. Maybe he has a dirty diaper." We'd stopped twice and checked it, but it'd been wet, that was all. Thomas worried his lip. "Do you think he has a fever?"

"Why don't you come inside for a second? Your little first aid kit is still here. We can check it."

"Okay." He stared at me with wide eyes.

"What?"

"It's one of those baby ones."

"Well, yeah. I'd expect it to be."

"It's a rectal one," he said.

"Oh." I leaned into the passenger door. "Well, dude. You're the dad. That's where I draw the line."

"Shit. Okay, let's do this."

I went to unlock the front door as Thomas freed a still-crying Milo from the car, and led the way to the dining table.

"You haven't put anything away," Thomas said.

My cheeks heated. "No."

Thomas hesitated as he looked at me, then dug through the little first aid kit and produced a tiny thermometer.

"No, I'm googling this first." He pulled out his phone and made a series of faces I'd have found hilarious if I weren't becoming more and more worried about Milo squirming in his arms. "Right. I got this. We have to take off his diaper."

I held back the *duh* and put Milo on the towels. "It's okay, little fella," I told him as he tried to throw a punch. "Good thing your arms are so short or I'd have two black eyes right now."

Thomas worked him out of his onesie and diaper, then picked up the thermometer. "Can you hold his legs? Tight, so he can't kick loose." He paused. "But not too tight. We don't want to hurt him."

"Thomas," I said, "I've got this end. You deal with the other end."

"Okay." He blew out a deep breath, dabbed some Vaseline on the tip of the thermometer, and pinched his lips together.

Milo's face drew in like a thunder cloud. "I know, buddy. It's not fair, is it? Oh look, he's really getting mad now, Thomas. Look at that, his face is going all re—"

"Oh God." Thomas straightened quickly.

"Well." I made a face, reached for a box of wipes, and handed them to Thomas. When I looked down at Milo, he was smiling. "I guess now we know why you were crying, huh?"

"No fever," Thomas said weakly, and I laughed.

The crying must've worn Milo out, because he fell asleep in Thomas's arms not long after.

"Do you think he can nap in his crib here for a while?"

It made my heart hurt that he thought he had to ask. "Of course."

# CHAPTER NINETEEN

I hadn't seen Thomas or Milo in two days. I hadn't slept, had barely eaten. My house felt like an echoing cave in its silence, and I ached for Thomas so much. Maybe a year was fast to move on, but I couldn't help how I felt. I loved Thomas, and I wanted to live with him. If that meant selling this house, I would. He was right. The past stuck to me like cling film, and while I adored this place, at the end of the day it was only a house.

"You need to sit down or I'm shoving a Xanax down your throat."

I glared at Cleo, walked into the hallway, peered through the frosted glass oval in my front door, saw nothing but pouring rain, and twisted around to face the tall mirror beside the coatrack. When Thomas had texted me this morning asking if the date was still on . . . Well. There had been squealing.

My hair was perfect, for once. I'd gone to my hairdresser right after work, and she had performed a miracle. She'd managed to make it smooth and soft on the sides, and swept my bangs back in some sort of bump that veered off the right. I looked stylish and fabulous, so of course it was raining like it hadn't rained in weeks. I was wearing a new pair of tight, distressed jeans that hugged my ass lovingly; a crisp, gray, short-sleeved button-down; and a thick burgundy cardigan with large buttons. I'd taken it off for now because all the pacing was making me hot.

Cleo was right. I needed to sit down before I began to sweat. I glanced at the overnight bag I'd packed and suppressed the urge to run my hands through my hair. I didn't know if we were still going to spend the night at his house, but I wanted to be prepared.

"He's fifteen minutes late," I told Cleo, who was lounging on my sofa, ready for babysitting duties. "What if he changed his mind? What if he's not coming? What if he *is* coming and I'm such a disappointment he never wants to see me again?"

She sat up quickly and pointed at the other end of the couch. I hurried to go sit.

"Okay, here's the thing: he's been in love with you for so long, you could have a tiny dick, and he wouldn't care." I squawked, but she held up a hand. "By now we all know that's not the case, thanks to Sam's talented hands." She gave me a stern look. "He has a baby, Ollie. A baby he's been alone with for a week. People with babies are never on time."

"Okay."

"Aw, Ollie." She scooted over and put her hand on my leg. "You'll be fine."

I covered her hand with mine. "I'm sorry. I'm being a total insensitive ass, aren't I? How's it going with you? Imran decided he didn't want to babysit?"

She shrugged. "We broke up."

"Oh no, Cleo . . ." I straightened, ready to hug her if she needed me to, but she looked surprisingly calm and collected.

"I'm okay with it, actually. I think . . . I have some things I need to work through. And I think I want to be single for a while. We were good together, but . . . I fell from one relationship into the next. I've never been alone, and I think I want to be."

I knew what she meant. "When did you see him last?"

"He moved out on Sunday night. I haven't seen him since. He calls every day though. The hardest thing will be giving up the apartment. I love that place, but I can't pay for it by myself. I'll have to give the landlord my month's notice."

"Oh, babe." I put my arm over her shoulder and pulled her close. She might not need a hug, but I did. Everything was changing. "You know you can stay here for as long you need to if you can't find anything better."

"With you and Thomas and a baby?"

"Fingers crossed, right? I mean it. There's plenty of room. And if things don't work out with Thomas, I might need you here to console my inconsolable self."

She rolled her eyes at me.

"Are you sure you're done with Imran?"

"I'm not sure, no. But I don't see how I can forgive him making me feel bad over what happened with Thomas while he has 'commitment issues.'" She finger quoted the last bit. "It's such a clusterfuck, but I still love him."

"You have to do what's right for you though," I told her and squeezed her tighter. "Even if it's difficult right now."

She nodded. "I know."

The doorbell rang, and I sprang up so fast I nearly dumped Cleo on the floor. "Oh my God, I'm sorry, I'm sorry."

"You're fine." She laughed, then stared at me. "Well?" She widened her eyes. "Are you going to let him stand out there in the rain?"

"Oh shit!" I sprinted to the door and yanked it open. "Hi," I said breathlessly. Disappointment nearly strangled me when I saw that he didn't have Milo with him. I stepped aside automatically to let him in. "Is . . . Are we changing plans?"

"A little bit," Thomas gave me a dark look, and had opened his mouth to say something else when Cleo appeared in the hallway.

"Well, I'll be on my way. Have a good time, boys." She winked, pushed open the umbrella she'd left by the door, and disappeared into the rain.

I stared after her. "But . . ." I looked at Thomas. "Where's Milo? Why is Cleo not babysitting him? Did you change your mind?"

Thomas crowded me against the front door, tilted my chin up, and kissed me. He nipped at my mouth and sucked on my tongue, bit the edge of my jawline, and licked the tendon stretching taut at the side of my neck.

He looked a little dazed when he came up for air. "What did you ask me?"

"Why Milo isn't babysitting Cleo. Or . . . something along those lines." I surreptitiously let the door take my weight because my knees felt like they were made from marshmallows.

"Oh." He rested his head on my shoulder. "Fuck, I really missed you. I'm not used to being at my own house by myself anymore." He nuzzled my neck, and I had trouble focusing. "Your mom has Milo for the whole weekend, and Cleo is going to keep her company tonight.

Cleo called your mom to see if that was okay, since she didn't want to do it by herself. Did she tell you she broke up with Imran?"

I nodded. "Yeah. It's sad. But maybe for the best."

"I think so too. And then I thought we'd probably be more comfortable in your house since mine is an epic mess right now." He laughed reluctantly. "I survived with Milo, but that's pretty much it."

"That's . . . that's fine with me." I ran my fingers gently through his hair. "So you did okay these last few days?"

"I . . . Yeah." He lifted his head and looked at me, then cupped my face and kissed me lightly. "I wanted to see if I could do it alone. Be with Milo all by myself. And I could. It was exhausting, but doable. But I kept wondering why I was alone in my house while you were alone in your house, and I missed you so much."

"I missed you too," I whispered, and we stood there, foreheads pressed together in silence for a long time.

"I gave my landlord my notice," he said. "So if you changed your mind about us moving in here, please tell me now so I can get the panicking out of the way."

"Are you serious?" I straightened and nearly brained him. "I pretty much decided to sell this place and move wherever you wanted." I paused. "Within reason. I don't do rural life."

Thomas laughed, and he sounded as giddy as I felt. "You'd sell the house?"

"Yes. You were right. I was hung up on the idea of this place meaning something because of Sam. But it's you and me now. You and me and Milo."

Thomas closed his eyes and crushed me tight. "This place does mean something," he said. "And it's a beautiful house. I want to live here. Together we can take care of the mortgage easily. If that's okay with you."

"Of course I'm okay with that. Oh my God. Really?" I sobered. "You're not feeling obliged to help me pay for this house, are you? We can wait. Not too long, though. I missed you like crazy. But we could if you wanted to."

"I'm doing it because I love you and I missed you like crazy too. And so did Milo. So what do you say? Roomies?"

"Roomies," I whispered, and then, because I wanted him to know exactly what I meant by that, "Joint homeowners."

He grinned at me. "Boyfriends."

"Yeah, that too."

"I'm pretty tempted to just stay here," Thomas said. "But you look so good, it'd be a real waste."

"No, it wouldn't." I ran my hands down his chest, felt the rise and fall of his pecs, the bumps of his nipples. "We could totally stay in."

"I want to have that date." He caught my hands and held them before they could trail too low. "A real first date, like we were meant to have."

My knees still felt a little weak. "That sounds nice." I squirmed against him, then bit the bullet. "I guess we should talk about expectations." He frowned at me, and I waved a hand in the air. "You know. Sex-wise. I mean . . . I've topped once or twice in my life, but I could, you know. Live without it. You?"

He leaned so close I saw the striations in his irises. "Can I live with fucking you?" he murmured, and lightly pressed his lips to mine. "Oh fuck yeah."

Thomas took me to Het Gerecht, a restaurant where Sam and I used to go for special occasions, but I didn't tell him that. In a way that made it even nicer to be there, as if Sam were looking down on us and giving his blessing. I sent him some kind thoughts and then gently pushed him from my mind.

The interior was crisp and clean, but warmed through with a dark wooden floor and vibrant red paintings on the white walls. We drank excellent wine and ate even better food. The dishes were deliberately small, with the intention that the diner would choose four or five, and we shared baby lobster with asparagus, lamb with beans, beets and aubergines, trout with hummus, an assortment of breads and cheeses that was to die for, and in the end a delicate vanilla ice cream with red fruits. Every plate was presented so beautifully, it was almost a shame to touch it.

We tried talking about lots of things, but kept coming back to Milo, and that was okay. We were a family. And families talk about their kids.

When Thomas led me to his car, he held me close and kissed my temple. "Did you have a good time?"

"The best," I said. I tried not to watch the shadows as we walked, but felt relief when we climbed into his car regardless. I wondered if that was a fear I was going to carry for the rest of my life. Maybe it would be, but I wasn't about to let it stop me from living my life.

"You okay?" Thomas asked. He took his hand off the gear stick for a second and squeezed my knee.

"Yeah. Just remembering things." I smiled to make sure he knew I wasn't hurting.

"It's okay to think about him, you know."

"I know."

We drove home in silence, and nervous anticipation about how the night would continue tickled my spine. Until now we'd always sort of landed on the couch in desperation when we thought we had a moment to ourselves. This deliberate drive toward an empty house, with only one plausible outcome, was something else altogether.

I tried not to fidget, but my palms were damp and I felt a little claustrophobic.

Thomas must've noticed, because by the time I was unlocking my front door, he asked me again, "Are you sure you're all right?"

I stepped aside and let him in, then turned on the hall light and took off my shoes. Thomas looked absolutely divine. He hadn't had a lot of wine to drink during dinner, but what he'd had left a rosy blush on his cheeks. His thick hair was layered over the right side of his forehead, and his eyes sparkled, although he did look worried.

"I guess I'm nervous." I laughed. He gazed at me intently, and I looked at my feet. "It's been, you know . . ." I fluttered my hand and said nothing else.

Thomas stepped closer and pulled me into his arms. Without my shoes on, he was even taller, and I leaned against his chest. "Ollie, you know we don't have to—"

"I know. And it's not about *having* to. It's been a while, and apart from Peter, there was only—"

"Don't talk to me about *Peter*," Thomas growled in my ear. I looked up at him, startled. "All I ever wanted was you, and then you went out with this stranger. Texting me you were going home with him. You were dating him. I was going out of my *mind*."

I cupped his face. "I didn't know. I didn't know I was hurting you."

He held my hands against his cheeks and smiled. "I know that. I'm not mad about it now. But at the time I was ready to yank my hair out."

"You never said anything."

"What was I meant to say?" He took off his coat, and I went a bit woozy seeing those thick biceps roll under his sweater. "'Oh, by the way, Ollie, now that you're single in the most horrific way, fancy giving me a go? I've been pining for you since the day we met.'"

I raised my eyebrow at him. "That was you pining? Going home with someone else every weekend?"

He laughed and put his hands on my shoulders. "Well, I could either pine and be miserable or live with it and have some fun. We were never meant to be. I knew that."

"And yet here we are."

He bit his lip, and his gaze zeroed in on my mouth.

"Here we are," he whispered, and he used me for balance as he stepped out of his shoes, then drew me closer again and kissed me. I felt the bulge in his pants, but I also noticed the tremor in his hands.

"You're nervous too," I whispered.

"Of course I am. You're all I've ever wanted. What if—what if—"

I pressed my mouth to his to silence him. "I know," I said against his lips. "I know."

We fumbled our way upstairs. I took off his sweater and floundered over the buttons of his shirt. His hands got stuck in both sleeves because I'd forgotten to take off his cuff links, so there was awkward bumping together halfway up the steps, trying to untangle him. When we reached the bedroom, he helped me undress, but I attempted to take off my socks before he pulled my pants down and ended up tripping over my own feet. I landed on the bed in an ungraceful heap and tried to laugh my way through it, but on the inside my heart hammered nervously.

Thomas kissed me, and caressed me, and did everything right. I loved the feel of his skin, the rise and fall of the landscape of his body, the scritch of his chest hairs against my palm. When I took his briefs off, his cock slapped against his belly, and I licked at the wet tip, just once. Thomas's breath shuddered out of his mouth, and I reached for him, drew him down between my legs.

We kissed and held each other, and when he peeled off my underwear, I told myself I wanted this. And I did. I *did*. But my body felt like a live wire, and Thomas's touch sparked me like static wherever he touched.

I could feel him tremble. We were too quiet. Our eyes were too wide when we dared to look at each other. When he reached for the lube, I made an involuntary noise, and he put the bottle away again.

He pulled me against him and hugged me tight. "Not like this," he whispered in my ear. "I don't want it to be like this."

I nodded against his neck and tried not to cry.

We lay in silence like that for a long time, until eventually Thomas sighed and rolled onto his back. He covered his face with his elbow, but drew me close with the other arm so I didn't feel like he'd shut me out.

I stroked his chest, slipped my fingers through the hairs, rubbed my thumb lightly over his nipple. "Are you okay?"

He let his arm fall away, turned his head, and smiled at me. "Yeah, I'm okay. You?"

I nodded.

"I think we worked ourselves up too much and our expectations were too high."

"Yes, I think so too. But that's okay, right? I mean, we have the whole weekend. It felt so weirdly . . . planned."

"I think that's how it goes when you have kids, but yeah. Usually by that time you've already had all sorts of sex together." His deep laugh rumbled under my ear, and I smiled, pressing my cheek closer to his heart. It thumped evenly, and I closed my eyes.

I was almost dozing off when he said, "So you're sure you're okay with Milo and me living here with you?"

"Yes, of course. Why do you ask?"

"Just making sure you haven't changed your mind about having a baby and his dad messing up your house now that you've had some time to let it sink in."

"Oh, please," I said, waving my hand in the air. "It's not the baby who messes up my house."

Thomas made a mock-outraged face and rolled over and pushed me back into the bed. "I see how it is," he said, his eyes twinkling in the soft moonlight. "You're using me for my adorable son."

"You got that right."

I laughed when he began to kiss-bite my neck, and we kissed lazily after that until I fell asleep.

It was barely dawn when I struggled out of sleep. Very pale sunlight touched my closed eyelids, and I cursed the curtains I'd forgotten to close the night before. I was also chilly since I'd managed to lose all the covers. For a second I thought about groping around to wrap myself back up, but the effort seemed too much. I was lying half on my stomach, half clutching a pillow, one leg pulled up. I had morning wood a lumberjack would be jealous of. My brain felt foggy with lust, and remnants of a very weird erotic dream clung to the edges of my memory. Something to do with being comfortably adrift in warm water, where a very friendly, tentacle-y plant was getting closely acquainted with my— *Oh my God.*

Something wet touched my asshole, and I squeaked, but a pair of firm hands came down on my buttocks and held me fast. I looked over my shoulder to see Thomas lying between my spread legs, and he licked me again.

"Jesus," I whispered weakly. A hot flush raced up my body, and I buried my face in the pillow. He spread my cheeks farther, languidly sliding his tongue over my asshole, and I quivered all over. "Ah, God." He did it again, and then again, and then he speared his tongue into me. "Oh my God, *Thomas.*"

I scrabbled at the sheets, bit the pillow, bunched up the covers with my toes. His fingers gave my ass a light squeeze, the is-this-okay kind, and my entire body heated with embarrassment and arousal.

He hesitated. I opened my mouth to say *Don't stop*, but no sound came out. So instead, I lifted my hips a little and pushed back against his mouth. My face flushed even hotter.

No one had ever done this to me. For me. *No one.* I moaned when he licked me again, tickled me with his tongue, nibbled on my taint. He touched my balls, and I made a bewildered, turned-on noise. I heard the click of a cap over the harshness of my own breathing, and spread my thighs farther.

"Fuck, Ollie." Thomas bit the swell of my ass, and I was glad to hear he sounded as wrecked as I felt. "This okay?"

I nodded into the pillow because deliberate words were still beyond my brain capacity. He held my ass spread with one hand, pushed his tongue into my hole, and followed it with a slick, thick finger. I moaned brokenly as he worked his way inside, and white light exploded behind my eyelids. Every time he moved, I thought I'd come, but I didn't. Instead he expertly kept me on the edge of the abyss, opening me up in ways I couldn't even keep count of, until all I knew was that I needed him, and I needed him in me right this second.

"Fuck me," I croaked. "Thomas, I want it. Now."

"Ollie . . ." he whispered almost reverently. I heard the crinkle of a condom wrapper, the slick noise of more lube, and then blunt pressure I'd learned to breathe through, yet it felt so different. He entered me slowly, and I couldn't hold back the guttural moan as he bottomed out. I kept breathing evenly as my body adjusted to him. He ran a hand over my flank, down my spine, over my arm, until he could lace our fingers together. "You okay?"

"Yeah." I reached down and rubbed my free hand along his thigh, felt the flex of his muscles, and twisted my head to the side. The kiss he offered was slightly awkward, but I didn't care. He stared into my eyes and began to move, slowly. He never looked away. I saw everything: how vulnerable he was, how awed, how in love. A reflection of what I felt on the inside, right there so clear in his gaze.

He fucked me tenderly at first, finding his way, learning my body, then a little harder when he understood how I liked it.

It didn't take long before we were covered in a sheen of sweat, and the friction on my cock became almost too much to bear.

"I'm going to come soon," I whispered, "if you keep going like that."

"Not yet," he said and took his weight off me. At first I didn't get what he wanted, but he guided me with soft touches until we were both sitting up, me in his lap, and understanding dawned. "This okay?" he asked.

I turned my head and looked at him. Thomas still wasn't hiding anything. He was worried and a little scared, and God—I loved him.

"Oh yeah," I murmured and lifted my arm so I could cup the back of his head. I kissed him deeply, and he began to fuck me harder, flesh on flesh, the slapping noise unmistakable, but I was too far gone to care. A hot burn raged in my belly, and pleasure sparked up my spine and down my legs. My cock hung too heavy and thick to stand upright, and was dripping a steady thread of clear liquid onto the sheets. We were slick with sweat now, and I had a fraction of awareness left to be really impressed with how Thomas had managed to keep his rhythm for this long and this hard.

He had his hands on my chest, holding us both upright. "Make yourself come," he panted in my ear.

I shook my head. "Don't need to."

I keened when his rhythm faltered for barely a second, and then he kept going, harder than before, the tempo nearly punishing. I wanted to say *almost* and *that's it* and *oh God*, but I didn't have the breath for it. Broken, cut-off moans kept falling from my mouth, but I was almost—there—

"Jesus fuck, you're killing me here," Thomas croaked, and I tensed all over, gripping his hair too hard and pulling his face into my neck, but I couldn't help it. My body seized, my cock jumped and pulsed, and my ass squeezed around Thomas's cock as I finally started coming. His thrusts turned sharp and frantic. He cried out between his teeth, for he'd clamped them down on my neck, and pushed hard and deep, staying pressed into me and forcing another jet of come from my balls.

I didn't know where he got the strength from, but he managed to extract himself gently and lower me onto the bed. A few oblivious minutes later, the come and lube had been wiped from my body, and he'd wrapped himself around me, tight, like he never wanted to let go.

"Ollie . . ." he whispered. "That was really . . ." He fell silent, and I smiled. I wanted to make a joke, but my brain was too orgasm-addled.

"Yes," I said, turning over so I could kiss him. "Yes, it really was."

 **EPILOGUE**

"**N**ow this," I told Milo, "is much more exciting than that baby oatmeal stuff. See?" I held up a spoon of goop. "It's squishy and green, and so much fun to stick your hands in." I paused. "But I suggest you only do that with Daddy. With me, you can eat nice and clean, can't you, you big boy?"

He'd changed so much, I found it hard to believe he'd been such a tiny baby only a few months ago. I wouldn't miss the interrupted nights—he'd started sleeping for ten hours at a time about a week ago—but he already didn't fit into the crook of my arm anymore, and I missed holding him like that.

"Da da," Milo said, and he bounced in his high chair.

"Yes! Daddy, that's right. He should be home any minute. And we'll tell him we've missed him lots and lots, won't we? Because we did. Now, how about we surprise him and show how well you can eat, huh? This is avocado. Can you say that? A-vo-ca-do."

I held up the spoon, and Milo looked at it. He looked back at me. Back at the spoon. Then opened his mouth.

"Yay, see? Easy peasy." I gave him the spoonful of avocado I'd pureed. He held it in his mouth. His face scrunched. I braced myself, ready with a paper towel, but he swallowed it down. "All right! Fist bump, little man. You are the best." We bumped fists.

"Da da," Milo said again, and he giggled and kicked his legs. He was looking over my shoulder, so I spun around. Thomas was leaning against the doorframe, arms crossed over his broad chest. He looked windswept and slightly chilled from the December cold. His hair was starting to grow again, and it fell loosely against his cheekbones. I wanted to climb him like a tree.

"Oh, hi," I said. "How long have you been standing there?"

"Long enough to hear how well you can say 'avocado.'" He grinned, and I rolled my eyes.

"Your son is eating new things. He said, 'No more baby oatmeal! That stuff is boring and for ordinary babies, not for special babies like me.' Isn't that r—" I turned to look at Milo just in time to see him stuff his hand in the bowl. Before I could even blink, I got a face full of avocado. He stared at me for a second, his blue eyes wide, then shrieked with laughter. His hands flailed about, more avocado going everywhere. When he caught sight of his green fingers, he stopped laughing and happily stuffed them in his mouth.

"Well," Thomas said as I plucked goop from my eyebrow. "At least he seems to like it."

"Har har. How did it go?" At this point I was pretty unfazed by anything that wasn't bodily fluids flying in my direction, so I reached for the paper towel and cleaned my face.

Thomas loosened his tie, looked at the chair, gave it a quick wipe, and sat down. "The contracts are signed," he said. "Milo will officially be with us every other week from January onwards."

"And Liesbeth is happy with that?"

"Yep."

I took in the sadness in his smile. "How about you? Are you happy with that?"

He sighed and stroked his thumb over Milo's chubby arm. The baby had put on a lot of weight over the past two months, so much that we'd brought it up during his last wellness visit. The doctor had assured us the weight would drop once he started crawling instead of flailing in place like a tiny and adorable beached whale.

"I'm going to miss him like crazy, but I'm happy he'll be with his mom," Thomas said. He put his other hand on my arm. "And I'm happy I'll get to spend more time with just you."

I covered his hand, squeezed it, and asked, "So you ready for our trip this weekend?"

"Oh yeah, so ready. Do I need to do any more packing for Milo?"

"No, it's all done. He doesn't need much anyway. Mom has plenty of baby stuff at her place now." Thomas kept looking at Milo, his eyes gentle and a little wet. "We can always change our minds, you know. We can easily take him with us. We have that travel cot and—"

"No. I want this weekend with you. It's another month before Liesbeth has him half the time, and . . ." He bit his lip. "I've really been looking forward to some alone time."

"Yeah?"

"Oh yes."

I studied my nails. "We could go kayaking while we're in the Ardennes."

Thomas narrowed his eyes at me. "Don't even go there," he said, voice low.

"Okay, that's fine. I mean, there's always the lovely heights of the mountains. Nice, steep paths we could climb, all the way up to the towering peaks, with staggering views of deep valleys below— Don't you dare!" Thomas had lifted Milo's spoon and aimed a heap of avocado at me. "You are setting an example for your son! If you throw food at me, he will think he can—"

Splat.

The avocado hit me right between the eyes. Thomas dropped the spoon and covered his mouth. Silence fell. Then Milo began to laugh so hard, we had to scramble so his high chair didn't fall over.

"I really didn't aim for your face," Thomas said, trying not to laugh. "I'm so sorry."

I rose slowly to my feet, grabbed another paper towel, and with all the dignity I could muster, cleaned my face again.

"Well," I said to Milo. "You'll be happy to know you'll at least grow up with one responsible parent while you live in this house."

Milo smiled, stuck out his arms in my direction, and said, "Da."

Thomas froze, and I froze. "He called you Dad," Thomas said.

"No, I'm sure that was just a noise. And he calls you 'Da da.' I'm sure it didn't mean anything."

"Ollie." Thomas rounded the table and hugged me. "I'm not jealous. I think that's great. I want you to be his dad. I mean . . . if that's what you want too."

I pressed my face against Thomas's chest, then sneaked a peek at Milo. His face was scrunched up, and he held out his arms as he kicked his legs. I worked myself loose from Thomas's grip, lifted Milo out of his seat, and didn't care he was covered in food. I hugged him tight, and he swung his little arms around my neck. With my free hand, I drew Thomas closer, and he engulfed us both.

"Two dads and a mom, huh," I croaked. I hid my face again when tears stung my eyes. "That has to beat growing up with only one parent."

"Da," Milo said again, and he put his head on my shoulder.

I lifted my face to Thomas's. "You've made me so happy," I said to him. His eyes were a little damp too. "Both of you. When Sam first died, I thought I'd never be happy again. I didn't think I could ever feel like this again, and look at us now. Thank you for being there for me."

"I was *always* there for you, Ollie," Thomas said. He kissed me lightly on the mouth and smiled. He held us closer. The three of us stood in the kitchen that had once been mine and Sam's and was now the heart of this patchwork family. "And I always will be."

Dear Reader,

Thank you for reading Indra Vaughn's *Patchwork Paradise*!

We know your time is precious and you have many, many entertainment options, so it means a lot that you've chosen to spend your time reading. We really hope you enjoyed it.

We'd be honored if you'd consider posting a review—good or bad—on sites like **Amazon, Barnes & Noble, Kobo, Goodreads, Twitter, Facebook**, **Tumblr,** and your blog or website. We'd also be honored if you told your friends and family about this book. Word of mouth is a book's lifeblood!

For more information on upcoming releases, author interviews, blog tours, contests, giveaways, and more, please sign up for our weekly, spam-free newsletter and visit us around the web:

Newsletter: tinyurl.com/RiptideSignup
Twitter: twitter.com/RiptideBooks
Facebook: facebook.com/RiptidePublishing
Goodreads: tinyurl.com/RiptideOnGoodreads
Tumblr: riptidepublishing.tumblr.com

Thank you so much for Reading the Rainbow!

RiptidePublishing.com

ALSO BY
INDRA VAUGHN

The House on Hancock Hill
Fated (Shadow Mountain, Book 1)
Fragmented (Shadow Mountain, Book 2)
Dust of Snow
Vespertine, with Leta Blake
The Winter Spirit

ABOUT THE AUTHOR

After living in Michigan, USA, for seven wonderful years, Indra Vaughn returned back to her Belgian roots. There she will continue to consume herbal tea, do yoga wherever the mat fits, and devour books while single parenting a little boy and working as a nurse.

The stories of boys and their unrequited love will no doubt keep finding their way onto the page—and hopefully into readers hands—even if it takes a little more time.

And if she gleefully posts pictures of snow-free streets in winter, you'll have to forgive her. Those Michigan blizzards won't be forgotten in a hurry.

Facebook: facebook.com/indra.vaughn.7
Twitter: twitter.com/VaughnIndra
Goodreads: goodreads.com/author/Indra_Vaughn

Enjoy more stories like
Patchwork Paradise
at RiptidePublishing.com!

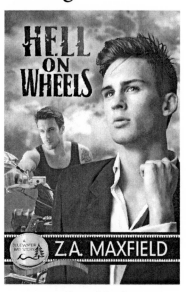

Until September
ISBN: 978-1-62649-356-8

Hell on Wheels
ISBN: 978-1-62649-173-1

Earn Bonus Bucks!

Earn 1 Bonus Buck for each dollar you spend. Find out how at
RiptidePublishing.com/news/bonus-bucks.

Win Free Ebooks for a Year!

Pre-order coming soon titles directly through our site and you'll
receive one entry into a drawing for a chance to win free books for
a year! Get the details at RiptidePublishing.com/contests.

CPSIA information can be obtained at www.ICGtesting.com
Printed in the USA
LVOW08s1625020516

486275LV00006B/389/P